Greatest Cat Stories

Greatest Cat Stories

Edited by

Lesley O'Mara

Michael O'Mara Books Limited

This paperback edition published in 1997 by
Michael O'Mara Books Limited
9 Lion Yard
Tremadoc Road
London SW4 7NQ

First published in Great Britain in 1995 by
Michael O'Mara Books Limited

Illustrations on p. i, iii, 7, 11, 12, 28, 47, 48, 58, 61, 64, 69,
70, 85, 93, 101, 102, 110, 111, 128, 135, 139, 140, 147, 148,
165, 166, 170, 171, 182, 183, 187, 188, 190, 192, 208, 209, 225,
226 by William Geldart

A CIP catalogue record for this book is available from the
British Library

ISBN 1-85479-699-2

5 7 9 10 8 6

Edited by Lesley O'Mara

Typeset by CentraCet Ltd, Linton, Cambridge
Printed and bound by Cox & Wyman, Reading

Contents

That Damned Cat

TERESA CRANE

It really wouldn't have been so bad if the cat hadn't been such an unabashed bully. From day one he positively terrorized my poor little Tabs – who could never be called the most assertive of cats and who had quite enough on her plate already, thank you, what with the move and the uncomfortable adjustment to unfamiliar surroundings. Every time she set foot out of the door the damned thing pounced on her. It was a brazen thief, too; twice I found the wretch on the kitchen table feasting in princely style on left-overs that my well-behaved Tabs wouldn't have dreamed of touching. It was a huge and I have to admit handsome animal, as black as sin, with bright green eyes that shone like lamps in its wicked face, and a plume of a tail that it carried like a banner. Oh, there was no doubt as to who was Tom Cat in the gardens of Hill View Cottages.

I had been living at Number Five, the end of the terrace, for three weeks now, and was still in a fearsome muddle. The cottage was tiny; two rooms and a bathroom upstairs, one room and a kitchen down. After the claustrophobic and gardenless town flat that had been our home for the past couple of years Tabs and I loved it.

The one and only drawback was that damned cat.

He came from Number One, at the far end of the terrace;

disdaining any such convention as a cat flap he was often to be seen scaling the small apple tree and nipping through the kitchen window – obviously his preferred method of entry, since that was how he had twice managed to plunder my left-over supper. His owner wasn't around much during the week, though I had caught the odd glimpse of him at the weekends, mostly sprawled in an ancient deckchair, feet up in the summer sunshine in a cleared spot in the tangled undergrowth that passed for a garden, his head in a book and a very large glass of beer beside him. No wonder the blessed cat was a thug.

By that third weekend, having spent the best part of Saturday morning bathing Tabs's torn ear and soothing her understandably jangled nerves, my patience had been so badly tried that, walking back from the village shop and seeing the young man in the garden, I was truly tempted to tackle him about his pet's terrorist activities. However good manners – with perhaps a small salting of cowardice – won the day and I contented myself with returning his wave and his cheerful grin with what I hoped was the mere trace of an exceedingly frigid smile and stalking on to my own gate. Never a great one for confrontations unless my temper really blows I reasoned that, after all, it would hardly be appropriate to begin my life at Number Five by having a storming row with one of my neighbours; though the sight of Tabs's ragged ear and forlorn expression when I walked in through the kitchen door tested my resolution sorely.

I spent the day – as I had spent every day of each weekend since I had moved in – unpacking the tea-chests that were still stacked in every spare inch of the cottage. I couldn't move without falling over something. The one thing my old flat had had was shelves; the one thing that Number Five *didn't* have was shelves. There were books, magazines and piles of paper just everywhere. I was on the tiny landing doing something fairly constructive with some bricks and a couple of planks that I had found in the shed when a crash from downstairs made me all but jump out of my skin. The bricks tottered. The plank I had so carefully balanced slipped to the floor, tearing at the skin of my hands as it did so. I yelped, swore and stuck a finger full of splinters into my mouth. A second or so later Tabs was up the stairs and streaking past me as if the hounds of hell were on her tail. I clattered down the narrow staircase and into the kitchen; and there, as I had suspected, was the enemy, large as life and twice as cocky, lapping at the milk that dripped from an over-turned glass jug on the table on to the flagstoned floor.

'Bloody cat!' I started toward him.

I swear he grinned at me before, a black streak, he was through the door, round the side of the house and up the front path to the gate. Shrieking like a fishwife and intent upon vengeance, I grabbed the nearest weapon – a large wooden spoon – and followed. 'Damn you! I'll have your guts for garters, you fiend – !' I stopped.

Across the narrow lane from Number Five was a small, neat, brick-built cottage with picket fence and gate. It was the home of a charming elderly lady who had shown me nothing but kindness since I had turned up three weeks before with two large and inexpertly driven hired vans and assorted noisy friends to move myself into Number Five. It had occurred to me at the time that, even as she had with great goodwill plied us with cups of tea and platesful of Nice biscuits, she might have had her doubts as to my suitability as a neighbour; the thought occurred again now as, scarlet with effort and rage, I skidded to a halt at the gate.

Secateurs in hand Mrs Lovelace looked up and smiled, affably.

'Good morning,' I said, brightly, struggling for breath. 'What lovely weather, still.'

The cat lifted its arrogant plume of a tail, smirked, and stalked gracefully off down the lane.

'It certainly is, my dear.' The old lady was imperturbable.

3

One might have thought she spent most mornings being confronted by dishevelled, grubby and furious young women brandishing wooden spoons with obvious malicious intent.

The cat leapt effortlessly upon the gate of Number One, stepped with the balanced delicacy of a tight-rope walker along the top and settled itself upon the gatepost, tail curled neatly, the very picture of innocence in the sunshine.

From behind me, from the kitchen, came the sound of a small, tinkling crash. Too late I realized that in my desire to strangle the cat I hadn't stopped to pick up the jug. Now, from the sound of it, there was no jug to pick up.

That was enough. Grimly I tucked the wooden spoon into the pocket of my jeans, opened the gate, smiled as pleasantly as I could at Mrs Lovelace – no mean feat considering that I had nothing less than murder on my mind – and set off down the lane towards Number One.

The cat sat cool as a cucumber and watched me come. Only at the very last minute did it decide that perhaps discretion was after all the better part of valour, and with a small disdainful swish of its tail it leapt from gatepost to apple tree and disappeared through the kitchen window.

'Hello there.' The voice, at least, was pleasant, as was the smile that accompanied it. The young man took his feet from the upended beer crate upon which they had been resting, swung long legs to one side and unravelled himself from the deckchair. His hair was brown, untidy, and a little too long, his eyes were blue and he was tall, and slim; a combination that might under other circumstances have impressed me. I was not, however, at that moment, in any mood to be impressed. 'You're the new neighbour, aren't you? From Number Five?' He grinned again, engagingly. 'What can I do for you? The traditional cup of sugar? A pint of milk? Or – ' he gestured to the glass beside the chair, and again that disconcerting smile flickered, ' – would you settle for a beer?'

'No,' I said, repressively. 'No, thank you. I haven't come to borrow anything. And I certainly haven't come for a beer. In fact, much as I dislike to, I've come to complain. About that – that terrorist that I suppose you call a cat.'

The smile vanished. He looked innocently blank.

'The black devil that's sitting not a million miles from here – on your kitchen windowsill in fact – looking as if butter wouldn't melt in its mouth,' I added, helpfully sweet.

'Ah,' he said. 'Ah, yes.' He eyed me warily. 'He can be a bit of a pest, can't he?'

'A bit of a pest?' I was outraged. 'If that isn't the understatement of the year then I don't know what is! He's bullied my poor little Tabs from pillar to post, torn her ear to shreds, stolen my food, wrecked my kitchen, broken my favourite jug – !' I ran out of steam and breath at approximately the same time, and stopped. 'You call that being a bit of a pest?'

He was watching me with suspiciously bright eyes.

'You think it's funny?' I asked, as quietly as I could manage.

'No. No, of course not!' The words were hasty. Too hasty. The laughter he was perfectly obviously trying to suppress suddenly got the better of him. I stood, icily unamused, as he almost choked.

'You do think it's funny,' I said at last, so collectedly that I was positively proud of myself.

'No. Honestly, I don't.' He managed to inject a mollifying modicum of sincerity into the words. 'It's just – well, amongst other things I wondered what you were thinking of doing with that?' He pointed.

I had forgotten the wooden spoon. With as much dignity as it was possible to muster, which admittedly wasn't much, I pulled it from my pocket. 'I was going to hit the cat with it,' I said.

'Well of course. What else would you do with a spoon that size?'

This time, oddly, it was I who, infuriatingly, had to resist laughter.

He spread large, appealing, long-fingered hands. 'Look – can't we start from the beginning again? I'm Tom Marsden. And I'm pleased to meet you. In fact, frankly, I've been trying to meet you for the last three weeks. And I'm sorry about the hooligan cat, I honestly am. I'll take him to obedience classes or something. Most people just belt him and sling him out; though I know better than most that you have to catch him first. Now, look – please – won't you stay and have a beer? Or a glass of wine? It isn't exactly vintage stuff but it's very drinkable.'

I held out for all of ten seconds. He really did have a very nice smile. 'Well – perhaps just a small glass of wine – '

One small and two rather larger glasses of wine later we had established a certain pleasant rapport. By the time he invited me to stay for lunch we were almost friends. It was with real regret that I declined.

' – honestly, I've got so much to do. There isn't a single shelf in the entire house, there are curtains to put up – and although my old flat wasn't exactly enormous I suppose I acquired bits and pieces as I went along and always found somewhere to put them. Here – ' I shrugged, ' – it's a shambles. I'm sorry, but I really do need to get myself sorted out, or I'll find myself disappearing down the hole in the middle – '

We were standing by the gate. 'Well. Perhaps another day?'

I nodded. His eyes really were very blue.

'Give me a shout if you need a hand.'

I nodded again.

'Perhaps we could go for a drink some time? There's a good pub in the village.'

'Yes. That would be nice.' For some strange reason I appeared to be rooted to the spot. It was the wine, of course. I really shouldn't drink more than one glass on an empty stomach. 'I'll be going then.'

'Right.'

This time I did manage to turn away and set off down the lane. The sun was warm on my back, a blackbird sang in the apple tree. I returned Mrs Lovelace's smile with a grin as broad as the Cheshire Cat's. At my gate I paused and looked back. Tom was still standing, watching me. As I turned he lifted a hand. I returned the wave.

He certainly seemed to be a very interesting young man.

Mind you, I told myself as I stood at the kitchen door surveying the wreckage, I still haven't forgiven that damned cat.

I didn't even pretend to be surprised when he turned up later in the afternoon.

I was back on the landing, doing a precarious balancing act with a pile of books and my makeshift shelves when I heard his voice from below in the kitchen. 'Hello? Anyone there?'

'Up here.'

His head and shoulders appeared. 'You forgot something.'

'Oh?'

'One rather large wooden spoon. You left it behind.'

I couldn't help smiling. 'Thank you.'

'And – ' he came up another couple of steps and with a flourish produced from behind his back a bunch of fresh-picked roses wrapped in newspaper. 'An apology. From the terrorist. He promises to behave himself in future.'

Something about his smile, the bright gleam of his eyes, seemed to be having a distracting effect on my concentration. 'I'll believe that when I see it,' I said, and let go of the books.

Predictably my carefully constructed edifice of bricks and planks collapsed around me. Books slid and scattered across the floor, avalanched through the banisters and down the stairs. We watched in silence until the earth-quake had subsided and the last volume had settled.

Tom lifted his head and looked at me, eyebrows raised. 'Back to the drawing board,' I said.

He contemplated the chaos about him. Pushed me the roses through the banisters. 'I think,' he said, 'that you need a hand. Don't you?'

Well, I suppose you could say that was that, really. He spent the afternoon doing clever things with brackets and bits of wood while I scrubbed floors and cleaned windows. We ate a Chinese takeaway at the kitchen table and discovered a shared passion for Dvořák and Dire Straits. We argued, amiably, about politics, religion and the best way to cook spaghetti, and with more passion about the wretched performance of the England cricket team. I accepted his invitation to lunch the following day. On the Monday night he came to supper with me, and on the Tuesday he kissed me as we strolled home from the White Hart.

It just shows – you never know what's round the corner. When I think of what I'd always said about the obviously idiotic concept of love at first sight . . .

The following weekend the weather changed and it became unseasonally cold. I came home to a note through my door, *'Fire's alight, supper's in the oven. Coming? T.'*

I grabbed a bottle and a couple of candles and went.

Tom's small, untidy sitting room with its rugs and books and its old, squashy furniture looked cosy as a Christmas card. The curtains were closed, the fire roared up the chimney.

The cat, sleek and black and sleepy eyed sat, lord of all he surveyed, on the hearth.

'I suppose,' I said, looking at it through my wine glass, 'that under the circumstances you and I should bury the hatchet?'

The cat said nothing.

'I have to admit you've been a bit better behaved lately. Though I have my suspicions about the sardines that went missing from the pantry on Thursday.'

He lifted a paw, contemplated it, licked it with precision and delicacy.

I raised my glass to it. 'So. Here's to new beginnings. I know I owe you a favour, but just don't push your luck, OK?'

The cat stood, yawned, stretched, claws unfurled.

'You know the silly thing?'

The animal looked at me, eyes gleaming.

'I don't even know your name. What is it? I must say you don't look much like a Tiddles.'

Silence. Then, from behind me Tom said, 'Well, go on. Tell the lady. What's your name?' He rested a hand on my shoulder and, smiling, I covered it with my own.

'He's doing a Rumpelstiltskin,' I said. 'He's not going to tell me. Do I have to spend all night guessing?'

'You may have to,' Tom said, 'since he certainly doesn't seem about to let it slip. Why don't we just call him Cupid and be done?' Still holding my hand he came round the settee and settled himself beside me.

'Yes, but – what is his real name?'

Tom slipped an arm about my shoulders and snuggled closer. 'I don't know,' he said, and kissed me.

'What do you mean, you don't know? How can you not know the name of your own cat?'

He put his lip to my ear, and whispered.

'If you can possibly bring yourself –' I said after a moment, interrupting his laughter, ' – to spare me the lecture about jumping to conclusions, then I might consider forgiving you for lying to me.'

'I didn't lie, my darling.' His breath was warm and gentle in my ear. 'If you remember, I never said he was my cat. You did. I just didn't deny it, in case you took your wooden spoon elsewhere. Now, come on – admit it – that would have been a pity. Wouldn't it?'

Undeniably true. And while we set about proving it that nice Mrs Lovelace's great hooligan of a cat warmed its wicked back at our fire and looked on with positively proprietary satisfaction.

The Fat of the Cat

GOTTFRIED KELLER

I

In Seldwyla, when someone has made a bad bargain, people say, 'He has tried to buy the fat off the cat!' It is a queer saying and a puzzling one. But there is an old, half-forgotten story which tells how it first came to be used and what it really means.

Several hundred years ago, so runs the tale, there lived in Seldwyla an old, old lady whose only companion was a handsome grey cat. This fine creature was always to be seen with his mistress; he was quiet and clever, and never harmed anyone who let him alone. 'Everything in moderation' was his motto – everything, that is, except hunting, which was his one great enjoyment. But even in this sport he was never savage or cruel. He caught and killed only the most impudent and troublesome mice; the others he merely chased away. He left the small circle in which he hunted only once in a while, when some particularly bold mouse roused his anger. Then there was no stopping him! He would follow the foolhardy nibbler everywhere. And if the mouse tried to hide at some neighbour's place, the cat would walk up to the owner, make a deep bow and politely ask permission to hunt there. And you may be sure he was always allowed to do so, for he never

12

disturbed anything in the house. He did not knock over the butter-crocks, never stole milk from pails, never sprang up on the sides of ham which hung against the wall. He went about his business very quietly, very carefully; and, after he had captured his mouse, disappeared just as quietly as he came. He was neither naughty nor wild, but friendly to everyone. He never ran away from well-behaved children and allowed them to pinch his ears a little without scratching them. Even when stupid people annoyed him, he would simply get out of their way or thump them over the hand if they tried to take liberties with him.

Glassy – for this was the name that was given him on account of his smooth and shiny fur – lived his days happily in comfort and modesty. He did not sit on his mistress's shoulder just to snatch a piece of food from her fork, but only when he saw that it pleased her to have him there. He was neither selfish nor lazy, but only too happy to go walking with his mistress along the little river that flowed into the lake near by. He did not sleep the whole day long on his warm pillow behind the stove. Instead, he loved to lie wide-awake, thinking out his plans, at the foot of the stairs, or prowling along the edge of the roof, considering the ways of the world like the grey-haired philosopher that he was. His calm life was interrupted only in spring, when the violets blossomed, and in autumn, when the warm days of Indian summer imitated Maytime. At such times Glassy would stroll over the roofs like an inspired poet and sing the strangest and most beautiful songs. He had the wildest adventures during these nights, and when he would come home after his reckless wanderings, he looked so rough and towsled that his mistress used to say, 'Glassy, how *can* you behave that way! Aren't you ashamed of yourself?' But Glassy felt no shame; he thought he was now a regular man-of-the-world. Never answering a word, he would sit quietly in his corner, smoothing his fur and

13

washing himself behind the ears, as innocently as if he had never stirred from the fireside.

One day this pleasant manner of life came to an unhapy end. Just as Glassy became a full-grown cat, his mistress died of old age, leaving him an unprotected orphan. It was Glassy's first misfortune, and his piercing cries and long wailing showed how deep was his grief. He followed the funeral part of the way down the street and then returned to the house, wandering helplessly from room to room. But his good sense told him he must serve the heirs of his mistress as faithfully as he did her – he must continue to keep the mice in their place, be ever watchful and ready, and (whenever necessary) give the new owners good advice. But these foolish people would not let Glassy get near them. On the contrary, whenever they saw him, they threw the slippers and the foot-stool of his departed mistress at his bewildered head. After eight days of quarrelling among themselves, they boarded up the windows, closed the house, and – while they went to court to see who really owned it – no one was allowed to set foot inside the doors.

Poor Glassy, thrown into the street, sat on the doorstep of his old home and no one took the slightest notice of him. All day long he sat and he sat and he sat. At night he roamed about the roofs and, at first, he spent a great part of the time hidden and asleep, trying to forget his cares. But hunger drove him to people again, to be at hand whenever there might be a chance of getting a scrap of something to eat. As food grew scarcer, his eyes grew sharper; and, as his whole attention was given to this one thing, he ceased to look like his old self. He ran from door to door and stole about the streets, sometimes pouncing gladly upon a greasy morsel that, in the old days, he would never even have sniffed at. Often, indeed, he found nothing at all. He grew hungrier and thinner from day to day; he who was once so plump and proud became scraggy and timid. All his courage, his dignity, his wisdom and his philosophy vanished. When the boys came from school, he crawled behind a barrel or into an old can, daring to stick his head out only to see whether one of them would throw away a crust of bread. In the old days he could look the fiercest dog straight in the eye, and many was the time he punished them severely. Now he ran away from the commonest cur. And while, in the times gone by, he used to run away from rough and unpleasant people, now he would let them come quite near, not because he liked them any better, but because – who knows? – they might toss him something to chew on. Even when, instead of feeding him, coarse men would strike him or twist his tail, still he would not cry. He would just sit there and look longingly at the hand which had hurt him, but which had such a heavenly smell of sausage or herring.

The wise and gentle Glassy had, indeed, come down in the world. He was starving as he sat one day, on his stone, dreaming and blinking in the sunlight. As he lay there, the town-wizard, a sly magician by the name of Pineiss, came that way, noticed the cat and stopped in front of him. Hoping for something good, Glassy sat meekly on his stone, waiting to see what Pineiss would do or say. At the first words, Glassy lost hope, for Pineiss said, 'Well, cat, would you like to sell your fat?' He thought that the magician was only making fun of his skinny appearance. But still he answered demurely, 'Ah, Master Pineiss likes to joke!'

'But I am serious!' the wizard replied, 'I need cat's fat in my witchery; I work wonders with it. But it must be taken only if the cat is willing to give it – otherwise the magic will not work. I am thinking if ever a cat was in a position to make a good bargain, you're the very one! Come into my service; I'll feed you as you never have been fed. I'll give you the richest of warm milk and the sweetest of cakes. You will grow fat as a dumpling on juicy sausages, chicken livers and roast quail. On my enormous roof – which is well known as the greatest hunting-ground in the world for cats – there are hundreds of interesting corners and inviting dark holes. And there, on the top of that old roof, there grows a wonderful grass, green as an emerald. When you play in it, you will think you are a tiger in the jungle, and – if you have eaten too many rich things – a few nibbles of it will cure the worst stomach-ache. My mice are the tenderest – and the slowest – in the country, and catnip grows in the back of my garden. Thus, you see, *you* will be happy and healthy, and *I* will have a good supply of useful fat. What do you say?'

Glassy had listened to this speech with ears pricked up and his mouth watering. But he was so weak that he did not quite understand the bargain, and he said, 'That isn't half bad, Master Pineiss. If I only understood how I could hold on to my reward! If I have to lose my life to give you my fat, how am I to enjoy all these fine things when I am dead?'

'Hold on to your reward?' answered the magician, impatiently. 'Your reward is in the enjoyment of all you can eat and drink *while* you are alive. That ought to be clear enough. But I don't want to force you!' And he shrugged his shoulders and made as if he were going to walk off.

But Glassy cried, quickly and eagerly, 'Wait! Wait! I will say yes on one condition. You must wait a few days *after* I have reached my roundest and fattest fullness before you take my life. I must have a little time so that I am not torn away too suddenly when I am so happy, so full of food and contentment.'

'So be it!' said Pineiss with seeming generosity. 'Until the next full-moon you shall enjoy yourself as much as you like. But it cannot last a minute longer than that. For, when the moon begins to wane, the fat will grow less powerful and my well-earned property will shrink.'

So they came to an agreement. Pineiss disappeared for a moment. Then he came running back with a great quill-pen and an enormous roll of paper. This was the contract, and it was so large because it was full of queer words that lawyers are fond of – words like 'whereas' and 'notwith-standing' and 'herinbefore' and 'thereunto' and 'party-of-the-second-part' and others too long and expensive to print here. Without stopping to read it through, Glassy signed his name neatly on the dotted line, which proved how well he had been brought up.

'Now you can come and have lunch with me,' said the magician. 'We dine at twelve, sharp.'

'Thanks,' replied the famished cat, 'I will be pleased to accept your invitation,' and a few minutes before noon he was waiting at the table of Master Pineiss.

From that moment Glassy began to enjoy a wonderful month. He had nothing else to do but to eat all the delicate dishes that were put before him, to watch the magician at work and go climbing about the roof. It was really a most heavenly sort of roof – dark, high and pointed like a steeple – just the sort of a top for a house of magic and mystery.

II

But you should know something about the town-magician. Master Pineiss was a jack-of-all-trades. He did a thousand different things. He cured sick people, removed warts, cleared houses of rats, drove out roaches, pulled teeth, loaned money, and collected bills. He took charge of all the orphans and widows, made black ink out of char-coal and, in his spare time, cut quill-pens, which he sold twelve for a penny. He sold ginger and pepper, candy and axle-grease, shoe-nails and perfume, books and button-hooks, sausages and string. He repaired clocks, extracted corns, painted signs, delivered papers, forecasted the weather, and prepared the farmer's almanac. He did a great many good things in the daytime very cheaply; and, for much higher prices, he did other things (which are not spoken about) after it grew dark. Although he was a magician, his principal business was not witchcraft; he made magic and worked spells only for household use. The people of Seldwyla needed *someone* who would do all sorts of unpleasant jobs and mysterious things for them, so they had elected him town-wizard. And, for many years, Pineiss had worked hard, early and late, to do whatever they wished – and a few things to please himself.

In this house, full of all sorts of curious objects, Glassy had plenty of time to see, smell, and taste everything. Tired out with doing nothing, he lay on large, soft cushions all day long. At first he paid attention to nothing else but eating. He devoured greedily whatever Pineiss offered him and could scarcely wait from one meal to the next. Often, indeed, he ate too much, and then he would have to go and chew the green grass on the roof to be well enough – so he could eat still more. His master was well pleased with this hunger, and thought to himself, 'That cat will soon be round and fat – and the more I give him now the less he will be able to eat later.'

So Pineiss built a little countryside for Glassy. He planted a tiny forest of a dozen baby pine-trees, made a few hills of stones and moss, and scooped out a hole with water so there would be a lake. In the trees he stuck sweet roast finches, stuffed larks, baked sparrows, and small potted pigeons. The hills were full of the most exciting mouse-holes; and inside them Pineiss had hidden more than a hundred juicy mice, which had been fattened on wheat-flour and broiled in bacon. Some of these delicious mice were easily within reach of Glassy's paw; others (to give him more of an appetite) had to be dug for, but all were on strings so that Glassy could play he was chasing without losing them. The little lake was filled with fresh milk every morning and, as Glassy was fond of fishing, young sardines and tender goldfish floated in that delightful pool.

It was Glassy's idea of Paradise, a cat's heaven on earth. He ate and ate and ate. And in between his meals, he nibbled. When he did not eat, he rested. And *how* he slept! It got so that the mice began to gather about his pillow where he lay and mock at him. And Glassy never stirred – not even when their tails whisked across his whiskers! Now that Glassy could eat all he wanted and whenever he wished to, his whole appearance changed. He looked like his old self: his fur became glossy and smooth again, his eyes grew large and fiery, and his mind acted more cleverly than before. He stopped being greedy; he no longer stuffed himself just for the pleasure of eating. He began to think seriously about life in general – and about his own in particular. One day, as he was thoughtfully tearing apart a cooked quail, he saw that the little insides of the bird were packed with unspoilt food. Some green herbs, black and white seeds, a few crumbs, grains of corn and one bright red berry were crowded together – just as tight as a mother packs her boy's lunch-basket when he goes off for the day. As Glassy saw this, he grew still more thoughtful. And the more thoughtful he grew, the sadder he became. At last he began to think out aloud. 'Poor bird,' he said, scratching his head, 'what good did all this fine food do you? You had to search so hard for these crumbs, fly who knows how many miles to find those grains of corn. That red berry was snatched at great risk from the bird-catcher's trap. And all for what? You thought you ate to keep yourself alive, but the fatter you grew, the nearer you came to your end. . . . Ah, me,' he sighed deeply, 'why did I ever make such a wretched bargain! I did not think – I was too foolish with hunger. And now that I can think again, all I can see is that I will end like this poor quail. When I am fat enough, I will have to die – for no other reason except that I will be fat enough! A fine end for a lively and intelligent cat-of-the-world! Oh, if I could only get out of this fix!'

He kept on brooding and worrying, yet he could think of no way to escape his fate. But, like a wise man, he controlled himself and his appetite and tried to put off the final day as long as possible. He refused to lie on the great cushions, which Pineiss had placed all over so that he could sleep a great deal and get fat quicker. Instead of soft places, he rested himself on the cold sill or lay down on the hard stones whenever he was tired. Rather than munch the roasted birds and stuffed mice, he began to hunt in earnest on the tall roof-top. And the living mice he caught with his own efforts tasted far better to him than all the rich goodies from Pineiss's kitchen – especially since they did not make him so fat. The constant exercise made him strong and slender – much to Pineiss's astonishment. The magician could not understand how Glassy remained so active and healthy; he expected to see a great clumsy animal that never moved from its pillows and was just one enormous roll of fat.

After some time had passed and Glassy, instead of wallowing in fat, grew still stronger and handsomer without losing his slender figure, Pineiss determined to do something. 'What is the matter, Glassy?' he harshly inquired one day. 'What is wrong with you? Why don't you eat the good things that I prepare for you with such care? Why don't you fetch the roast birds down from the trees? Why don't you dig the dainty broiled mice out of their holes? Why have you stopped fishing in the milky sea? Why don't you take better care of yourself? Why do you refuse to lie on the nice, soft cushions? Why do you wear yourself out instead of resting comfortably and growing good and round?'

'Because, Master Pineiss,' answered Glassy, 'I feel much better this way! I have only a little while to live – and shouldn't I enjoy that short time in the way it suits me?'

'Not at all!' exclaimed Pineiss. 'You should live the sort of life that will make you thick and soft! But I know what you are driving at! You think you'll make a monkey of me and prevent me from doing what we have agreed upon. You think I'll let you go on like this for ever? Don't you believe it! I tell you it is your duty to eat and drink and take care of yourself so that you'll grow layer upon layer of fat! I tell you to stop behaving the way you have been doing! And if you don't act according to the contract, I'll have something still more serious to say!'

Glassy stopped purring (which he had begun only to show how calm he was) and said quietly, 'I don't remember a single word in the contract against my being healthy or living the kind of life I liked. There was nothing in the agreement that did not allow me to eat whatever food I wished, and even chase after it if I cared to! If the town-magician took it for granted that I was a lazy, greedy, good-for-nothing, that is not my fault! You do a thousand good things every day, so do this one also – let us remain good friends as we are. And don't forget that you can only use my fat if you get it by fair means!'

'Stop your chattering!' cried Pineiss angrily. 'Don't you dare to lecture me! Perhaps I had better put an end to you at once!' He seized Glassy sharply, whereupon the surprised cat struck out and scratched him sharply on the hand. Pineiss looked thoughtful for a moment. Then he said, 'Is that the way things are, you beast? Very well. Then I declare that, according to our agreement, I consider you fat enough. I am satisfied with the way you are, and I will act according to the contract. In five days the moon will be full, and until then you can live the way you wish, just as it is written down. You can do exactly as you please until then – and not one minute longer!'

With this, he turned his back and left the cat to his own thoughts.

These thoughts, as you can believe, were painful and gloomy. Was the time really so near when Glassy would have to lose his skin? And, with all his cleverness, was there nothing he could do? What miracle could save him now? Sighing, he climbed up to the roof, whose pointed ridge rose like a threatening sign against the happy autumn sky. It was early evening and the moon began to climb up the other side of the roof. Soon the whole town was flooded with blue light and a sweet song sounded in

21

Glassy's ears. It was the voice of a snow-white puss whose body was shining like silver on a neighbouring roof. Immediately Glassy forgot the thought of death and answered with his loudest and loveliest notes. Still singing, he hurried to her side and soon was engaged in the most terrific battle with three other gallant cats. After he had defeated his rivals, he turned to his lady, who met his ardent glance with a modest but encouraging miaow.

Glassy was charmed. He remained with the white stranger day and night, and was her devoted slave. Without giving a single thought to Pineiss, he never came home, but remained close to his lady-love. He sang like a nightingale every moonlight night, went on wild hunts with his fair companion, and was in continual fights with other tom-cats who wanted to come too close. Many times he was almost clawed to pieces, many times he was tumbled from the roof; but he only shook his towsled fur and came back to the struggle as hardy as ever. All these adventures – moments of peaceful talk and hours of angry quarrels, love and jealousy, friendship and fights – all of these exciting days made a great change in Glassy. The wild life showed its effects. And finally, when the moon was full, the poor animal looked wilder, tougher and thinner than ever.

At this moment, Pineiss (who had not seen his cat for almost a week) leaned out of the window and cried, 'Glassy, Glassy! Where are you? Don't you know it's time to come home!' And Glassy, leaving his partner, who trotted off contentedly, came back to the magician's house. It was dark as he entered the kitchen and Pineiss came towards him, rustling the paper contract, and saying, 'Come, Glassy, good Glassy.' But as soon as the magician had struck a light and saw the cat sitting there defiantly, nothing but a bundle of bones and ragged hair, he flew into a terrible rage. Jumping up and down with anger, he screamed, 'So that's the way you tried to cheat me! You villian, you ragamuffin! You evil parcel of bones! Wait! I'll show you!' Beside himself with fury, he seized a broom and sprang at Glassy. But the desperate cat was no longer frightened. With his back high in the air, he faced his maddened owner. His hair stood up straight, sparks flew from his green eyes, and his appearance was so terrifying that Pineiss retreated two or three steps. The town-wizard began to be afraid; for it suddenly struck him that this might also be a magician, and a more powerful one than himself. Uncertain and anxious, he asked in a low voice, 'Is the honourable gentleman perhaps in the same profession as myself? Ah, it must be a very learned enchanter who can not only put on the appearance of a cat, but change his size whenever he wishes – large and strong one minute, then suddenly as skinny as a skeleton!'

Glassy calmed himself and spoke honestly. 'No, Master Pineiss, I am no magician. It is nothing but my wildness, my love of life, which has taken away my, I mean your, fat. Let us start over again, and this time I promise you I will eat anything and everything you bring me. Fetch out your longest sausage – and you will see!'

Still angry, Pineiss picked Glassy up by his collar and threw him into the goose-pen, which was empty, and cried, 'Now see if your love of life will help you. Let's see if your wildness is greater than my witchcraft! Now, my plucked bird, you'll remain in your cage – and there you will eat or die!'

Pineiss began at once to broil a huge sausage that had such a heavenly flavour that he himself had to taste it before he stuck it between the bars. Glassy finished it, skin and all, without stopping for breath. And, as he sat comfortably cleaning his whiskers and smoothing his fur, he said to himself, 'Ah, this love of life is a fine thing, after all! Once again it has saved me from a cruel fate. Now I will rest awhile and keep my wits about me. This prison is not so bad, and something good may come of having nothing to do but to think and eat for a change. Everything has its time. Yesterday a little trouble; today a little quiet; tomorrow something different. Yes, life is a very interesting affair.

Now Pineiss saw to it that no time was wasted. All day long he chopped and seasoned and mixed and boiled and basted and stewed and baked and broiled and roasted and fried. In short, he cooked such delicious meals that Glassy simply could not resist. The delighted cat ate and ate until Pineiss was afraid that there would not be enough left in the house for the smallest mouse to nibble at.

When, finally, Glassy seemed fat enough, Pineiss did not delay a moment. Right in front of his victim's eyes, he set out pots and pans and made a great fire in the stove. Then he sharpened a large knife, lifted the latch of Glassy's cell, pulled the poor cat out (first taking care to lock the kitchen door) and said cheerfully, 'Come, my young friend. Now to business! First, we shall cut your head off; then, when that's done, we shall skin you. Your fur will make a nice warm cap for me and maybe even a pair of gloves. Or shall I skin you first and then cut off your head?'

'No,' answered Glassy meekly, 'if it's the same to you, I'd rather have my head off first.'

'Right you are, poor fellow,' said Pineiss, putting some more wood on the big fire, 'I don't want to hurt you more than necessary. Let us do only what is right.'

'That is a true saying,' said Glassy, with a deep sigh, and hung his head. 'Oh, if I had only remembered that – if I only had done what was right, I could die with a clear conscience, for I die willingly. But a wrong which I have done makes it hard for me.'

'What sort of a wrong?' asked Pineiss inquisitively.

'Ah, what's the use of talking about it now,' sighed Glassy. 'What's done is done, and it's too late to cry over it.'

'You rascal!' Pineiss went on. 'You must indeed be a wicked scoundrel who richly deserves to die. But what did you really *do*? Tell me at once! Have you hid anything of mine? Or stolen something? Have you done me a great injury which I know nothing about? Confess your crimes immediately or I'll skin and boil you alive! Will you talk – or die a horrible death?'

'But you don't understand,' said Glassy. 'It isn't anything about you that troubles my conscience. It concerns the ten thousand gold guldens of my poor dear mistress. . . . But what's the sense of talking! Only – when I look at you, I think perhaps it is not too late, after all. When I look at you, I see a handsome man still in the prime of life, wise and active and . . . Tell me, Master Pineiss, have you never cared to marry – to come into a good family and a fortune? But what am I talking about! Such a smart and busy man as you has no time for such idle thoughts. Why should such a learned magician think about silly women! Of course, it's no good denying the fact that a woman is very comforting to have around the house. To be sure, a wife can be a great help to a busy man – obliging in her manner, careful about his tastes, sparing with his money and extravagant only in his praise. A good wife will do a thousand things to please to her husband. When he is downcast, she will make him happy; when he is happy, she will make him happier. She will fetch his slippers when he wants to be comfortable, stroke his beard and kiss him when he wants to be petted. When he is working, she will let nobody disturb him, but go quietly about her household duties or tell the neighbours what a wonderful man she has. . . . But here I am talking like a fool at the very door of death! How could such a wise man care for such vanities! . . . Excuse me, Master Pineiss, and cut my head off.'

But Pineiss spoke up quickly, 'Wait a moment, can't you! Tell me, where is such a woman? And are you sure she has ten thousand gold guldens?'

'Ten thousand gold guldens?' asked Glassy.

'Yes,' answered Pineiss, impatiently. 'Isn't that what you were just talking about?'

'Oh, those are two separate things. The money lies buried in a certain place.'

'And what is it doing there? Who does it belong to?' Pineiss asked eagerly.

'To nobody – that's just what is on my conscience! I should have seen to it that the money was put in good hands. Really, the guldens belong to the man who marries the woman I have described. But how is a person to bring those three things together in this stupid town: a fair white lady, ten thousand guldens, and a wise and upright man? That is too hard a task for one poor cat!'

'Now listen,' advised Pineiss. 'If you don't tell me the whole story in the proper order, I'll cut off your tail and both your ears to start with! So begin!'

'Well, if you wish it, I will go ahead,' said Glassy, and sat down on his haunches, 'although this delay only makes my troubles worse. But still, I am willing to live a little longer – for your sake, Master Pineiss.'

The magician stuck his sharp knife in the bare boards between Glassy and himself, sat down on a barrel, and the cat told the following story.

III

'You may know, Master Pineiss,' he began, 'that the good lady who used to be my mistress died unmarried. She was a quiet person – people knew her only as an old maid who did good to a great many and harm to none. But she was not always so plain and quiet. As a young girl, she was the most beautiful creature for miles around and young men came flocking from far and wide. Everyone who saw her dancing eyes and laughing mouth fell in love with her at once. She had hundreds of offers of marriage and many a duel was fought on her account. She, too, had decided to marry – and she had enough candidates to choose from. There came bold suitors and shy ones, honest lovers and sly ones, merchants, cavaliers, landowners, loud wooers and silent adorers, suitors who were boastful, suitors who were bashful – in short, the lady had as great a choice as any girl could wish. But she had one great fault: she was suspicious of everybody. Besides her beauty, she had a fortune of many thousand gold guldens – and it was just because of this that she never could decide which man to marry. She had managed her affairs so shrewdly that her property had grown still larger, and (as people always judge others by themselves) she thought that the suitors only wanted her because of her fortune. If a man happened to be rich, she thought, "Oh, he only wants to increase his wealth. He wouldn't look at me if I were poor." If a poor man proposed to her, she would think, "Ah, he's only after my gold guldens." The foolish lady did not realize that she was thinking about her money much more than the suitors did, and what she believed to be *their* greed for gold was really something in her own nature. Several times she was as good as engaged, but at the last minute something in her lover's face would convince her that he, too, was only after her wealth. And so, with a heavy heart, but a stubborn will, she would have no more to do with him.

'When they brought her presents or gave feasts in her honour, she would say, "I am not so foolish a fish to be caught with such bait!" And she would give their gifts to the poor and send the givers off. In fact, she put them to so many tests and treated them so badly that after a time, all of the right sort of men stayed away. The only men that came to win her were sharp and cunning fellows, and this made her more suspicious than ever. So, in the end, she who was only looking for an honest heart, found herself surrounded by mean and dishonest persons. She could not bear it any longer. One day she sent all the grasping suitors from her doors, locked up the house and set out for Italy, for the city of Milan, where she had a cousin. Her thoughts were heavy and sorrowful as she travelled across the Alps, and her eyes were blind to those great mountains, standing like proud kings with sunset crowning their happy

heads. Even in Italy, beneath the bluest skies, she remained pale; no matter how light the heavens were, her thoughts were dark.

'But one day the clouds began to lift from her heart, and the winds (which had never spoken to her before) whispered little songs in her ear. For a young man had come to visit at her cousin's house, a young man who looked so fair and talked so pleasantly that she fell in love with him at once. He was a handsome youngster, well educated and of fine family, not too rich and not too poor. He had just ten thousand guldens (which had been left to him by his parents) and with this sum he was going to start a silk business in Milan. Highly educated though he was, he seemed as innocent as a child, and, though only a merchant, he carried his sword with a knightly air. All of this so pleased the fair lady that she could scarcely contain herself. She was happy again – and if she had little moments of sadness, it was only when she feared that the young man might not return her affection. The lovelier she grew, the more she worried whether or not she made a good impression on him.

'As for the young merchant, he had never seen anyone so charming and (to tell the truth) he was even more in love with her than she was with him. But he was very shy and most modest. "How can any man," he said to his anxious heart, "hope to win such beauty for himself? How can I expect one so far beyond me even to consider me? No, no, I must not think of it; it is impossible." For several weeks he tried to conquer his love or, at least, to hide it from the world. But his nature was so warm and sincere he could not disguise it. Whenever he was near his adored one, or even when her name was mentioned, he trembled, grew confused; and it was easy to see where his thoughts were. His very timid manner made my mistress still fonder of him – especially since he was so different from all her other suitors of the past – and her love grew greater with every day.

'Here was a peculiar situation. Two hearts were on fire; cupids were fanning the blaze – and yet nothing happened. Here were two people head-over-heels in love with each other – and remaining as distant as strangers. He, for his part, was too bashful to declare his desire; she, naturally, was too modest to speak of hers. It was a curious comedy, and the people of Milan watched it being played with keen enjoyment. It must be confessed that she helped him a bit – not, of course, with words, but with smiles and little expressions of pleasure whenever he gave her some trifle, and with a hundred unspoken hints that women understand so well. Things could not go on like this much longer. Finally the day came. People were beginning to gossip, and he felt it was not fair to her to let matters stand as they were. "Better put an end to it," he thought, "even though it will kill my last hope!" So he came to her and, frightened but desperate, blurted out his love in a few words. He gave her little time to consider, his sentences came so fast. It never occurred to him that a young lady might like to delay the happy moment before answering; he did not know that women, even when they are most in love, say "no" at first when they expect to say "yes" afterwards. He just poured out his heart in one burst, ending with, "Do not keep me in agony! If I have spoken rashly, let the blow fall at once! With me it is one thing or the other: life or death, yes or no! Speak – which is it to be?"

'Just as she was about to open her arms to him as an answer, her old distrust overcame her. The old suspicion flashed on her that, maybe, like all the others, he only cared for her fortune. "Possibly," an evil thought nudged her, "he is only saying this to get your money into his business. Don't yield to your impulse too quickly. Think it over. Test him first!" Therefore, instead of telling him the truth and completing her happiness, she listened to the voice of doubt and decided to put her lover to a severe test. As he stood waiting for her answer, she put a sad expression on her face and made up the following story.

'She was sorry, she said, that she could not say "yes" to him because (here she blushed at her falsehood) because she was already engaged to marry a man in her own country. "I am very fond of you, as you can tell," she continued, "and you see I confide in you. I regard you as a brother – but my heart belongs to the man who is waiting for me in my own land. It is a secret that nobody knows – how deeply I love this man and how impossible it would be for me to marry anyone else. We would have been married long ago, but my lover is a poor merchant and he expected to start in business with the money I was to bring him as a bridal gift. Everything was ready; he had started a shop; our wedding was to be celebrated in a few days – when hard times came and, overnight, most of my fortune was lost. My poor lover was beside himself; he did not know where to turn. As I said, he had already made preparations for a large business, and ordered supplies, had bought goods, and he owed for all of it, mostly to merchants in Italy. The day of payment is close at hand, and that is the reason I came here – in the hope of getting help from my relatives. But I see I have come at a bad time; nobody here can do anything for me – even my uncle will not risk his money. And if I return without assistance, I think I will die."

'She finished and buried her face in her hands, but watched between her fingers to see what effect this tale would have on the young man. During her story, he had grown pale and, as she ended, he was as white as a new napkin. But he did not utter a sound of complaint or speak another word about himself or his love. He only asked, with a sadness he tried to hide, what was the amount of money owed by her fiancé? "Ten thousand gold guldens," she answered, in a still sadder voice. The young merchant stood up, advised her to be of good cheer, and left the room without telling her how deeply her story had moved him.

The poor fellow, of course, believed every word of it and his affection for her was so great that he made up his mind to help her, even though she was (as he thought) going to marry another. Her happiness – not his – was the only thing he now considered. So he gathered together everything he possessed – all the money with which he was going to start in business – and in a few hours' time he was back again. He offered the money and asked her, as a great favour to him, to accept it until things improved after her marriage and her husband could afford to pay it back.

'Her eyes danced and her heart beat faster with a joy such as she had never felt before. She did not doubt any longer. "But where," she inquired, as if she could not imagine, "where did you get all this money?"

'"Oh," he replied, "I have had a lot of luck lately. Business has been very good with me, and I can spare this amount without any trouble."

'She looked closely at him and knew at once that he was lying: she realized it was his entire fortune he was sacrificing for her sake. Still, she pretended to believe him and thanked him heartily for his kindness. But, she said, she would accept his generous offer only on one condition: that, on a certain day, he would come to her wedding, as he was her best friend and, also, because he had made her marriage possible.

"No, no; do not ask me that," he pleaded, "ask me anything else!"

'"And why not?" she inquired, looking offended.

'He grew red and could scarcely speak for a moment. Finally, he said, "There are many reasons why I cannot come to your wedding. In the first place, my business demands me here. In the second place, I haven't the time to go to Switzerland. And," he added honestly, "there are other reasons."

'But she would not listen to him. "Unless you do as I ask, I will not accept a single one of these gold-pieces," she said firmly, and pushed the money towards him.

'So finally he consented, and she made him give her his hand in promise. As soon as he left her, she locked the treasure in her trunk and placed the key in the bosom of her dress. She did not stay in Milan more than a few days more, but travelled quickly back to Switzerland. Crossing the Alps was a far different experience than the first time; instead of shedding tears or carrying a dark expression, she laughed and sunshine leaped out of her eyes. It was a happy voyage and a happier home-coming. She aired the house from top to bottom, threw the doors wide open, had the floors polished and decorated the rooms as if she were expecting a royal prince. But at the head of her bed she placed the precious bag with the ten thousand gold gulden, and every night her happy head rested on it as comfortably as though the hard bundle were stuffed with the softest feathers. She could scarcely wait until the day came when he was expected, the day of beautiful surprises, when she would give him not only his own ten thousand gold guldens, but many times that amount, as well as her whole household and (here she must have blushed sweetly) herself. He would surely come; for she knew, no matter what happened, he would never break his word.

'But the day came and her beloved did not appear. And many days passed and many weeks, and still he did not come. She began to tremble, and all her hours were filled with fear. Her messengers searched for him on every highway. She stood at the window of her topmost balcony from daybreak till night blotted out the whitest roads. She sent despatches to Milan, letter after letter – to him, to relatives, to strangers – all without result. No answer came; no one could tell where he was to be found.

'At last, quite by accident,' continued Glassy, taking a breath in the midst of his long story, 'she learned that her belovèd had gone to the wars and that his body had been found, full of wounds, on the field of battle. Just before he died, he had turned to the man lying next to him – a Swiss soldier who happened to come from Seldwyla and who had not been so badly hurt – and had given him this message. "If you ever return to Seldwyla," he said, "seek out my love and ask her to forgive me for breaking my word. Tell her I loved her so much that I could not bear to go to her wedding and see her married to another. She will forgive me, I know – if she still remembers me – for she has also suffered because of love. Tell her I wish her a long lifetime of happiness."

'As soon as the soldier from Seldwyla reached home, he repeated these words (which, like a true Swiss, he had carefully put down in his note-book) to my mistress. The poor girl scarcely listened till he had finished the sad message. She beat her breast, tore her clothes and began to cry in such a loud voice that people far down the street thought that someone was being murdered. Her reason almost left her. She carried his bag of gold guldens about with her as tenderly as if it were a baby. At other times she would scatter the coins on the ground and throw herself, weeping, upon them. She lay there, day and night, without eating or drinking, kissing the cold metal, which was all she had left of him. Suddenly, one dark midnight, she gathered the treasure together, tied up the bag, and, carrying it into her garden, threw it down a deep well so that it should never belong to anyone else.'

As soon as Glassy had finished this sorrowful tale, Pineiss broke in eagerly, 'And is the money still there?'

'Yes,' replied Glassy, 'it is lying just where she dropped it. But don't forget that I am the person who was supposed to see that it was given to the right man – and my conscience is troubled because I have failed to do this.'

'Quite right,' Pineiss added hastily, 'your interesting story made me forget all about you. What you say makes me feel that, after all, it might not be a bad thing to have a wife with ten thousand guldens around the house. But she would have to be very pretty! . . . But there must be more to your story. Go on with the rest of it so I can see how it hangs together.'

Glassy continued, 'It was many years later that I first came to know the unfortunate lady I have been telling you about. She was a lonely old maid when she took me into her household, and I allow myself to believe that I was her best friend and her only comfort to the end of her days. As she saw this end drawing near, she related the whole story of her youth to me and told me, with many tears, how she had lost her whole life's happiness because of suspicion and distrust. "Let it be a warning to others," she said to me. "Ah, if I could only save some other girl from my fate!" It was then that she thought of a way to use the gold guldens lying in the well. "Promise me, Glassy, you will do just what I tell you?" she said to me one day, as I sat perched on her work-basket. And when I had promised, she spoke as follows: "Look around, keep your eyes open, until you find a beautiful girl who has no suitors because she is too poor. Then, if she should meet an honest, hard-working, handsome man – and the man loves her for herself alone – then you must help her. If the man will take an oath always to cherish and protect the girl, you are to give her the ten thousand gold guldens which are in the well; so that, on her wedding-day, the bride can surprise her husband by giving him this wedding-present." Those were almost the last words of my dear mistress. She died soon after speaking them. And, because of my bad luck, I have never been able to carry out her wishes.'

IV

There was a moment's silence as Glassy finished. Then Pineiss, with a greedy look and a distrustful voice, said, 'I'd like to believe you were telling me the truth. And maybe I *would* believe it – if you could let me have a peep at the place.'

'Why not?' answered Glassy. 'Only I warn you not to try to take the treasure out of its hiding-place. In the first place, the gold can only be removed at the right time; in the second place, it lies in a very dangerous part and you would be sure to break your neck if you tried to go after it.'

'Who said anything about taking it out?' protested Pineiss, somewhat frightened. 'Just lead me there so I can see whether you are telling the truth. Or, better still, I will lead you on a stout string so that you won't try to run away.'

'As you like!' replied Glassy. 'But take a long rope and a lantern with you, for it's a very deep and dark well.'

Pineiss followed this advice and led the cat to the garden of his dead mistress. They climbed over a crumbling wall and through an overgrown path which was almost blotted out by bushes and weeds. Finally they reached the spot. Pineiss tied the lantern to the rope and dropped it part of the way down the well, still holding Glassy with the other hand. Pineiss leaned over and trembled as he caught the glint of something shining in the depths.

'Sure enough!' he cried, excitedly. 'I see it! It's there, all right! Glassy, you are a wonder!' Then, looking eagerly down again, 'Are you sure there are ten thousand?'

'I can't swear to that,' replied Glassy, 'I have not been down there and I have never counted them! Also, the poor lady may have dropped a few when she carried them here, as she was so worried and nervous at the time.'

'Well, if there are two or three less,' said Pineiss, rubbing his chin, 'I will have to be satisfied.' He sat down on the rim of the well; Glassy also seated himself there and began to lick his paws. Pineiss scratched his head and began again. 'There is the treasure, and here is the man. But where is the girl?'

'What do you mean?' inquired Glassy.

'I mean there is only one thing missing to fulfil the old lady's wishes – the girl who is to give her husband the ten thousand guldens as a wedding-present and who has also all the other good qualities you spoke about.'

'Hum!' replied Glassy, with a wide yawn. 'The facts are not exactly the way you state them. The treasure is there, as you have seen, and the girl is ready, for I have already found her. But where can I find the right man who will marry under such conditions? For he will come into a great deal of money, and money brings with it a lot of cares and troubles. The man who has such a fortune has so much to keep him busy. He will have fine horses and many servants. He will have velvet suits and fresh linen sheets, cattle and hunting-dogs, oak furniture and a kitchen full of copper pots. He will have to remember what to tell his gardener to plant, will have to think of his property, his flowers, his wife, his crops, his armour, his old wines, his carriages, his rare books, his games – always his and his and his, from dawn till dark. Yes, owning things is a lot of trouble for a wealthy man. Then there are his rich clothes, his fat cows, his – '

But Pineiss interrupted him. 'Enough, you chatterbox! Will you ever stop babbling?' he cried, tugging at the string until Glassy miaowed with pain. For, you can imagine, Pineiss would gladly have had all these 'troubles' – and the more he heard about what such a fortune would bring, the more his mouth watered. 'Where is the young woman you have found?' he asked, suddenly.

Glassy acted as if he were astonished. 'Would you really care to try it? Are you sure?'

'Of course I am sure! Who else but *I* should have the fortune? Tell me, where is she?' demanded Pineiss.

'So that you can go there and be her suitor?' inquired Glassy.

'Absolutely.'

'Understand, then,' Glassy declared, 'the business can only be conducted through me. You must deal with *me*, if you want the gold and the girl!'

'I see,' said Pineiss slowly. 'You are trying to get me to give up our contract so you can save your head?'

'Is that so unnatural?' inquired Glassy, and began to wash his ears with wet paws.

'You think, you sly scoundrel, you'll cheat me in the end!' cried Pineiss.

'Is that possible?' mocked Glassy.

'I tell you, don't you dare betray me!'

'All right, then I won't,' said Glassy.

'If you do!' threatened Pineiss.

'Then I will.'

'Don't torture me like this!' said the excited Pineiss, almost crying.

And Glassy answered seriously. 'You are a remarkable man, Master Pineiss! You have me on a string and you pull on it until I can scarcely breathe. You have kept the sword of death hanging over me for two hours – what am I saying! – for two years, for two eternities! And now you say, "Don't torture me like this!" You ask that of *me*! . . . With your permission, let me tell you something,' Glassy continued in a calmer key. 'I would be only too happy to carry out the wishes of my late mistress and find the man fit for the lovely girl I spoke of – and you seem to be the right sort in every way. But it will not be easy for me to persuade the young lady. It is a difficult task. And if I must die . . .! No, I tell you frankly, Mr Pineiss, I must have my freedom before I speak another word. Therefore, take the cord from my neck and lay the contract here on the well-curb, or cut my head off – one or the other!'

'Why so excited and hot-headed?' asked Pineiss. 'Let us talk this thing over.'

But Glassy sat there, motionless, and for three or four minutes neither uttered a word. Then Pineiss, afraid that he might lose the fortune, reached into his pocket, took out the precious piece of paper, unfolded it, read it through once more and put it slowly down in front of the cat. The paper had scarcely reached the stone-curb before Glassy pounced upon it, chewing up every morsel. And, although he almost choked on some of the large words, he still considered it the best, the most wholesome meal he had ever enjoyed – and hoped it would make him healthy and fat!

As he finished this very satisfying dish, he turned to

the magician ceremoniously and said, 'You will hear from me without fail, Master Pineiss. I promise to deliver the treasure as well as the lovely lady. Therefore, make yourself ready: prepare to receive your future wife, who is as good as yours already, and be happy. Finally, allow me to thank you for your care and hospitality, and kindly excuse me while I take leave of you for a little while.'

So saying, Glassy went his way and rejoiced at the stupidity of the town-wizard who thought he could fool everyone. This man even tried to fool himself, thought Glassy, by declaring he was going to marry the girl for herself alone, whereas all he cared about was the sack of money. Glassy was already thinking of who the bride would be as he passed the street where the magician lived.

V

Across the way from the worker-in-magic, stood a house whose plaster front was whiter than milk and whose windows were always washed till they shone. The curtains were equally white and prim, and everything that one could see was as clean and stiffly ironed as the linen head-dress and collar worn by the woman who lived in this house. She was an old woman, very pious and very ugly. The starched edges and corners of her clothes were sharp; but they were no sharper than her long nose, her pointed chin, her spiteful tongue or her cutting glance. Yet she scarcely ever spoke to people, for she was so stingy she would not even spend her breath on them. Her neighbours disliked her intensely, but they had to admit she was religious – at least she seemed to be. Three times a day they watched her go to church; and every time the children saw her long nose coming down the street, they ran to get out of her way. Even the grown people ducked behind their doors if they had time. But still, even if nobody cared to go near her, she had a good reputation because of her continual prayers and church-going. So the strict old woman lived – never smiling, never mingling with other people – from one day to the other, at peace and utterly alone. And if the neighbours had nothing to do with her, she, for her part, never concerned herself about them. The only person she ever paid any attention to was Pineiss – and him she hated. Whenever he appeared, she would throw a terrible look and pull her curtains together quickly; while he, who feared her like fire, hid himself away from her.

As I have said, the part of her house that faced the street was neat and clean. But as white as was the front, so dark, so gloomy, so queer and so evil-smelling was the back. Built in the corner of an old wall, it was so black and lost in shadows that it could only be seen by the birds in the air and the cats on the roof. Under the eaves, in a place that no man had ever seen, hung filthy bundles, torn scraps of clothing, ragged underwear, broken baskets, bags of strange herbs. On top of the roof was a little forest of thorn-bushes and mosses, from the centre of which a thin chimney stretched its length like a lean and wicked finger. And out of this chimney, when the nights were darkest, a witch would often rise – young and fair and without a stitch of clothing – and go riding about on a broomstick. Thus, by the power of her secret magic, the old woman would disguise herself as a young girl. She would laugh lightly as she galloped through the air on her one-footed steed; her lips would shine like polished cherries and her long, black hair would flutter in the night-wind like a flag.

In a hole in the chimney sat an old owl. And it was to this wise bird that Glassy came as soon as he was freed, carrying a fat mouse in his jaws.

'Good evening, dear Madam Owl,' said Glassy. 'Still busy keeping watch?'

'I have to,' replied the owl. 'And good evening to you. You have not given your friends the pleasure of your company for a long time.'

'There were reasons, as I will tell you. Have you had

your supper yet? No? Here is a mouse; nothing much, but it is all I could find on the way. I hope you won't refuse it. And has your mistress gone out riding?'

'Not yet,' answered the owl. 'She will wait another hour until it is almost morning. Thanks for the fine mouse. And here I have a small sparrow laid aside; it happened to fly too close to me. Try it, just to please me. And how have things gone with you?'

'Wonderfully. You would hardly believe it. If you care to listen, I'll tell you.' And so, while the two good friends enjoyed their little meal, Glassy told the whole tale how he came to make the fearful contract, how Pineiss had almost killed him, and how, in the end, he had saved himself.

After Glassy had finished, the owl said, 'Well, I congratulate you! And I wish you the best of luck. Now you are a free man again; you can go where you please and do whatever you wish!'

'But not right away,' objected Glassy. 'First, Pineiss must have his lady and the ten thousand gold guldens.'

'Are you crazy?' screamed the owl. 'Surely, you are only joking! You certainly are not going to reward the man who wanted to take the very skin off your back?'

'Yes, he was about to do that. But if I can pay him back in the same coin, why shouldn't I? The story I told him was a pure fairy tale; I made the whole thing up myself from beginning to end. My mistress was a simple body; she was quite plain, had never been in love, and no suitors ever came near her all her life. As to the treasure, there really are some guldens at the bottom of the well. But it is stolen money, and my mistress would never touch it. "Let it lie there," she used to say to me, "for there is a curse on it. Whoever takes it out and uses it will be unlucky!" That shall be Master Pineiss's "reward"!'

'Ah,' the owl chuckled, 'that's different! You're a deep one! But where is the promised lady going to come from?'

'From this chimney!' answered Glassy. 'That is the reason I came here. Let us talk it over like two sensible people.

41

Wouldn't you like to be free of this witch who is always making you work for her? And wouldn't it be a lovely thing to get these two old villains married to each other? But first, we must catch our witch. And that's no easy matter. Stir your brains; think how we can manage it!'

For a while there was nothing but silence in the night. Then the owl whispered, 'I think I have it! As soon as you are here with me, my brain begins to work!'

'Good,' said Glassy. 'Soon we will have a plan.'

'I have a plan already,' continued the owl. 'Everything joins together nicely.'

'When do we begin?' asked Glassy, eagerly.

'At once!' said the owl.

'And how are we going to catch her?' inquired Glassy, with eyes that burned like green fire.

'With a net for catching snipe, a fine new net made of the toughest hemp. It must have been woven by a twenty-year-old hunter's son who has never once looked at a woman. The night-dew must have fallen three times upon it where it lay without having caught a single snipe. And it must have lain there because of three good deeds. Only such a net is strong enough to catch witches!'

'But I am curious to know where such a net can be found,' said Glassy. 'There must be one somewhere in the world, I suppose, because I have never known you to say a foolish thing. But where,' repeated the puzzled animal, 'are we ever to find such a remarkable affair?'

'It has been found already, just as if it were made for us,' replied the owl. 'Listen. In a wood, not far from here, there sits the twenty-year-old son of a hunter who has never looked at a woman as much as once. He was born blind. There's your first requirement. Being blind, he cannot do much except weave yarn and, a few days ago, he finished a fine net for catching snipe. As the old hunter was about to spread it out to trap the birds, a woman came along who wanted him to go with her and join a band of wealthy robbers. But she was so hideous that he dropped

42

everything in fright and ran away. So the hempen net lay in the dew without catching a snipe, and a good motive was the cause of it. The next day, as the old hunter returned to stretch the net, a horseman rode past carrying a heavy bundle behind him. In this bundle was a small hole, and, from time to time, a gold-piece fell out of it. The hunter dropped the net again and ran hotly after the horseman, picking up the gold pieces and putting them in his own hat – until suddenly the horseman turned around, saw what the hunter had been doing, and charged angrily down upon him. Fearing for his life, the hunter bowed suddenly, snatched his cap from his head and said, "Allow me – you have been losing your money, and I have run all the way after so I could give it back to you." This was the second "good" act, and, as the hunter was by this time far away from the net, it lay a second night without being used as a trap. Finally on the third day, which was yesterday, as he came to the place, he met a young woman who carried a basketful of delicious home-cooked sausages and cakes. She was a pleasant girl, and when she invited the hunter to come to her sister's wedding, where there was to be a great feast that evening, he accepted gladly and said, "Oh, let the snipes go! One ought to take pity on the animals! Besides, who cares for snipes when there's a goose?" And because of these three good acts, the net has lain for three nights in the dew without being used – quite ready for us. All I have to do is fetch it.'

'Fetch it quickly, then,' cried Glassy. 'It is the very thing we need!'

'I will get it at once,' said the owl. 'You keep watch for me here, and if my mistress should call up the chimney asking if the coast is clear, answer her in my voice and say, "No, it is not foul enough!"'

Glassy thereupon took his friend's place, and the owl flew over the town towards the wood. In fifteen minutes she was back, carrying the snipe-net in her beak. 'Has she called out?' asked the owl. 'Not yet,' said Glassy.

Then they stretched the closely woven trap over the chimney and sat down to wait for whatever might happen. The night was pitch dark and an early morning wind blew out two or three pale stars. Suddenly they heard the witch's voice: 'Is the coast clear?' And the owl answered, 'Quite clear. The air is fine and foul!'

As soon as the words were said, a white form rose from the chimney – and the next moment the witch was squirming in the snare, while the two animals pulled and tied it together. The witch raged and kicked and flopped and floundered like a gleaming fish in a net, but 'Hold fast!' cried the owl, and 'Tie it tight!' called Glassy. And the net held. Finally, seeing she was helpless, the witch grew quiet and asked, 'What do you want of me, you strange creatures?'

'Let me leave your service and give me my freedom,' said the owl.

'Such a great boast for such a little roast!' said the witch, using an old Swiss proverb. 'Why all this trouble? You are free. Now open the net.'

'Wait a moment,' cried Glassy, 'before we let you out you must promise to marry the town-wizard, Pineiss, in the way we shall explain to you.'

'Marry that man? Never!' replied the witch, and began to fume again.

But Glassy continued quietly. 'Would you like the whole town to know who you are? If you don't do exactly as we say, we will hang the net – and all that is inside of it – right under the part of your roof which faces the street. Tomorrow morning the villagers will pass this house on their way to work. When they look up, they'll see you caught here and everybody will know who the witch is! Besides,' Glassy went on in a more persuading tone of voice, 'just think how easily you will be able to rule Master Pineiss after you are his wife!'

It is hard to say which of these two arguments convinced the witch. At any rate, after a long pause, she said with a sigh, 'Tell me, then, what you want me to do.' And Glassy told her the plan he had in mind and explained to her exactly how it was to be carried out. 'Very well, then, as I cannot help myself, I agree,' said the sorceress, and pledged her word with the strongest magic known to witchcraft. Then she mounted her broom, the owl settled herself on the handle, Glassy perched securely behind on the straw bottom, and so they flew through the air to the old well. The witch descended it, took out the treasure, and the three parted company for the time being.

Early next morning Glassy appeared before Pineiss and informed him that he could see the promised lady. She was so poor and lonely that she had no suitors and was sitting underneath a willow in front of the town-gate, crying bitterly. As soon as Pineiss heard this, he was overjoyed and his dark room seemed lighter. He ran to his mirror, took off his shabby working clothes, put on his yellow velvet doublet (which he only wore on holidays), his silk hose (which he always thought too good to wear), his best fur-cap, and stuck a coloured handkerchief in his pocket. As if this were not enough, he sprinkled perfume on himself, sent a boy out for a big bouquet of flowers, carried a pair of green gloves, and, thus magnificently attired, went with Glassy to the town-gate. There he saw a girl seated under a willow-tree weeping as if her heart would break. She was the loveliest person he had ever seen, even though her dress was so torn that it barely covered her. Pineiss could scarcely take his eyes off her, and it was some time before he could speak. The girl was really too beautiful. But she dried her eyes as he comforted her, and when he asked her to marry him, she even laughed in musical tones and said yes. Quickly Pineiss provided her with a wedding-dress and a bridal veil as long as a waterfall. She looked lovelier than ever, so radiant that when they passed the town the men sitting outside raised their glasses and cheered. Afraid that she might change her mind, Pineiss hurried to an old hermit and, within an hour, the town-magician and the fair unknown were made man and wife. Candles were lit, merry cupids seemed to be singing in the air, and, with downcast eyes, the lovely bride entered her new home. The wedding-feast was celebrated in the wizard's house without any other guests except the owl and the cat, who had asked permission to come. The ten thousand gold guldens were in a bowl upon the table and Pineiss's greedy eyes kept looking from his beloved gold to the lovely girl and back again from the girl to the gold. She sat, in sea-blue velvet, with pearls around her slender neck and her eyes brighter than diamonds. But Pineiss cared most for her piled-up yellow hair, for it looked to him like a great mass of glittering gold-pieces.

It was a merry dinner, spiced with Glassy's witty remarks, flavoured with the owl's wise sayings and sweetened with the smiles of the beautiful bride. When the meal was over, the two animals sang a few duets and, as it was beginning to grow dark, prepared to leave their host. Pineiss took them, with a light, to the door, thanked Glassy again and wished them both goodnight. Then, gleefully rubbing his hands together, he went back to the room, congratulating himself on his clever bargain. He closed the door, letting his greedy eyes drink in the happy sight.

There, in the bowl, sparkled the yellow money. But, as his eyes went further, his heart almost stopped beating. Something had gone wrong! There, at the head of the table, instead of the young bride, sat his neighbour, the horrible old woman, frowning at him with a look of hate! She rose from her chair, picked up a broomstick and rode on it in all her hideousness. Imps and demons appeared in every corner, goblins ran about, kobolds sprang on top of the stove. The room was full of strange sounds and queer lights. The very air flickered. Dazzled and scarcely able to see, Pineiss let the candle fall and leaned, trembling, against the wall. His jaw dropped and his whole face grew as white and sharp as the old witch's. They were two of a kind – and the town-wizard richly deserved his 'reward'.

When the marriage became known, the townspeople said, 'Still waters run deep! Who would have thought that the pious old lady would have married the master-magician! Well, they are a well-matched pair – if not very handsome!'

From that time on, Pineiss lived a hard life. His wife learned all his secrets and kept him busy from morning to night. She ruled him with an iron hand; there was not an idle minute he could call his own. And whenever Glassy happened to pass by, the cat would smile cheerfully and say, 'Always busy – eh, Master Pineiss? That's the way – always keep busy!'

And so in Seldwyla, even today, whenever a person has made a bad bargain, they say, 'Too bad! But he should never have tried to buy the fat off the cat!'

The Suburban Lion

STELLA WHITELAW

The whole street panicked. Mothers rushed out to drag children from the playground. The milkman thrust his float into gear and retreated tensely at eight miles per hour. Men stopped gardening, threw down their spades and hurried indoors. Mrs Parker even brought in her washing. She wasn't having a lion eating her best undies.

Fear swept through each household. This was real cold fear, not the synthetic thrill of a horror movie on the box. They could almost hear the crunch of jaws on bones and the tearing of flesh.

A police car began touring the area, lights flashing. 'PLEASE STAY INDOORS. THIS IS AN EMERGENCY,' 'boomed the loudspeaker.

'What's he saying?' asked Donald Miles, cupping his ear. 'Get down on the floor? Is it the IRA?'

'No, grandpa,' said Alison. 'They're telling us to stay indoors. It's just a precaution.'

'I wasn't going out anyway.'

Alison stood at the window watching the helicopter buzzing overhead. It was searching the canal and the railway sidings with long swoops like a tipsy dragonfly. Alison wanted to go out. She wanted to go out and find Rufus. He'd make a tasty snack for a hungry lion. She shuddered, imagining the worst, seeing Rufus's beautiful tail hanging from the lion's huge jaws, blood and saliva dripping down its shaggy fur.

She turned on the news. There it was, sandwiched between a protest march about student grants and a post office robbery. A lion had been spotted near Lufton Marshes, marshes which had long since been drained for a Victorian development. It had been seen in various places, sunning itself on a locomotive shed, prowling along the canal path, foraging among the allotments on the hill, roaring in the municipal park.

A big cat expert from London Zoo had been called in. He was standing by with his team, armed with a tranquillizer gun.

'It looks to me like a young lion,' he said with confidence to the reporter. A shaky amateur video was shown, all fuzzy and out of focus, zooming in to a blurred shape. 'We're checking out private zoos. We haven't lost a lion in years.'

Superintendent John Foster of Lufton Marshes police held a news conference. 'We are satisfied that this is a young animal of the lion variety. The public are warned not to approach. It could be dangerous.'

Mrs Parker was interviewed. She'd seen the creature while she was perched on the top of a ladder, cleaning the upstairs windows. 'It's definitely a leopard or a puma. It was stalking a dog in the park. Huge, it was . . . striped. And I think I heard it roaring. Perhaps it's escaped from a circus.'

'Police are warning householders to stay indoors,' said a newsreader from the safety of an air-conditioned studio. 'Now over to you, Gargy.'

'Thank you, Tim.'

Alison switched off. Rufus haunted the canal. He thought it was full of fresh fish, not old bikes and tyres and rubbish. He'd once caught a plastic bottle and brought it home for Alison to cook.

He was also an addicted train spotter. The day didn't

sit right until Rufus had spotted at least three trains in either direction. He was probably a reincarnation of a grubby note-book. Alison took care never to make fun of his fixation. He was entitled to watch anything. And the park . . . he collected birds. Not in reality, but mentally. Rufus imagined he was a great white hunter.

'I'm going out,' she said, pulling on her anorak.

'What about the IRA?' said grandpa.

'Don't worry about them. I'll be back in time to make your supper.'

Alison was an unpaid carer. She also worked full-time in an office, typing meaningless letters about matters that could have been resolved with a phone call. She said nothing. She was paid to take dictation from her boss and type it up. She could have done all the work herself in half the time.

She went out into the sunless evening. She could smell next door's Evening Primrose plant throwing out its daily dose of tranquillity. From the nearby Thames, grey and sluggish, she smelled escape to the sea. Kitchens spewed out cooking smells . . . curries, chips, chilli, Irish stew, pizzas. Surely Rufus would be making his way home by now? He was always hungry. He'd sell his soul for a slice of pizza with melted cheese.

Alison could believe there was a very big cat out there. Hadn't there been sightings in Devon, on Bodmin Moor, Shropshire, Worcestershire? So why not London? The foxes had become urbanized and roamed among the dustbins for the pickings. Why not big cats?

A neighbour had his television on loud. 'At least seven foot long from nose to tail. It could slash your throat,' she heard a commentator pronounce.

'Rufus, Rufus,' she moaned. 'Where are you? I must find you.'

It was not easy looking after her grandfather but she would not dream of putting him into a home. It would be too unkind. She remembered when he had been agile and funny and she had sat upon his knee while he read her stories. And he had played ball with her in the garden, teaching her how to catch. Those kind of memories couldn't be trashed. It wasn't his fault that he'd grown old.

But he was exhausting. He drained her energy. Even in sleep, she stayed alert, in case he got up and began to wander.

'Good heavens, what are you doing out here?'

The man was tall and tense. He wore glasses and was carrying a gun. Alison almost stopped breathing, wondering if she could get past him and make a run for it.

'I don't know what you're up to,' she breathed. 'But I'll go away, say I never saw you. I'm only out looking for my cat.' Alison zipped up her anorak like body armour. It was suddenly very cold.

'I'm also looking for a cat, puma, leopard, lion. I get a different description every other minute. Black, striped, spotted. London is apparently teeming with big cats, prowling the streets. It's been spotted a dozen times in the last hour,' he said, resting the gun on his hip.

'Oh, you're the Zoo man on television.'

'Ewan Proposki. It's Welsh and Russian. Some mixture. My parents were both immigrants.'

'Mr Prop . . . Prop . . .?'

'Call me Ewan. Listen, you shouldn't be out here, young lady. It's too dangerous.'

'It's Rufus,' said Alison, falling into step with him. 'He's not just any old domestic cat. He's very special. In a funny way, he keeps me sane. They say cats are therapeutic if you've had a heart attack or are ill. Well, I'm not sick but my life is difficult, stuck in a groove. And he's my lifeline. I don't know what I'd do without him. He's the only friend I have time for.'

Ewan looked at her more closely in the gathering gloom. 'Then you must do something about your life, find some friends. Time rushes by.'

'I know. But I'm a prisoner in my own home,' said

Alison. She knew it sounded over dramatic. 'OK, I go out to work but that's just kind of another prison. I come home as fast as I can, hoping grandpa hasn't set fire to the kitchen or left the tap running or fallen down the stairs.'

He understood without her saying any more. 'So, tell me about Rufus.'

Alison's face lit up and even in the gathering darkness, he could see the warmth in her eyes.

'He's more than a cat. He's like a real person, a member of the family. I've had him since he was a kitten. We've grown up together. I pretend he understands what I say . . .'

'Perhaps he does.'

They had walked a full circle and were back at Alison's house. There had been no sign of Rufus, not a whisker. Alison was prepared to continue her search.

'No,' said Ewan firmly. 'It's very dangerous. Big cats are at their most active at dawn and dusk. Go indoors, please. Believe me. You must let Rufus take care of himself.'

*

Rufus had a lovely day. It had been the kind of bright, clear sunlight he liked best with a slight wind to ruffle his long fur. No rain. He hated rain. Bath stuff.

Alison had been in a terrible rush that morning. The old man had been more difficult than usual. She'd opened two tins of mashed rabbit without thinking, working on automatic pilot. Rufus did not bother to alert her to the fact. Why cause trouble? He'd cleared both dishes to save her any bother.

The morning was glorious. Rufus watched the 8.15, the 8.45 and the 9.10 on their way to London, crowded with commuters. Big rattly snakes, he thought, strapped to lines. It made him feel safe, watching how they never made any unexpected move despite all the huff and the puff. They were trapped snakes, tamed by the rails. He'd never seen one get off and go a different way.

He growled loudly at the 9.10 but it didn't miss a single beat. So what? It was no big deal.

He wandered down the path beside the ribbon of water they called a canal, checking it was still there. He'd once seen a fish in the water, a gleaming silver missile darting, succulent and wet. He lived in hope of seeing another. Several times he almost thought he saw one. He stared hard into the water, the hairs on his spine starting to rise, sensing fear, smelling horror. Something was wrong. Two huge green eyes stared back at him. He leaped up in alarm, fur starched stiff, whiskers quivering. He looked behind him but there was nothing there.

He hurried away, heart pounding.

None of his friends were working on the allotments today. He wondered why. He could usually rely on a few tit-bits from their elevenses. He chewed thoughtfully on a crust of stale ham sandwich. Where had they gone?

He had the place to himself except for those pesky pigeons attacking the pale tops of newly planted greens. The birds were pulling up the plants, tossing them about with extravagant abandon.

Rufus felt the indignation rising inside his throat. With a leap worthy of Superman he flung himself among the pigeons, claws windmilling. The pigeons shrieked, flapped upwards in distress, feathers falling to the ground. One bird took the full force of a blow and staggered along a row of lettuces.

Rufus looked at it in surprise. He'd never actually caught a bird before and was not sure what to do next. His natural instinct was to go home and tell Alison. The pigeon solved matters by flopping over, dying of fright.

It was a shock, too, for Rufus. He hadn't meant to kill it, only scare it off the tender plants. Still, there it was, warm and smelling tantalizingly of fresh meat. It wouldn't hurt to taste, would it? Remove the rancid ham flavour from his mouth . . .

Later, he waddled away, his stomach swaying, feathers stuck in his whiskers. He needed to sleep off his gargantuan meal. He climbed, with difficulty, on to the roof of a shed and fell asleep in the warmth of the sun, stretching himself out to catch the maximum rays.

The Nine O'clock News was short of hard news that night so it led with the lion roaming Lufton Marshes. Ewan Proposki was interviewed again and Alison thought how sensible he sounded. But he looked tired.

'Of course, at the end of the Sixties a black leopard was popular as a status symbol,' he was saying. 'It was a mark of wealth and power. People paraded them like poodles. Then they grew tired of them and set them free. Some leopards may then have mated with domestic cats and produced a new species.'

There were more sightings of the lion. The animal was on the move and kept disappearing. There were rumours that a child had been attacked. The boy had been taken to the Accident and Casualty Department with long scratch marks on his arm and he said he had tried to pick up a very big furry creature.

'It was 'normous,' he hiccuped to a swarm of reporters. He stretched his arms wide. 'This 'normous.'

'And what did it look like?'

'It was spotted and striped,' said the boy, warming to the attention. 'And it was black and orange. With a tail.'

'A spotted, striped, black and orange lion?'

'Yes.'

And a group of foreign tourists were being terrorized. One of them had spotted the lion prowling outside a hotel window. They were all too terrified to leave the hotel despite the fact that they had tickets for *Sunset Boulevard*.

'We're taking the first flight home,' said a spokesperson.

Ewan Proposki finished his interview with a warning. 'Don't use flash photography on this animal. It's probably disorientated. This creature, lion, leopard, or puma, whatever it is, does exist. Stay at home and leave this to the experts.'

Alison settled her grandfather in front of the television, putting a dish of his favourite humbugs near him.

'Now you watch the television, grandpa,' she said. 'Here're your sweets. I'll be back soon. I have to go out again for a short time.'

'Have I had my supper?' he asked.

'Yes, you've had your supper.'

Alison pulled herself together, gathered her courage. A curfew had been imposed on the area for the night but she didn't care. She was beside herself with worry. Rufus had never been so late before. He was usually curled up on the boiler by now, basking in the heat.

A helicopter was still sweeping the skies, its searchlight probing the dark hiding places like an angel of light. Trees loomed silvery and ethereal. Cut-out shapes of roof-tops and chimneys were etched against the sky.

Alison did not know where to search first. She went carefully along the railway embankment. He loved trains. It was easy to wriggle under the barrier or climb over the fence.

'Rufus, Rufus,' she called.

The canal was a dark swathe of water, eerie and stinking of unmentionable refuse. But she walked the path, head held high, back straight, holding on to her courage.

'Rufus, Rufus.'

She climbed over the gate into the allotments. She knew Rufus had friends here. They had told her. The old men and the lonely widowers. 'Your cat's a real character,' they often said. But it was deserted. Ghosts of diggers from the past straightened up as she walked by. They sensed her distress, dissolved into the night-drinking mist, could not help.

'Rufus, Rufus.'

The park was closed but not locked. They had forgotten to lock it. Perhaps the warden had fled, alarmed by sightings of the lion.

Once she had walked this park with a young lover but he had long gone, was less than a shadow now. But memories rushed in, disturbing her with the thought of ardent kisses and a man's strong arms around her.

'Rufus, Rufus,' she whispered. 'Please come home . . .'

A huge shaggy shape leapt out of a tree and landed on her chest. Alison was thrown to the ground by the momentum and the weight. She screamed, gasping, smothered.

'Don't move! Don't move!' Armed police appeared from nowhere. Lights flashed on. The whole area was illuminated like a scene in a movie.

'Don't move,' Ewan shouted. 'I've a tranquillizer gun. Don't be afraid. I'm going to dart it.'

The noise and pandemonium were horrendous. Alison closed her eyes to the cameras popping and television crews reeling in their footage for a late news flash.

'Don't be stupid,' she cried, wiping strands of long fur out of her mouth. She knew the shape, the feel, the throbbing purr of the animal wrapped round her. 'This isn't a lion. This is my Rufus. He wouldn't hurt anyone or anything. He wouldn't know how.'

She struggled to her feet still holding the huge ginger tom. Rufus was magnificent. A long-haired, tawny cat with vivid green eyes, whiskers like windscreen wipers, fangs borrowed from Dracula, a tail that thrashed the air with vigour and ecstatic pleasure.

'That's your Rufus?' asked Ewan incredulously, coming out of the trees.

'Of course, this is Rufus. And he's safe, thank goodness.'

She buried her face in the long thick fur and was lost in the bliss of the familiar smell. He was all that mattered.

'You can all go home now,' said Superintendent John Foster, dismissing his men. 'I think we have found the lion of Lufton Marshes.'

Ewan walked Alison home, trying to make himself heard over Rufus's outrageous purring. The cat was wrapped round her neck like a fur stole, feathery tail thrashing her waist.

'You didn't tell me he was so big,' he said loudly.

'You didn't ask me.'

'I thought I was hunting a lion.'

'Rufus has the heart of a lion,' said Alison, rubbing her face against the soft head.

They reached her house. The purring subsided into a throaty grumble as sleep overcame Rufus and he rode into his dreams of bravery and great deeds.

'Would you like to come in for some coffee?' Alison asked hesitantly. 'You must be exhausted. It's been a long day. All that television.'

'I would like that more than anything,' said Ewan.

They were going to face change, get out of grooves but they were prepared for it and smiled at each other.

Rufus dug his claws into her hair and growled to himself as he relived his glorious day as a lion. He loved trains. Tomorrow he'd roar twice as loud at that impudent 9.10.

Puss in Boots

CHARLES PERRAULT
(translated by G. M. Gent, 1802)

There was a miller, who had left no more estate to the three sons he had, than his mill, his ass, and his cat. The partition was soon made. Neither the scrivener nor attorney were sent for. They would soon have eaten up all the patrimony. The eldest had the mill, the second the ass, and the youngest nothing but the cat.

The poor young fellow was quite comfortless at having so poor a lot. 'My brothers (said he) may get their living handsomely enough, by joining their stocks together; but for my part, when I have eaten up my cat, and made me a muff of his skin, I must die with hunger.' The Cat, who heard all this, but made as if he did not, said to him with a grave and serious air, 'Do not thus afflict yourself, my good master; you have nothing else to do, but to give me a bag, and get a pair of boots made for me, that I may scamper through the dirt and brambles, and you shall see that you have not so bad a portion of me as you imagine.'

Though the Cat's master did not build very much upon what he said, he had, however, often seen him play a great many cunning tricks to catch rats and mice; as when he used to hang by the heels, or hide himself in the meal, and make as if he were dead; so that he did not altogether despair of his affording him some help in his miserable condition. When the Cat had what he asked for, he

booted himself very gallantly; and putting his bag about
his neck, he held the strings of it in his forepaws, and
went into a warren where there was great abundance of
rabbits. He put bran and sow thistle into his bag, and
stretching himself out at length, as if he had been dead,
he waited for some young rabbits, not yet acquainted
with the deceits of the world, to come and rummage his
bag for what he had put into it.

Scarce was he laid down, but he had what he wanted;
a rash and foolish young rabbit jumped into his bag, and
Monsieur Puss, immediately drawing close the strings,
took and killed him without pity. Proud of his prey, he
went with it to the palace, and asked to speak with his
Majesty. He was shown upstairs into the King's apartments, and making a low reverence, said to him, 'I have
brought you, Sir, a rabbit of the warren, which my noble
Lord, the Marquis of Carabas (for that was the title which
Puss was pleased to give his master) has commanded me
to present to your Majesty from him.'

'Tell thy master, (said the King) that I thank him, and
that he does me a great deal of pleasure.'

Another time he went and hid himself among some
standing corn, holding still his bag open; and when a
brace of partidges ran into it, he drew the strings, and so
caught them both. He went and made a present of them
to the King, as he had done before of the rabbit which he
took in the warren. The King, in like manner, received
the partridges with great pleasure, and ordered him some
money for drink.

The Cat continued for two or three months thus to carry
his Majesty, from time to time, game of his master's
taking. One day in particular, when he knew for certain
that he was to take the air, along the river-side, with his
daughter, the most beautiful princess in the world, he said
to his master, 'If you will follow my advice, your fortune is
made; you have nothing else to do, but go and wash
yourself in the river, in that part I shall show you, and

leave the rest to me.' The Marquis of Carabas did what the Cat advised him to, without knowing why or wherefore.

While he was washing, the King passed by, and the Cat began to cry out as loud as he could, 'Help, help, my Lord Marquis of Carabas is going to be drowned.' At this noise the King put his head out of the coach window, and finding it was the Cat who had often brought him such good game, he commanded his guards to run immediately to the assistance of his Lordship the Marquis of Carabas.

While they were drawing the poor Marquis out of the river, the Cat came up to the coach, and told the King, that, 'While my master was washing there came by some rogues, who went off with his clothes, though he cried out, "Thieves! Thieves!" several times, as loud as he could.' The cunning Cat had hidden them under a great stone. The King immediately commanded the officers of his wardrobe to run and fetch one of his best suits for the Lord Marquis of Carabas.

The King caressed him after a very extraordinary manner; and as the fine clothes he had given him extremely set off his good mien (for he was well made and very handsome in his person), the King's daughter took a secret inclination to him, and the Marquis of Carabas had no sooner cast two or three respectful and somewhat tender glances, but she fell in love with him to distraction. The King would needs have him come into the coach, and partake of the airing. The Cat, quite overjoyed to see his project begin to succeed, marched on before, and meeting some countrymen who were mowing a meadow, he said to them, 'Good people, you who are mowing, if you do not tell the King that the meadow you mow belongs to my Lord Marquis of Carabas, you shall be chopped as small as herbs for the pot.'

The King did not fail of asking of the mowers, to whom the meadow they were mowing belonged; 'To my Lord Marquis of Carabas,' answered they all together; for the Cat's threats had made them terribly afraid. 'You see, Sir

(said the Marquis), this is a meadow which never fails to yield a plentiful harvest every year.' The Master Cat, who went still on before, met with some reapers, and said to them, 'Good people, you who are reaping, if you do not tell the King that all this corn belongs to the Marquis of Carabas, you shall be chopped as small as herbs for the pot.'

The King, who passed by a moment after, would needs know to whom all that corn, which he then saw, did belong; 'To my Lord Marquis of Carabas,' replied the reapers; and the King was very well pleased with it, as well as the Marquis, whom he congratulated thereupon. The Master Cat, who went always before, said the same words to all he met; and the King was astonished at the vast estates of my Lord Marquis of Carabas.

Monsieur Puss came at last to a stately castle, the master of which was an Ogre, the richest that had ever been known; for all the lands which the King had then gone over belonged, with this castle, to him. The cat, who had taken care to inform himself who this Ogre was, and what he could do, asked to speak to him, saying, 'I could not pass so near the castle without having the honour of paying my respects to him.'

The Ogre received him as civilly as an Ogre could do, and made him sit down. 'I have been assured (said the Cat) that you have the gift of being able to change yourself into all sorts of creatures you have a mind to; you can, for example, transform yourself into a lion, or elephant, and the like.' 'This is true (answered the Ogre very briskly), and to convince you, you shall see me now become a lion.' Puss was so sadly terrified at the sight of a lion so near him, that he immediately got into the gutter, not without abundance of trouble and danger, because of his boots, which were of no use at all to him in walking upon the tiles. A little while after, when Puss saw the Ogre had resumed his natural form, he came down, and owned he had been very much frightened.

'I have been moreover informed (said the Cat), but I know not how to believe it, that you have also the power to take upon you the shape of the smallest animals; for example, to change yourself into a rat or a mouse; but I must own to you, I take this to be impossible.'

'Impossible! (cried the Ogre) You shall see that presently,' and at the same time changed himself into a mouse, and began to run about the floor. Puss no sooner perceived this, but he fell upon him and ate him up.

Meanwhile the King, who saw, as he passed, this fine castle of the Ogre, had a mind to go into it. Puss, who heard the noise of his Majesty's coach running over the drawbridge, ran out, and said to the King, 'Your Majesty is welcome to the castle of my Lord Marquis of Carabas.'

'What! my Lord Marquis (cried the King), and does this castle also belong to you? There can be nothing finer than this court, and all the stately buildings which surround it; let us go into it, if you please.' The Marquis gave his hand to the Princess, and followed the King, who went up first. They passed into a spacious hall, where they found a magnificent colation, which the Ogre had prepared for his friends, who were that very day to visit him, but dared not to enter, knowing the King was there.

His Majesty was perfectly charmed with the good qualities of my Lord Marquis of Carabas, as was his daughter, who was fallen violently in love with him; and seeing the vast estate he possessed, said to him, after having drank five or six glasses, 'It will be owing to yourself only, my Lord Marquis, if you are not my Son-in-Law.' The Marquis, making several low bows, accepted the honour which his Majesty conferred upon him, and forthwith, that very same day, married the Princess.

Puss became a great Lord and never ran after mice any more, only for his diversion.

Olly and Ginny

JAMES HERRIOT

It irked me, as a cat lover, that my own cats couldn't stand the sight of me. Ginny and Olly were part of the family now. We were devoted to them and whenever we had a day out the first thing Helen did on our return was to open the back door and feed them. The cats knew this very well and were either sitting on the flat top of the wall, waiting for her, or ready to trot down from the log shed which was their home.

We had been to Brawton on our half-day and they were there as usual as Helen put out a dish of food and a bowl of milk for them on the wall.

'Olly, Ginny,' she murmured as she stroked the furry coats. The days had long gone when they refused to let her touch them. Now they rubbed against her hand in delight, arching and purring and, when they were eating, she ran her hand repeatedly along their backs. They were such gentle little animals, their wildness expressed only in fear, and now, with her, that fear had gone. My children and some from the village had won their confidence, too, and were allowed to give them a careful caress, but they drew the line at Herriot.

Like now, for instance, when I quietly followed Helen out and moved towards the wall, immediately they left the food and retreated to a safe distance where they stood, still arching their backs but, as ever, out of reach. They regarded me without hostility but as I held out a hand they moved further away.

'Look at the little beggars!' I said. 'They still won't have anything to do with me.'

It was frustrating since, throughout my years in veterinary practice, cats had always intrigued me and I had found that this helped me in my dealings with them. I felt I could handle them more easily than most people because I liked them and they sensed it. I rather prided myself on my cat technique, a sort of feline bedside manner, and was in no doubt that I had an empathy with the entire species and that they all liked me. In fact, if the truth were told, I fancied myself as a cats' pin-up. Not so, ironically, with these two – the ones to whom I had become so deeply attached.

It was a bit hard, I thought, because I had doctored them and probably saved their lives when they had cat flu. Did they remember that, I wondered, but if they did it still didn't give me the right apparently to lay a finger on them. And, indeed, what they certainly did seem to remember was that it was I who had netted them and then shoved them into a cage before I neutered them. I had the feeling that whenever they saw me, it was that net and cage which was uppermost in their minds.

I could only hope that time would bring an understanding between us but, as it turned out, fate was to conspire against me for a long time still. Above all, there was the business of Olly's coat. Unlike his sister, he was a long-haired cat and as such was subject to constant tangling and knotting of his fur. If he had been an ordinary domesticated feline, I would have combed him out as soon as trouble arose but since I couldn't even get near him I was helpless. We had had him about two years when Helen called me to the kitchen.

'Just look at him!' she said. 'He's a dreadful sight!'

I peered through the window. Olly was indeed a bit of

a scarecrow with his matted fur and dangling knots in cruel contrast with his sleek and beautiful little sister.

'I know, I know. But what can I do?' I was about to turn away when I noticed something. 'Wait a minute, there's a couple of horrible big lumps hanging below his neck. Take these scissors and have a go at them – a couple of quick snips and they'll be off.'

Helen gave me an anguished look. 'Oh, we've tried this before. I'm not a vet and anyway, he won't let me do that. He'll let me pet him, but this is something else.'

'I know that, but have a go. There's nothing to it, really.' I pushed a pair of curved scissors into her hand and began to call instructions through the window. 'Right now, get your fingers behind that big dangling mass. Fine, fine! Now up with your scissors and – '

But at the first gleam of steel, Olly was off and away up the hill. Helen turned to me in despair. 'It's no good, Jim, it's hopeless – he won't let me cut even one lump off and he's covered with them.'

I looked at the dishevelled little creature standing at a safe distance from us. 'Yes, you're right. I'll have to think of something.'

Thinking of something entailed doping Olly so that I could get at him, and my faithful Nembutal capsules sprang immediately to mind. This oral anaesthetic had been a valued ally on countless occasions where I had to deal with unapproachable animals, but this was different. With the other cases, my patients had been behind closed doors but Olly was outside with all the wide countryside to roam in. I couldn't have him going to sleep somewhere out there where a fox or other predator might get him. I would have to watch him all the time.

It was a time for decisions, and I drew myself up. 'I'll have a go at him this Sunday,' I told Helen. 'It's usually a bit quieter and I'll ask Siegfried to stand in for me in an emergency.'

When the day arrived, Helen went out and placed two meals of chopped fish on the wall, one of them spiked with the contents of my Nembutal capsule. I crouched behind the window; watching intently as she directed Olly to the correct portion, and holding my breath as he sniffed at it suspiciously. His hunger soon overcame his caution and he licked the bowl clean with evident relish.

Now we started the tricky part. If he decided to explore the fields as he often did I would have to be right behind him. I stole out of the house as he sauntered back up the slope to the open log shed and to my vast relief he settled down in his own particular indentation in the straw and began to wash himself.

As I peered through the bushes I was gratified to see that very soon he was having difficulty with his face, licking his hind paw then toppling over as he brought it up to his cheek.

I chuckled to myself. This was great. Another few minutes and I'd have him.

And so it turned out. Olly seemed to conclude that he was tired of falling over and it wouldn't be a bad idea to have a nap. After gazing drunkenly around him, he curled up in the straw.

I waited a short time, then, with all the stealth of an Indian brave on the trail, I crept from my hiding place and tiptoed to the shed. Olly wasn't flat out – I hadn't dared give him the full anaesthetic dose in case I had been unable to track him – but he was deeply sedated. I could pretty well do what I wanted with him.

As I knelt down and began to snip away with my scissors, he opened his eyes and made a feeble attempt to struggle, but it was no good and I worked my way quickly through the ravelled fur. I wasn't able to make a particularly tidy job because he was wriggling slightly all the time, but I clipped off all the huge unsightly knots which used to get caught in the bushes, and must have been horribly uncomfortable, and soon had a growing heap of black hair by my side.

I noticed that Olly wasn't only not moving, he was watching me. Dazed as he was, he knew me all right and his eyes told me all. 'It's you again!' he was saying. 'I might have known!'

When I had finished, I lifted him into a cat cage and placed it on the straw. 'Sorry, old lad,' I said, 'but I can't let you go free till you've wakened up completely.'

Olly gave me a sleepy stare, but his sense of outrage was evident. 'So you've dumped me in here again. You don't change much, do you?'

By teatime he was fully recovered and I was able to release him. He looked so much better without the ugly tangles but he didn't seem impressed, and as I opened the cage he gave me a single disgusted look and sped away.

Helen was enchanted with my handiwork and she pointed eagerly at the two cats on the wall next morning. 'Doesn't he look smart! Oh, I'm so glad you managed to do him, it was really worrying me. And he must feel so much better.'

I felt a certain smug satisfaction as I looked through the window. Olly indeed was almost unrecognizable as the scruffy animal of yesterday and there was no doubt I had dramatically altered his life and relieved him of a constant discomfort, but my burgeoning bubble of self-esteem was pricked the instant I put my head round the back door. He had just started to enjoy his breakfast but at the sight of me he streaked away faster than ever before and disappeared far over the hill-top. Sadly, I turned back into the kitchen. Olly's opinion of me had dropped several more notches. Wearily I poured a cup of tea. It was a hard life.

The Amethyst Cat

MARGERY SHARP

Everyone knows that in 1860 far too much looting went on at the Summer Palace in Pekin. Bric-a-brac carved from jade and crystal proved in particular irresistibly attractive to an acquisitive if not licentious soldiery. (Today, of course, such objects would probably be described as having been liberated.) The result was the dispersal through Western Europe of a great number of miniature Chinese masterpieces; and Sherrard, some hundred years later, thought he had his eye on one of them.

Sherrard looked through the plate-glass window at the cat, and the cat, or so it seemed, looked back through the window at Sherrard.

It was a portly and sagacious creature; couchant in an attitude of great comfort and dignity; about nine inches long by five high, carved from a block of amethyst quartz which must thus have been considerably larger. The body was light grey, striated with crystal, the mask and ears violet – almost Siamese colouring; but the broad complacent face, sunk so reposefully upon the broad chest, had nothing of a Siamese's nervous tension. It was a Chinese cat – and, in Sherrard's opinion, a masterpiece.

Sherrard at this juncture, it so happened, greatly

desired to make a gift of surpassing beauty to a young Chinese lady, resident in New York. He therefore entered the shop, and a moment or two later balanced the creature on his palm.

He could just manage it. For its size, it was astonishingly heavy. It must have weighed about seven pounds. It was also astonishingly cold – like wet ice.

'Amethyst quartz?' suggested Sherrard.

'Amethyst quartz,' agreed the proprietress, with a polite smile for her customer's knowledgeableness. She was a small, elegant woman, thus matching her establishment, which was situated in Piccadilly; for his pocket's sake Sherrard would have preferred less *chic*, but at the same time recognized that one couldn't expect such a cat to turn up in – to put up with – any flea-market. 'Of the finest quality,' added the proprietress. 'So is the workmanship. Turn him over.'

Sherrard obeyed. The cat's underside was as exquisitely carved as the rest of him: four delicate paws, the claws withdrawn, were tucked neatly into a comfortable belly. Near the root of the tail Sherrard made out a small, faintly-incised Chinese ideogram.

'Have you its pedigree?' inquired Sherrard, without irony.

The proprietress shrugged.

'Chinese and, say, eighteenth century. Not that I'm an expert. I bought it at a sale in a country house, because I was lucky, there were no Chinese experts there. And, of course, I know what my eyes tell me, it's the work of a considerable artist.'

Sherrard's eyes told him the same thing. He appreciated it, it gave him confidence, that she didn't produce any tale of loot from the Summer Palace to put the price up. In any case, the price was quite high enough for Sherrard.

'Two hundred pounds,' murmured the proprietress indifferently.

'I'll have to think,' said Sherrard. 'May I let you know tomorrow?'

Indeed he had to think. He was a foreign correspondent, and a successful, even a celebrated one; on his pay and expenses he lived a thoroughly ample life; but to put down two hundred pounds cash – six hundred dollars, twenty thousand francs, three hundred and fifty thousand lire – wasn't a trifle to him. All the rest of that day, and well into the night, he mulled it over.

There were several reasons why he wished to make Maria in New York some exquisitely beautiful gift. In the first place she was herself exquisitely beautiful, and like to like. (Her Chinese name meant Small Pink Lotus Bud at Dawn, and it suited her. Maria discarded it to become Maria when she so thankfully and enthusiastically became an American citizen.) Had he been a millionaire, and had he known nothing of Maria but her appearance, Sherrard would have bought her the amethyst cat as a mere matter of artistic propriety. But he did, besides, know her, he'd known her off and on for some years, and had the greatest admiration for her character also. Educated in China, at a Quaker school, sent on a scholarship to an American university, it perhaps hadn't been difficult for Maria herself to acquire citizenship in the New World; but with incredible pains and persistence, as soon as she could support a dependant, she succeeded in bringing over her only living relative – an uncle so old and so useless that only a heart of gold could see him as anything but a burden. 'He was kind to me when I was little,' said Maria, 'and I've got him off opium on to Coca-Cola!'

For as well as being golden-hearted and beautiful, she was sensible and strong-minded. She had every feminine quality. Every time he left New York without asking her to marry him, Sherrard regretted it in the 'plane.

Why he didn't ask her to marry him was partly because he was so used to being a bachelor, and partly because

Maria kept him always, very slightly, at a distance. She kept everyone, Sherrard fancied, slightly at a distance. In the hospital where she worked as a masseuse she had dozens of friends, but no intimates; as she had dozens of escorts, but no one particular escort. Her reserve was like a delicate Chinese fan fluttering perpetually before her face, which she couldn't cast aside even though she wanted to. Sherrard thought that at the sight of the amethyst cat – so surpassingly beautiful, expensive and Chinese – perhaps that fan would for an instant drop; never, if he seized his chance, to be picked up again . . .

He went back to the shop next day, and wrote out a cheque.

Sherrard had known all along that he was buying no common cat; the personality it developed, on the flight out to New York, was none the less disconcerting. It created difficulties, and attracted attention, all the way.

To begin with, he hadn't cared to pack it in his luggage. It was too precious, and possibly too fragile. (It might have survived at least a century of racketing about, and perhaps a century before that; Sherrard still thought of it as fragile, because precious.) So he stuffed it into his overnight bag, where its weight, on the airport scales, produced a startled query from the officer in charge. 'It's a cat,' said Sherrard shortly. 'I've a cat in my bag.' Someone to the rear laughed, but the officer looked grim. 'Livestock?' he inquired sternly. 'No, quartz,' snapped Sherrard. He pulled it out; the officer grinned and passed him – on payment of excess; and as they were immediately marshalled to their 'plane, Sherrard boarded it with the cat under his arm.

Unusually, the seat beside him remained vacant. Having dumped the cat down on it, he left it there. The cat settled down very comfortably but continued to attract attention. Sherrard was reminded of the one and only flight he'd made with his Aunt Gertrude – a charming and sociable old lady who'd apparently regarded the whole trip as a nice At Home given by the airline. Like his Aunt Gertrude (which was something), the cat made contact only with the nicest people; chiefly elderly ladies travelling with their husbands. One such couple – whom Sherrard mentally christened The Texans, on no other grounds than the man's broad-brimmed hat and general air of prosperity – sat directly across the aisle; the lady in particular was perfectly charmed by the cat and the cat, it couldn't be denied, appeared most complacently to receive her attentions. It didn't purr, it couldn't, but it appeared to purr. Finally Sherrard who, unlike Aunt Gertrude, felt no social obligations whatever, covered it over with his scarf.

He was none the less roused from sleep, shortly before arrival, by the Texan.

'Pardon me, I thought you were awake,' the Texan apologized.

'At least I should be,' said Sherrard – his Aunt Gertrude, as it were reminding him of his manners.

'The fact is, my wife's taken a remarkable fancy to your cat. If I could get one similar for her, I'd be very glad to know where to go for it.'

'I'm sorry, I'm afraid this one's about two hundred years old,' said Sherrard.

The Texan looked at it respectfully. (Somehow, during the night, it had got its head out again.)

'You mean no one makes them nowadays?'

'Not that I know of,' said Sherrard.

'Too bad,' said the Texan regretfully. 'All the same, I'd like you to take my card – just to show Maisie I'm trying. If you ever run across another, and have the kindness to let me know, I'll be deeply obliged.'

Sherrard pocketed the bit of pasteboard and tried to doze off again. But he'd been disturbed, for a man of his fifty years, too thoroughly; instead he sat and thought about Maria.

The cat dozed off all right. Sherrard didn't remember pulling the scarf over its head a second time, but when he looked again, not an ear showed. It was thus in fine fettle to make an exhibition of itself at the customs; but, leaning on its age, carried Sherrard through without difficulty.

Sherrard reached Maria's flat about seven that evening. There were several professional contacts he had needed to make first; he'd had no time to get the cat wrapped, as he'd thought of doing, in some elegant packing. It was still simply muffled in his scarf. But as he set it down, so muffled, on the little table in the centre of her living room, it presented at least an intriguing shape.

Maria was there waiting for him. He'd cabled her. Actually he'd cabled her twice – once from London, once from Gander.

'You are the nicest friend in the world!' cried Maria. There was still, even in the pretty, affectionate phrase, a formality: as though she offered a little poem of welcome brushed across a fan. She stood before him none the less so exquisitely beautiful, so explicitly friendly, that his heart rose. 'And you've brought me a present from England!' cried Maria. 'Really, you're too good!'

Smiling and eager, she poked at the bundle with a tentative forefinger. It was another of her charming traits that she was readily pleased, and always showed her pleasure; yet Sherrard had no doubt that she reserved pleasure still in store, so to speak; that she would find the unimaginably right words of gratitude and admiration, when she saw his marvellous gift; that before the cat, her compatriot, in short, the fan of reserve would at last drop.

Already she was more eager, more caught up by a flow of pleasure and excitement, than he had ever seen her.

'Do I unwrap it, or do you show it me?' demanded Maria. 'I'm not going to guess, I'm too impatient!'

'Sit down, and I'll put it in your lap,' said Sherrard.

Obediently, Maria sat. She even (to give *him* pleasure) closed her eyes – and this momentarily distracted Sherrard, for he had never before seen Maria with her eyes shut. She looked at once ageless, and very young; her lids were the colour of tea-roses; and with irrational tenderness Sherrard realized that her lashes weren't long, as he'd always believed them to be, but quite short and scrubby, like little brushes . . .

'What are you waiting for?' urged Maria.

Sherrard pulled the cat out of its wrapping and set it down on her knee, between her slim welcoming hands.

For an instant, undoubtedly, as she opened her eyes, the fan dropped. But only for an instant. Almost immediately her features recomposed themselves into an expression of extreme politeness.

'How perfectly *lovely*,' said Maria.

Sherrard picked up the table-lamp and held it so that the light shone down through the violet ears.

'It's amethyst quartz.'

'I see it is. Lovely!' repeated Maria. With quick, intelligent fingers, she traced the curve from nape to tail, tipped the cat over, scrutinized its underneath, and settled it back between her palms.

'Oh, dear, I hope you didn't pay too much for it!' cried Maria uncontrollably . . .

Then Sherrard knew that the emotion she'd so briefly betrayed had indeed been what he'd fancied it. For a moment, incredulously, he'd fancied she was disappointed. Now he knew she was.

'Does that mean it's no good?'

'Of course not! It's beautiful! Only if they told you it was eighteenth century, you might have paid four or five hundred dollars.'

Sherrard was very quick-witted. He saw what was coming and got in first.

'Of course it's only a modern reproduction.'

Maria smiled with relief.

'I'm so glad you weren't robbed – as people can be,

76

quite shockingly! Now I can enjoy my present with a good conscience!'

She jumped up, and set the cat first on the table again, then on a tabouret, then on the mantelpiece, seeking where it would look best; she gaily and charmingly made a fuss of it, even giving it a vase of violets to smell at, a little silver box to play with. Nothing could have been prettier; but Sherrard remained unhappy. He was indeed in a most distressing quandary; the sheer costliness of the gift had been a large part of its point – a declaration, so to speak, of his intentions; yet he couldn't now admit to it without also admitting himself a sucker – worse, without bringing down on his head Maria's mingled sympathy and exasperation. She had always an acute dislike of any kind of waste – in her early days in America Sherrard recalled how she'd worried over the crusts cut off from sandwiches – and waste of money ranked next with her to waste of food. She was very nearly parsimonious. Considering her starveling infancy, the trait was a natural one; for the first time Sherrard found himself disliking it. He hadn't toted the cat halfway round the world to have its price asked! True, Maria hadn't done so yet, in so many words, but Sherrard strongly suspected her of wanting to, certain of finding it exorbitant in any case . . .

He also suspected – too late, too late! – that she didn't much care for the cat at all.

'Next time I'll bring you a cashmere twin-set,' said he.

Undeniably, her eyes sparkled.

'Will you really? I'll give you my size.'

It didn't soothe Sherrard's soreness that the cat meanwhile continued to sit handsome and complacent as ever, looking every minute of two hundred years old. It met Sherrard's gaze affably. 'All right, so you fooled me,' thought Sherrard. (It didn't, oddly enough, occur to him that he might have been fooled by the shopkeeper; he was convinced that the cat had fooled them both.) 'But now you've run into an expert,' thought Sherrard nastily, 'and as soon as I'm out of town you'll be put in your proper place . . . which is probably the back of a clothes-closet.'

Naturally the cat's expression didn't alter. Maria exclaimed afresh, that very moment, at its air of aplomb. Sherrard gave the imposter another dirty look, for his own aplomb left much to be desired – he having not realized the implications of his hasty threat. *'As soon as I'm out of town,'* he'd warned the cat; did he then mean to leave cat and Maria together behind him? Wasn't he after all going to ask Maria to be his wife? And if not, why not? Because she'd wanted to know how much he'd paid for her present? Put so, the thing was ridiculous; there stood Maria just as exquisite as he remembered her, just as charmingly affectionate, having moreover, and at last, dropped the fan of her reserve – to reveal behind it the admirable wifely quality of concern for a man's pocket . . .

What an admirable wife she would make!

She'd probably run a wonderfully economical kitchen.

Not impossibly, when he wanted to go out on the town, she'd have something in the oven.

She'd certainly want to see any dinner-bill.

Sherrard glanced again at the amethyst cat, and the cat with ancient wisdom gazed back at Sherrard. (With *fictitiously* ancient wisdom, Sherrard reminded himself.) It was shocking, and it was completely out of period, that the cat appeared to murmur something under its whiskers about wives to keep men steady, but concubines to keep them young. For a moment Sherrard felt he should absolutely apologize to Maria for the cat's immorality; but on second thoughts recognized that to her a lump of quartz, however masterly carved, remained simply a lump of quartz.

Which brought him to another point. Beautiful Maria – sensible and kind Maria – lacked imagination. 'And what else do I deal in?' Sherrard asked himself. 'I, the factual reporter, what else after all do I deal in? Don't I produce, for those who haven't the wit or opportunity to make them for themselves, the images of President, Prime Minister, statesman? Don't I image the whole world, or try to, in a column of print? Maybe it would be all right for me, maybe it would be even good for me, to marry a wife with no imagination at all; but somehow I don't think so . . .'

Complacently upon Maria's mantelpiece sat the amethyst cat.

Sherrard turned back to Maria. He didn't know how long the silence had lasted, only that it had lasted quite long enough. 'Where would you like to go for dinner?' he asked uneasily.

Now Maria, damn it, was looking uneasily at *him*.

'My dear, I hate to tell you,' she apologized, 'but actually I've a date already. And it's one I can't put off – with a boy from China, a boy who knew my family there . . . It's his first evening in New York, you see, without me he won't know what to do with himself. You do understand, don't you?'

'Perfectly,' said Sherrard. 'You'll see he isn't robbed.'

Maria laughed in happy relief.

'That among other things! Though tonight I think he wants to be rather grand and extravagant, to celebrate *getting* here!'

'Just for once I don't suppose it matters,' suggested Sherrard, 'if you keep him on a tight rein afterwards?'

'Oh, I mean to,' agreed Maria seriously. (No wonder the cat looked smug. 'That's the sort of lad for *her*,' it seemed to say, 'a lad she can boss about; see what I've saved you from!' Sherrard ignored the brute.) 'So I really ought to dress up a little,' added Maria, now glancing frankly at the clock, 'but won't you wait and meet him? He is studying medicine, and he seems to be really quite brilliant . . . Please wait!'

'If you want me to, of course I will,' said Sherrard amiably.

He felt suddenly flat – flat and sore. He wasn't yet grateful to the cat at all. He felt let down. For nothing had

turned out as he'd planned; even his own emotions had gone adrift, he didn't even feel jealous of the boy from China; and it wasn't exactly Maria's fault, so that he couldn't even feel angry with Maria. His anger turned itself upon the cat – upon the smug impostor he'd toted halfway round the world, with no other result than to put himself, Sherrard, in danger of looking a fool . . .

'What's the Chinese name that means Labour-in-Vain?' Sherrard mentally inquired of the amethyst cat. 'You should know; it's yours.'

He had been alone perhaps five minutes (while Maria dressed up) when the door discreetly opened. The old party who now joined him, however, was, in appearance at least, less discreet than showy. Maria's efforts to turn her uncle into a hundred per cent American had in one respect succeeded only too well: he wore a Palm Beach shirt. There were hibiscus blossoms upon it, also sea-horses, also bathing-beauties, but above its brilliant uninhibited colouring a face like an old walnut peered, incongruously diffident, humble and submissive.

'I beg pardon,' murmured Maria's uncle. 'I did not know anyone was present . . .'

'Don't go, come on in and keep me company,' said Sherrard. 'I'm just waiting to vet Maria's new beau.'

It was as incongruous to him, that slangy turn of phrase, as was the Palm Beach shirt on Maria's uncle. Sherrard recognized it at once, recognizing also that he wasn't quite himself. Fortunately the old man, it seemed, recognized nothing but a permission to enter; he sidled in bowing politely, with a smile that revealed a really splendid set of false teeth. Sherrard was again aware of an incongruity: they were so wonderfully confident, those splendid American dentures, yet the old man's smile remained humble . . .

'Your company will give me great pleasure,' Sherrard corrected himself. 'Perhaps you remember me? My name is Sherrard.'

Extraordinarily, to this overture there was no response at all.

The old man mightn't even have heard. It was extraordinary indeed – one moment all his attention was fixed on Sherrard, the next it had flown away; one moment his eyes dropped humbly before the stranger, the next they were riveted on the mantelpiece. With short, hasty steps he almost trotted across the room; pushed his wrinkled old face against the smooth complacent countenance of the cat, laid his fingers (like a bundle of bamboo twigs) to the curve of the cat's nape, tipped the beast over, scrutinized its belly – and only then turned back to Sherrard.

Maria had always insisted on her uncle speaking correct English, so that he could never say anything very quickly; but the words got out at last. 'How – came – this – object – here?'

'I brought it to give to Maria,' said Sherrard. 'D'you like it?'

'I *made* it!' proclaimed Maria's uncle triumphantly. 'See, under my mark!'

There was now naturally much Sherrard understood that he hadn't before. His thoughts raced. Poor Maria, to begin with! – had she recognized her uncle's mark too, or only his general style? Or even remembered, perhaps, sitting under his work bench as he chipped and polished and engraved at that very beast? In whichever case, what a facer for her, what a grotesquely absurd disappointment! And how well, in the circumstances, she'd behaved! Sherrard felt all his affection for her flooding back – not too strongly, not strongly enough to make him jealous of her Chinese beau – but with sufficient warmth to heal all soreness. 'Poor Maria, it's a wonder she didn't box my ears!' thought Sherrard and began to laugh.

Maria's uncle had been laughing for some time. He stood and rocked with silent, delighted laughter, the cat clasped to his bosom, all humility wiped from his face by an artist's giddy pride. Even his teeth looked very nearly natural.

'Listen,' said Sherrard, 'I'm taking that cat away from Maria and giving it to you. *Back* to you. You understand? It's yours. If you want to sell, I can give you an address where they'll probably pay anything you like to ask for it. And if you can lay hands on any more quartz, or whatever else you carve cats out of, I imagine you've a very rewarding future. I see I'll have to say all this over again,' concluded Sherrard, 'so in the meantime, instead of waiting for Maria's wonderboy, why shouldn't we go out to dinner ourselves?'

There was a response, all right, then. Half incredulous, half eager, like a very old tortoise sniffing the spring, Maria's uncle poked forth his head above the cat's. 'You and I go out to *dinner*?'

'Why not?' said Sherrard.

'Chinese style?'

'Why not? We needn't,' added Sherrard, as the old man appeared to turn something over in his mind, 'disturb Maria. We'll just leave her a note.'

But it wasn't Maria the old man was thinking of. Stroking a finger down the cat, nose to tail. 'You are certain,' he pressed, 'it can be sold for much? For how much? A – hundred dollars?'

'Six hundred,' said Sherrard – justifiably confident in his Texan.

Every tooth in the old head gleamed anew.

'Then *you* shall be *my* guest, not I yours,' pronounced Maria's uncle.

What an evening it was!

All the best dinners, Sherrard remembered once hearing, are eaten on credit; the old man's credit with a certain compatriot restaurateur appeared illimitable – especially after he had displayed the amethyst cat, which they bore with them. (It didn't even have to suffer the indignity of being left in pawn.) They dined, with intervals for conversation, while special dishes were being cooked, or special delicacies sent for, until well past midnight. Sherrard was rather queasy next day and so, as reported by Maria, was her uncle. 'Where did you two go for heaven's sake?' demanded Maria, over the telephone. 'And why didn't you stay to meet Harry? We were disappointed.'

'Didn't you and Harry have a good time too?' asked Sherrard.

'Yes, of course we did,' said Maria. 'We had a wonderful time; we ate steak. But my uncle tells me you've given him my cat, he says now it's his!'

'As you always knew it was,' said Sherrard.

There was a slight pause. Then to his immense satisfaction – what a splendid girl she was! – he heard Maria giggle. 'How could I tell you? But really it's the nicest thing that ever happened, my uncle is so pleased! And what do you think he means to do *now*?'

'I know; we spent last night planning it,' said Sherrard. 'He is going to go back to carving cats, and make hundreds of dollars, and put them all away in a box, and write on it, *"For Maria's Dowry"* . . .'

Sherrard himself boarded the east-bound 'plane as usually unwed – or affianced – but not unhappy either. He hadn't even the amethyst cat with him; but both felt better off as they were, and at least it made for a peaceful journey. He was indeed two hundred pounds to the bad, which he could ill afford; but there had been something to show for it. An old man's face of bliss, as he looked down at his no longer useless hands: an old man's joy in dowering the kind child who'd succoured him . . .

'Cheap at the price,' thought Sherrard; glared disagreeably at his neighbours, in case any should be minded to address him, and went to sleep.

The Wolf and the Cats

JANE BEESON

'Daddy – can I have a kitten?' asked the little girl, standing by his bed in the early morning holding a cup of tea.

Her father's eyes grew small and round, his ears grew longer and pricked, his teeth grew sharp and pointed.

'Daddy – what funny eyes you've got,' said the little girl.

'All the better to see you with,' said her father.

'Daddy – what big ears you've got,' said the little girl.

'All the better to hear you with,' said her father.

'Daddy – what sharp teeth you've got,' said the little girl.

'All the better to eat you with,' said her father, and jumped out of bed with a horrible howl.

The little girl was so frightened she spilt the tea on the carpet.

'Now look what you've done,' said her father – for it was indeed her father as he didn't have fur all over or a long tail – 'You've spilt tea on my Persian carpet. What do you think a kitten would do – eh? It would scratch it, rip it, make puddles. And what about my furniture?' Her father looked round at his priceless antiques, 'It would sharpen its claws on the legs. No,' he said. 'Quite definitely, no. Fetch a cloth and a bowl of cold water quickly to prevent a stain.'

So the little girl sadly went away and told her mother, 'He said, No, she said.

'Oh dear,' said her mother. 'I was afraid he would.'

'I spilt the tea,' said the little girl.

'Good heavens,' said her mother. 'Where?'

'On the carpet.'

'Oh *no*,' moaned her mother. 'He'll be terribly upset.'
And she hurried off to get a bowl of cold water and a cloth.

As a child I was appalled at my father's sense of priorities; once a year I plucked up courage and the same scene was re-enacted.

The break came at last; my mother relented because my father was stationed in Germany, and she and I were alone together in a rented farmhouse. In fact she only half-relented; the inculcation of my father's ruthless anti-cat regime had permeated my impressionable mother too deeply for her not to feel guilt at relaxing orders – to such an extent that my longed-for kitten was forced to live in a stable.

He was black and fluffy, rather large and not over friendly, I seem to remember, but as everyone told me, he would 'tame'. So numerous times every day, carefully carrying a very full bowl of milk, I would steal into the stable, squat on the floor, and watch ecstatically while Sooty lapped. (Yes, he was called Sooty – not very original, I admit, especially as he was a rather original cat, but it seemed all right to me then.) After he had had enough, he eyed me, then walked round the perimeter of the stable, back slightly arched, fluffy tail stuck straight up, purring and brushing against the wall. The only thing he wouldn't brush against was me, no doubt because of the hopeful lunges I made at him. Remember, I had been starved of cats, and as far as Sooty was concerned I was an unknown mistress importuning clumsily.

Soon Sooty was allowed out of the stable into the house, but only the back quarters – kitchen, scullery and coal shed. My mother made a big-hearted concession, she laid a thin cushion on a wooden chair for him to sleep on. He accepted it with his usual lack of charm, sniffing and declining, then settling for it with a slitty-eyed defiance as if embarrassed by luxury. At nights he stole in after I had gone to bed, and vanished again in the early morning before I got down; only black fluffy tufts on the cushion betrayed his weakness. Most of the rest of the time he lived out of doors, and as he grew larger and larger, disappeared for longer and longer periods of time.

At regular six-week intervals my mother would say: 'I'm afraid poor old Sooty's gone.'

I'd stare at her with woeful eyes over my bread and honey, 'Do you mean he's dead?' I'd ask anxiously.

To which my mother answered in suitably tragic tones that he hadn't been back for a long time. Whereupon I'd slip away to my bedroom and sob for unfriendly Sooty, only to see him a day or two later, standing on the wall opposite, tail up and well fluffed out, one eye closed, tufts of fur missing, and an ear oddly bent. I'd scamper downstairs, drag open the hefty front door; Sooty would hurry past straight to the cat bowl in his allotted quarters. So hungry was he that he ignored my tentative hand so I was able to stroke him as he ate. If I was unwise enough to continue after he had finished, he would give my hand a deft backward cuff, then leap on his cushion and sleep for three days.

'Dear old Sooty's back,' my mother would say. As if I didn't know. The odd thing was my mother seemed never to have heard of having a tom-cat fixed, or perhaps they didn't know how to do it in those days, or perhaps she just shrank from the idea of tampering with sex organs. Certainly such things were never discussed and, apart from my observing Sooty spraying bushes, he didn't add much to my sex education because his own rampant sex life was conducted off the premises. Nor, I think, had my mother ever heard of intestinal parasites because the poor cat grew rangier and more tatty-looking as the years passed, which couldn't have helped him in his obsessive pursuit.

To my knowledge, Sooty remains immortal. When, several years later, my mother announced that my father was back for good and we would be returning to our old house in Surrey, I immediately thought of Sooty. As the date grew near for our departure I became more and more anxious until eventually I braved it, asked my mother straight out if we were taking Sooty with us. Sooty had gone off on one of his six-week sprees. My mother left him with only conscience enough to ask the neighbouring farmer to put out milk for which she paid in advance. I gave the farmer Sooty's cushion and cried all night for three nights; my mother told me how 'adaptable' cats were, and that was the end of it – or Sooty. I've no doubt he did make the best of things, he was that sort of cat.

My next cat was a different story altogether. I was married, and living in Powell River, B.C., west of the Coast Range which is west of the Rockies for those whose geography is as poor as mine. Powell River was a one-eyed hole if ever there was one, worse than Lillooet and I'll come to that. It was a mill town, meaning it centred on a paper mill which blasted out sulphurous fumes day and night. We soon moved out of the sulphur range – except in a north wind – to a place named Grief Point. There I lived on cornflakes and rotten oranges that Simon proudly brought home as a bonus from the Company store in which he temporarily worked. I awaited our baby.

There was a little old lady who lived above us in the trees; I don't remember her house very clearly as she always came to ours when I was by myself – which was all day. She was very thin with spindly, slightly bowed legs, a shapeless print dress, and a lovely face that had seen a thing or two of life; she was English and longed to go back.. I was her 'missing link'. Anyway, one day she suddenly said: 'You ought to have a cat.'

'Yes,' I said. I wondered I had never thought of it before.

In no time at all some friends on a farm who owned habitually producing cats, presented me with a small tabby ball with beautiful grey-blue eyes. She slept on our bed and was christened Ouija. What possessed me to give it such an unpronounceable name I don't know, but Ouija was a startling success from the word go. She never 'smiled on the carpet' as John Lennon so aptly described such a misfortune; she was playful, affectionate, intelligent – I could sing her praises long enough to bore a patient cow. She didn't appear to be jealous of the baby, but tactfully moved off our bed and had a litter of her own – five of them. In many ways there was a lot to be said for her kittens, or perhaps she was just a better mother than I. Certainly she raised her family without noise or fluster, while by contrast, on the first evening the little old lady from the trees came to baby-sit the noise of our son was excessive. Off-shore in a canvas canoe Simon had thought-fully given me to celebrate the birth of Thomas, the sounds of baby cries filled me with alarm; we paddled hastily for the shore and I scrambled breathless up the hill to find my good friend's hair standing on end as she vigorously – very vigorously, actually – rocked the baby. 'I think he's hungry,' she said, which judging by the noise and Thomas's scarlet face, I agreed with and instantly remedied. The next thing, of course, was 'the colic', but I won't go into that . . . All I intended was to draw a comparison with Ouija who didn't appear to have any of these problems. Her family never made a sound except for a few delighted squeals as she climbed in the box to feed them; they settled to knead her with their tiny paws in an extraordinarily sensual manner while her loud purrs of content sounded through the log cabin – rhythmic, calming, altogether civilized. After that they slept, delightful little balls until the next feed time. I really think she helped restore my sense of proportion. Motherhood, I assured myself, was all common sense and being natural, but it didn't seem to work. Nevertheless it had taken a distinct upward curve by the time Thomas was three months old.

This coincided with a move. Simon, fed up with rotten oranges and cornflakes now that I was no longer in a state to fully appreciate them, decided to change jobs. We made a bonfire of our orange-crate furniture which had served its purpose very well, returned our bed springs to the dump from which Simon, always quick on to a good thing, had removed them; bade a lingering farewell to our little old fairy-godmother from the trees, and took our leave.

The carry-cot with Thomas in it, mostly, went in the back. Ouija, her family all sadly given away, wandered untethered round the back of the large Chevrolet station-wagon we had acquired. Its colour could only be described as underwear pink – a sort of cooked salmon – but it proved an excellent vehicle. Ouija, intelligent as ever, soon settled for her new home on wheels, jumping out at appropriate times to do her 'smiling', never running off, never sitting on the baby, never miaowing or being car-sick. In those days our cat experience was so limited we didn't really appreciate her in the way we should have done. Even so, she was very much one of us.

The first bad night came in Lillooet, B.C., set in one of those red sandy gorges for which north America is famous. Lillooet had one straight street running down the centre of about twenty-five wooden shacks; behind these and on either side, rose steep cliffs, or so they seemed to us, arriving in the last throes of dusk. Why did we go there? God knows! It was en route to Alaska, or the Yukon, or somewhere, places Simon seemed bent on visiting – 'bent' probably being the key word with a family consisting of an undomesticated wife, a three-month son, and a cat. The snows had already started, it would not be long before the Alaska Highway – a romantic name to describe a dirt road of vast potholes – was closed.

So we stopped at Lillooet, surrounded the only inhabitant we could find, who was sitting placidly on his veranda in a rocking chair, feeding himself snuff, making those amazing guttural sounds in preparation for a long-distance spit – that's how we located him in the fast-falling night – and followed him along the street until he stopped before an oddly lopsided shack which he said we might rent for a night, indeed for as long as we pleased. Eyeing it up, I thought probably one night would be long enough. There didn't seem to be many lights coming from the rest of the street, except for one building at the end I guessed to be the saloon bar – the sort with swinging double gates like in Westerns – perhaps all the inhabitants other than our landlord, who was counting out coins with Simon by matchlight, were in there?

They finished their transaction, we mounted the shaky steps to the creaking veranda where the landlord pushed open a door. Inside was the usual sort of accommodation we had come to expect, a large space in which was a basin, a gas ring, and a seamy-looking shower adjacent to what was described as 'the commode'. I was taken by the general spaciousness and the single window, even if the wooden planks had dropped so its angle was curious. The only problem was Ouija; we were on the main street whereas before we had generally been in auto courts which were built round central courtyards. We decided she would just have to stay in because the straightness of the main street meant the traffic took advantage to show off speed after the endless windings of the gorge road.

Things didn't begin well because Ouija was reluctant to enter her new abode, roaming round and disappearing under the house which, as was the custom, was set up about three-foot above the ground, to accommodate deadly spiders, snakes, skunks, or any other friendly species that liked the proximity of human neighbours. I went in, sat on the bed, the only object that could be called furniture, and fed Thomas. I left Simon to get Ouija out from underneath the house – fortunately he had a torch. Even so when he eventually came in carrying her he didn't seem in the best of tempers; in fact his ears seemed to have lengthened and be distinctly pricked.

'Don't let her out,' he commanded, and dropped her, less sensitively than usual, on the cringing floor. This meant shutting the door so we were now in almost total darkness because the light didn't work, which explained the unlit appearance of the street. 'Power cut,' announced Simon, but I wondered. The torch again came in handy. In bed between our spread double sleeping-bags to insulate us from the indigenous bedding, all seemed peace. Thomas was sleeping blissfully, only Ouija was more restless than usual but it was the first time we had had to shut her right in.

At 1 a.m. I woke to hear her scratching at the door. I sat up. She uttered a pathetic miaow leaving me in no doubt what was the matter, or so I thought.

'Simon,' I said, 'Ouija wants to go out.'

'No,' said Simon.

So I lay down. But not for long. Ouija was obviously desperate, she paced round the room, leapt up on the rickety windowsill, sat silhouetted in the light of the powerful moon from outside, then hastened back to scratch at the door.

'Simon,' I said, 'the poor cat's desperate.'

Simon pretended not to hear; I imagined his hands were covering his pricked ears. So I slid out of bed, opened the door a crack and listened. It was certainly a beautiful night, the street was all silver in the moonlight. A cat seemed to be yowling but there was no sign of traffic. Lillooet, in fact, was deathly still. I opened the door a fraction wider and Ouija pushed past, indeed made a dash for it very unlike her normal self. I left the door open a crack for her return, got back into bed and went to sleep.

The next thing I was aware of was a howling like a pack of hyenas – or what I thought a pack of hyenas must sound like – in the street outside, followed by a positive

thunder of multiple galloping paws, then an indignant screech I thought I identified as Ouija's.

'Simon,' I said, 'something's after Ouija. Listen.'

Simon rolled over. The moonlight glinted on his eyes that seemed to have grown very small and round. 'Where is she?' he demanded.

'Outside,' I said guiltily. 'I let her out, I had to. Will you go and see if she's all right. I can't very well go out in a nightshirt. Please,' I wheedled.

Simon got out of bed naked, because he always slept naked – and I was relieved to see there was no fur on his body – and looked out of the door. I joined him. Thomas, who was in that good period between three and nine months, slept. The moon was still shining helpfully over Lillooet Main Street which, as I have said, was Lillooet's only street, and as we looked we saw a startling sight. Ouija was sitting in the very middle of it surrounded by, at the very least, a dozen tom-cats, each one with an appropriately different voice. Instead of fighting each other they were all circling Ouija, making sudden approaches while she, demure cat that she was, rose at every sally, back arched, ears laid flat, striking out deftly at any potential lover that got within claws distance. Simon cursed and strode out into the moonlight. Shivering with apprehension and cold, I returned to bed, sat clutching my knees and watching through the open door. Suddenly there was a wild kerfuffle followed by an unearthly howl and the thud of numerous feline feet, followed by Simon's heavier ones, passed under the window and streamed on down Lillooet Main Street. I got to the window in time to see Ouija ahead, running like the mechanical dummy before a pack of greyhounds. Simon, stark naked and silver in the moonlight, but running magnificently, was last. It was a strange sight. In moments they vanished out of my vision into the back of beyond, or to be more precise, the nether regions of Lillooet. I thought the whole town would have waked, but apparently they took such night happenings in their stride and not so much as a window opened. Surprisingly quickly the absolute silence returned. I got back in bed again, lay down for warmth. After what seemed an eternity I heard Simon's feet come up the steps. The veranda creaked. He came in, closed the door, and dropped a damp cat on my neck.

'Take it.' I did. His voice was distinctly wolfish. Ouija slid out of my hands to settle tactfully at the end of the bed where she licked and repaired herself at great length.

'Where did you get her?'

'About half a mile down the street under a house.'

'Did anyone see you?' I asked, thinking of Simon's naked state.

'I don't care if they did. And *don't* go letting her out again.' He firmly turned his back.

'Is she all right?'

'I think I got her in time.'

*

In the morning I found Ouija had been amazingly circum-spect and 'smiled' in the shower. Well, under the circum-stances what else could the poor cat do. I dealt with the situation as I thought Simon had done his bit in the night, then fed Thomas who had slept peacefully through all the excitements, and we went on our way. Lillooet was recorded in our travel diary as a town populated by coarse cats.

The following night was not as relaxed as it should have been either. Simon decided to pitch our tent for a change – he liked tents and I didn't. So he took great care over choosing the site to try and encourage me, introduce me to the orgasmic pleasure he got from being zipped into canvas that I hadn't yet learnt to respond to. The site he selected was under yet another cliff with an overhang that he pointed out should give us quite a bit of protection if the wind got up. Being now a good deal further north, the temperature had dropped considerably, causing the exquisite icicles we gazed up at, awe-struck, before retiring.

I was wakened by Thomas's yells. His carry-cot was literally afloat, and steady drips were falling on his poor little face. Our air-mattress and our weight had kept us in position, but Ouija wasn't enjoying it any more than Thomas; she was sitting upright on the only remaining dry island of ground sheet. As I watched she made for the tent flap with a pathetic miaow, stopping to flick the wet off each paw. I woke Simon who couldn't understand how the tent could leak till he went out, whereupon all became clear. There had been a thaw in the night . . .

Ouija, Thomas and I took refuge in the car while Simon bravely struggled with the hideous performance of rolling up a wet tent. Once we were underway I grizzled shame-lessly for a 'proper' house, and Simon, salivating a little at the corner of his mouth for loss of his Alaskan dream, turned for home, or a home we anticipated in Vancouver. Ouija neither argued nor complained, she was a much nicer companion than I was. She curled by the back window, purring softly as the heat in the car increased, only opening her great ovals of green amber when spoken to. Thomas too, once reassured he wasn't a new Moses about to take off down the Frazer Canyon in his cot, behaved admirably.

Vancouver, as it lay beneath us in the mist, the mountains rising away where there wasn't sea, looked to me like heaven. Civilized. People, shops, doctors if needed for Thomas. Nowhere Simon could possibly find to pitch a tent.

We landed ourselves on some kind and hospitable friends we hardly knew: could they accept us, our cat, and our baby while Simon looked for a job? Of course they could, dear generous new world people. We could go in their newly done-up basement flat, self-contained. Just one problem, they had two Siamese cats who, unlike their owners, were not known for their hospitality.

The Siamese cats made an appropriate appearance at this moment as if to substantiate their owners' story – and indeed they were sleek, magnificent, with immense and impenetrable blue eyes, about a size and a half again the size of Ouija. Their pads, from which from time to time they extended long claws, were exceedingly large, I noticed. Our friends explained they weren't afraid for them, they could take care of themselves, but for any other cat . . . well, they wouldn't like to say.

We really didn't have much choice other than a boarding-house which might not accept baby or cat, so we said Ouija would be our responsibility. We went back to the car where she had been keeping an eye on what was going on and had squeezed herself under the back seat, her ears laid flat. When I bent to pick her up, she unusually evaded me and slunk to the back of the car. It didn't bode well for her town residence. However, our ever-thoughtful friends shut up Hector and Achilles, while I smuggled Ouija into the basement where she prowled round sniffing examining the window, the ground level and the further reaches of the basement. It was soon agreed the cat problem would be solved by our friends shutting their cats in at night, which in any case they always did, and Ouija being allowed to make any necessary exits through the open basement window. In the day when Hector and Achilles were roaming, Ouija would be firmly shut in. The arrangement seemed foolproof. Everyone relaxed; we went out and bought drink while our friends cooked dinner. We all got quite drunk, just happily so, said goodnight and retired to our respective quarters.

Perhaps it was the drink that made our friends forget a window; if it had made me forget to open ours, all might have been well. Ouija started the night as usual on the foot of our bed; the first warning I had that she had moved was a screech, followed by a thud as she leapt back through the window followed by two panther-like shadowy forms, Hector and Achilles. I couldn't find the light switch.

'Simon,' I shouted, 'quick – they're after her.'

Simon sprang to life, struck by the urgency in my voice. So was poor little Thomas who started to cry.

The cats tore round the basement, knocking over the odd cup and pot of flowers, kindly picked for us by our host – his lilies – and finally surrounded Ouija cowering beneath our bed, her tail to the headboard wall, her teeth bared in a fearful snarl, her fur on end, ears flattened, back arched. With Simon's torch, accompanied by Hector and Achilles, we surveyed her. I must say, tears of admiration came into my eyes. She made a perfect statue to feminine defensive aggression; now and again a frightening hiss escaped from somewhere deep inside her, I don't know how because her mouth remained in a classic snarl, the picture of poised savagery.

'Simon, can you reach her?' I asked. At that moment the door opened, the electric light switched on, our hosts arrived. We must have looked unusual, our heads under the bed, our two bottoms raised in the air, Hector and Achilles crouched beside us in similar positions, tails lashing, large claws ready for the kill. Our hosts realized in no time something was seriously amiss, grabbed Hector and Achilles, shut them out, and returned, noble saints, with glasses of brandy for us. I soothed poor Thomas who had fortunately found his thumb and was avidly sucking it. We left Ouija where she was to calm down.

After that everyone tightened up on the window routine and the nights passed restfully, Ouija's escapades only being registered by the small trail of muddy pawmarks under the window where she jumped in and out. We would wipe them up before we left, we decided.

The really terrible time came when Simon learnt his career in forestry would take him back to England, and then on to Sweden. At first it seemed exciting, then I suddenly thought of animal quarantine.

'Simon,' I said, 'what about Ouija?'

'We'll have to leave her behind,' he said heartlessly, but added 'until we come back.'

'We can't,' I said, horrified.

But Simon's eyes had grown round and small, his ears long and pointed, and his mouth was slightly open showing his sharp teeth. Saliva trickled from both sides of his mouth.

'With the quarantine it would be out of the question,' said the wolf.

'She'll be miserable without us,' I said.

'She would hate being shut up in a small cage for eight weeks, it would be cruel.' The wolf was panting unpleasantly.

'She'd get used to it,' I said.

'Besides, it would be incredibly expensive.' And the wolf leapt out of bed and ran out of the open door into the forest.

*

So we journeyed back to that one-eyed-hole, Powell River, where the coast road ended and hardly surprising, to leave Ouija where she was born. Our farm friends accepted her happily enough. She could live up in the milking parlour with two other cats, have plenty of milk, Graham tipped some out for the cats every day – there were plenty of rats and mice, she could earn her living, they laughed. What could I say other than she liked people, was used to being in the house . . . But that they couldn't promise, only that they'd take care of her till we got back. I distinctly felt my heart break.

And of course life being what it is, unpredictable when you're young if not always, we never returned to Canada, so I never saw Ouija again. They did assure us by letter from time to time she was happy and well, but who knows. I tried hard to believe them and that she got on well with the other cats, her kith and kin after all, but I'm not sure it works that way with cats.

Now I live on a farm with four cats. Frequently my adult family come to stay and bring their cats. They point out they only have them because I pressed them on them at the time of a cat population explosion. Now they have become too fond of them to be separated, and besides, catteries are expensive. I have learnt to welcome their cats: 'Of course,' I say when told they are coming to stay as well; I even inquire after them along with the babies. This means at Christmas and Easter when, as everyone knows, it is nice to get out of London, my three children, partners and cats arrive. The cat household goes up from four to nine – one has had a kitten that naturally has to come too. None of them really get on – the cats, I mean – the house is filled with repressed friction and stealthy cats stalking round suspiciously in fear of meeting their own mothers, wily mothers who have discarded all maternal sense; growling emits from under every bed. My own cats frequently retire to the barns.

These town cats are very well looked after, they eat lobster and crab, wear flea collars – especially for coming down here – have special cat trays for 'smiling' in with arched roofs. My cats' occasional flea, I am told, will give their refined cats tapeworm. And it is here we are faced with a family failing – all of us are distinctly nervous when faced with our cats' response to spray or pill. We've rolled them up like Tom Kitten, put them in canvas bags like the vet, three people have held one cat while the fourth drops a pill in between teeth that match the shark's in *Jaws*. Two minutes later the cat regurgitates the pill on the floor. We were nonplussed – yes, even Simon – until Emma came. Emnma was a tall, elegant blonde, altogether delightful and exuding the faintest trace of deliciously expensive scent. She had a distinct feel of London about her, I admit my prejudice.

So one day when discussing, while roasting a chicken, the problem of dosing cats, I was dumfounded when Emma said: 'If you mean you want your cats pilled, I'll do it.'

I looked at her long white fingers with perfectly shaped pearly nails, visualized our cats needle teeth and extending claws. 'No,' I said. 'It's sweet of you to offer but you've no idea what they're like.'

'If you tell me which one,' Emma said, 'I'll do it.'

'Two of us could hold it,' I offered, 'wrap a blanket round its legs to try to stop it scratching you.'

'I don't need help,' she said, 'just put it on my lap.'

Her confidence demanded instant obedience. Trance-like I placed a cat on her lap, handed her a pill. With a quick, deft squeeze of the jaw, a flash like a conjuror's hand, the pill vanished. Emma stroked the cat, put it down on the floor.

'Has it gone down?' I asked, disbelieving.

'Yes,' said Emma calmly. 'Do you want any more done?'

I handed her another five – not a scratch, not a scuffle, not a regurgitated pill.

And that just goes to show, I remarked to Simon in bed that night, how silly prejudices are.

'Who would have thought it of Emma,' he said.

'Yes,' I said, 'Who? She's obviously a genius with cats.'

So now I live amidst purring happy cats, with my family unafraid of the contamination their cats might suffer on a visit. The only downside, a telephone rings: 'It'll be all right, won't it, if I leave Domino and Cluedo with you while we're away – oh, and could Henry possibly leave his cat too?'

It's a chastening thought to realize I have come to resemble the Wolf who jumped out of bed to eat a little girl who wanted a kitten.

Cat Talk

LYNNE BRYAN

The cat has a shoulder joint which is extraordinarily mobile. It allows the foreleg to rotate in every direction.

The time I leave from work varies, which is why I can't always catch the 5.30. Some days this is a blessing. The 5.30 bus is packed, always full of smoke, always hell to get off.

The bus-stop nearest my house is the first after a roundabout. When the bus is empty there's hardly a problem. But when the bus is full, like the 5.30, it's murder. The standing passengers try to keep upright as the bus goes into a swerve: they won't budge to let you down the aisle.

The 5.30 has this attraction though: three women who talk about cats. They are all over fifty, dress in similar brown macs with tie belts. Two of them have the standard perm, whilst the one who does most of the talking models a tube-like bun. It sits on the top of her head, a beckoning receiver drawing and emitting news about cats.

The first time I heard them was on Day 1 of the Gulf War. The bus was unusually silent, except for a few voices worrying whether Saddam would send terrorists into Scotland, except for the women talking about cats. I was surprised nobody told the women to shut up. It seemed like they were committing a crime, bemoaning hair balls whilst young men prepared for death.

But I've begun to appreciate them. You can submerge yourself in cat flu, kitten fever, the merits of name tags and elasticated collars. You can forget the real crappiness of life.

The sanitary tray should be large enough for the cat to stand inside. It should be waterproof, and easy to clean.

I work in a department store behind a perfume counter. But I was made for better things. At school I was the brightest in the class, and the most popular. I had prospects. Then I met Danny. He was down from Scotland on holiday. I met him at a disco, and my hormones went wild. I gave up everything to move to Glasgow, to be with a twenty-seven-year-old turning to fat, a market trader into cracked crockery and melamine.

The marriage was OK for a while. But then I got bored. It's all routine: the missionary position, the sock-washing on Sunday, the fish supper on Friday. Danny has no idea. He thinks we're fine. He thinks I love him.

But for the past five years I've had affairs. I see the men at my work, as they pick out perfumes for their grannies, and I muscle my way in, offer more than a squirt of Obsession. I go for the weedy type, with hopeless hair. Because they let me get on top. Because they talk to me about life. Because they give me confidence.

My current lover is Bob. He's been around for a while, because he makes me laugh. At least he used to. But now the world is getting so unstable he's changed.

On Day 1 of the Gulf War he came into the shop to give me a box of chocolates. 'For you,' he said, 'because I love you in that white tunic, because I cherish everything about you.'

'Oh Bob,' I smiled. 'You should be a stand-up.'

'A stand-up?' he said.

'Comedian,' I explained.

'I'm serious,' he said.

*Whenever you notice a sudden change in your cat's behaviour
examine the cat carefully.*

Bob hung his angular face over the 99p toilet waters. He
was furious. 'Bob,' I said. 'The chocolates are lovely, you
are lovely, but I'm married.'

'But what if it comes to conscription?' he snarled. 'What
if I have to go away? I will want to know you're mine.'

'This is desperation talking, Bob,' I said. I felt as if I'd
entered a movie. 'There will be no conscription.'

Now, we're into Week 3 and Bob is almost manic. He's
obsessed with conscription, but more – a black hole has
entered him. He can no longer study. He has stopped
washing. He eats only bread, drinks only water.

Part of me enjoys his despair: the sex is amazing. But
mainly I can't do with it. He pesters me at work. He walks
me to the bus-stop, clutching tightly at my hands. I get
no relief unless I can catch the 5.30 and listen to the
women who talk about cats.

*Do not keep frail and senile cats alive merely because you cannot
face a trip to the vets.*

Bob comes into work. He arrives at twelve o'clock, which
is his regular time. He looks terrible. He wears his green
winter pullover; it has holes beneath the arms, and a large
oily streak runs from the neck edge across his chest. His
trousers are black, but even they look dirty. They hang
limp from his skinny frame. And he has shaved his head.
He hasn't touched his beard, but has removed his mop of
cotted hair. I feel sympathy for him, but also anger.
Everybody else manages to go about their own business,
to get on with life, why can't he? Why does he have to be
so melodramatic?

'Bob,' I say. 'I've had enough. I'm not cut out for this.'

'What?' he whispers. 'Are you dumping me?'

'I'm sorry, Bob. But it's not like it was. I used to look up to you. And we had fun. But now I feel so responsible. And I can't stand the gloom. I have problems of my own. I can't cope with yours too.'

This morning I tucked into my Rice Krispies, fuelling myself for another stretch in the shop. Rex strolled in to start his begging act. He's Danny's Alsatian and I loathe him. He has bad breath. He sat in front of me and thumped his large tail on the carpet. Little flecks of gravel jumped from the pile, and I was reminded of Danny's work boots; the sturdy steel-capped boots he wears in case rain or hurricane hits his stall. I shivered. I've seen lots of those boots, on the news. They belong to soldiers, the successful ones, who walk and run and tramp their boots over the bodies of others.

Danny cheers the news: he cheers the soldiers; and the images of oil wells alight; the bombed-out families; the Scuds; the POWs. He's a thug, which is why I'm still bound to him.

'So you're dumping me,' says Bob. He stands a while with his head cocked like some stupid bird, then he walks out of the shop.

'Thank God,' says Marjorie, the Max Factor woman. 'He gave me the creeps.'

Studs with defects such as ingrowing eyelashes, inverted eyelids, kinked tails or those that are rigged (having only one testicle present in the scrotum) should be neutered.

I catch the 5.30 bus, and the only seat spare is next to the women who talk about cats. I listen to their chat. I helps me forget Bob's naked head, his look of hurt.

'All I know is my Uncle George passes away, and the next minute this little ginger stray lands on my doorstep.

I pick him up, and what do I see? Uncle George's eyes. The same old gentleman eyes. "Well," I say to this kitten, "do you mind if I call you George?"' The woman with the tube-like bun taps her cigarette; the ash falls on her coat and she brushes it away. Her expression is serious. I want to hug her for it.

When I get home, Danny is waiting for me. I know something is wrong, because he has switched off the news. 'I've had a phone call,' he says, 'from somebody called Bob. Claims he knows you, and is madly in love with you.'

I try to keep calm, to act innocent. 'Bob?' I say. I shake my head. 'I don't know any Bob.'

Cats can be nervous. They are frightened by loud noises and bangs.

I go to bed early, leaving Danny to watch some newscaster move little plastic battleships over a map of the Gulf. He is raging, but he hasn't hit me. His hand has just hovered close to my face. 'You wouldn't live,' he said, 'if I started on you now.'

I slip off my work overall, and pull on my nightie. I curl into bed, and try to decide what to do. Nothing comes into my head except for Bob. 'You selfish fucker,' I say aloud. 'You selfish, selfish fucker.'

I sleep fitfully, my dreams frantic. I'm running down corridors, sliding down Helter Skelters. I'm a little brown sparrow being chased by a big brown eagle. I'm on fire. I toss and turn, and only really settle when I register that Danny won't be joining me.

There is a loud knock on the bedroom door in the morning. It wakes me, and I rise not in a sleepy way but tensed. 'Yes,' I say.

Danny saunters in. He seems pleased with himself. He holds a tray, piled with two plates and two cups of tea. On the plates are slabs of plain bread, and square sausage. I feel queasy, especially when he fixes this smile on me. 'I thought we could have breakfast together, have a little talk before you go to work. Sort out a few things.'

The skin of the cat is loose so it acts as great protection in combat or accident. Many a cat has soon recovered from severe lacerations after a fight, because only the loose skin has been torn and nothing vital has been damaged beneath.

'What's happened to you?' says Marjorie the Max Factor woman.

'Ran into a lamppost,' I reply, pulling down my overall sleeve to try to hide the bruises. They stand out red and impressive against my fair skin, and no amount of foundation will disguise them.

'Some lamppost,' says Marjorie, whistling.

I wait for her to pry further, but a customer interrupts. The rest of the day is lost, to sales, to stock-taking, to dusting the bottles of perfume which have stood behind the counter for years. At twelve o'clock I watch for Bob, expecting him to come with apologies, begging for forgiveness, and to start again. But there is no Bob.

I am not upset. I would've liked the chance to lay into him, but know he's not worth it. I imagine him cowering in the corner of his bed-sit, listening to the World Service, crossing his fingers that conscription is not an item. Poor Bob. I'm not as puny as him.

Cats are survivors.

I step on to the 5.30 and follow the queue of people up the metal stairs to the top deck. The bus is packed, but I get the seat I want, next to the three women who talk about cats. They are mid-way through a conversation on defleaing, and I interrupt.

The words tumble out. 'Hiya,' I say. 'Can I butt in? It's just that I have a cat and she's covered in ticks. I've tried all the powders, but they only make her sick. And I've washed her and washed her, and of course she doesn't like that.'

The three women look at me. They are on the defensive, suspecting ridicule. I try to appear harmless. I smile, with their acceptances.

'No cats don't like water,' says one of the women. She glances at her friends.

The woman with the tube-like bun backs her. 'But they are fascinated by it,' she comments. 'My Molly likes nothing better than to sit and watch me in the bath. She likes me to raise my knees, so she can see the water trickle off them. Sometimes she even licks the water off.'

'Well, what do you suggest I do?' I implore. 'I'm getting quite desperate. Should I have my whole house fumigated? Should I have Tinkerbell put down?'

'No. Never,' says the woman with the tube-like bun. She seems outraged. 'There's too much death and destruction in this world as it is. Just ask the vet for a lotion, not a powder. Lotions stay put.'

I feel the curving motion of the bus and look out of the window to see my stop go by. I feel sick, but do not move. Instead I peer at the familiar scenery of shops and Chinese Take-Away, and hold my breath.

'Excuse me,' says one of the women who talks about cats. 'I don't mean to pry, but I'm sure I've seen you on this bus before, and you've always got off at the roundabout.'

'No,' I say. 'No, I live in Greenock. And I usually travel by car, but it's broken down and my husband's not around to mend it. He's in the Gulf, you see.'

Hundreds of cats have disappeared never to be heard of again, and most of them go at night.

Danny was like a leech this morning, sticking to me as I prepared for work. I couldn't take a suitcase. I couldn't take my building society book, or the necklace my grandma left me. He checked my pockets, cleaned out my handbag before returning it to my shoulder. 'It's not that I don't trust you, Christine,' he said, handing me a lipstick, fifty pence and my travel card.

As the bus journeys to Greenock, I watch the unfamiliar territory, and refuse to feel frightened. The woman with the tube-like bun sits beside me. She waves goodbye to her companions as they get off at Woodhall. 'Ciao miaow,' she calls.

'Ciao miaow,' they reply.

'Now,' she says, turning to look at me. Her face is covered with a fine pink powder: it smells of baby talc. 'What do we do with you?'

Cats are perceptive. They have a sixth sense which enables them to read situations for what they really are.

The time I leave from work varies, but I always make sure I catch the 5.30. The 5.30 is always packed, always full of smoke. But it has this attraction. My three friends who talk about cats. Thelma, Jean and Doris.

Doris sports the tube-like bun. I have tried to persuade her to get rid of the bun. On my first night in her home I mentioned a good hairdresser's. She told me to lay off. She is blunt, but kind. She pulled the plug on the news when she saw it was bothering me, and she gave me comfrey ointment for my bruises. She also let me talk about Danny and Bob. But not now. 'There comes a point,' she says, 'when you have to change the record. Men don't make a conversation. Cats do.'

Piccolo Mac

DINAH LAMPITT

B*uon giorno, come stai? Bene, bene,* that *is* good news. Me? Why, in fine shape as always; fighting fit as the cats who frequent the alleyways of this beautiful city of ours would say. But then, of course, may I state, in modesty, that this is not a difficult condition for me to be in with a master like mine. Indeed no. I simply emulate him in everything he does and, ecco, here I am, a sleek and sinewy mass of rippling fur containing between my unbattle-scarred ears one of the sharpest brains in Florence, even though I do say so myself. You doubt this? Then let me explain further.

My name is Mac, Piccolo Mac to be precise, named after that very master of whom I have just spoken. He, of course, though his real name is Niccolo, is referred to as Grande or Big Mac to differentiate between us. We live, the two of us, plus some servants and my wife Carlotta, in a tall house, much embellished with wooden carvings, considered to be quite some of the finest in the city, not far from the Ponte Vecchio. Every day both Niccolo and Piccolo – me! – traverse this beautiful bridge, jostling amongst the merchants, ignoring the cries of the traders, crowded into their small shops on either side, acknowledging the many greetings that we receive with stately bows of our heads. Naturally, being my own person, I do not walk beside Grande Mac but follow at a discreet distance, keeping my counsel, watching all that he does and imitating, this being the sincerest form of flattery. Sadly, I must admit that my wife does not accompany me on these sojourns for, alas, the fact of the matter is that she has not weathered the passing of the years as well as I.

I will be honest with you for it is not my policy to lie about my age. Indeed I am so proud of my youthful appearance that, if anything, I would pretend to be some- what older than I am just to see the looks of amazement on people's faces. But the truth is that I am eight, forty in human terms, and in the very essence of my prime. Carlotta, however, saddened though I am to have to say it, is a different story. Too much pasta, years of kitten bearing, have taken their inevitable toll upon her figure and now she sits, fat, purring and contented just outside the kitchens – this in case she should need a small snack during the course of the day – whiling away her hours in the sunshine. When I bid her *arrivederci* Carlotta opens one eye, grunts a farewell and watches me as I saunter on my way, tail erect and whiskers gleaming. Then she goes back to sleep. This, I suppose, is as good an arrangement as any in view of the little secret I keep at the Medici Palace. But I progress too quickly! Let me return to the subject of my master.

As well as his town house Niccolo also has a country residence at San Casciano where, or so I am told, there dwells another cat. As I have never seen this individual and know nothing of him I am unable to comment, let me leave the situation at that. Yet I digress again. Some years ago my master was exiled to this country estate – before I was born, heaven be thanked – and it is only in my lifetime that he has been restored into the favour of the Medicis, a powerful Italian family of whom you may have heard, and allowed to return to Florence. They now use him, among other things, as tutor to the three children of the house, Ippolito, Alessandro and, of course, little

Catherine. But more of them later. Let me now return to where I started, the walk across the Ponte Vecchio.

Greeted on all sides, we make our way, stopping now and then to talk to an acquaintance or two. As is the manner of all great men, Grande Mac has few close friends, though many would claim to be so. Nor has he ever taken a wife, so wrapped up is he in the world of politics. Naturally, I know the secrets of his boudoir, have glimpsed through a crack in the door the sheen of taffeta, the opalescence of silk, where a lady visitor has casually cast aside her garments. But my lips are sealed. The identity of these intimates will never be revealed and I will take on in fair fight anyone who would dare to breathe their names.

On the particular day I have in mind to tell you about, it was sunny and warm in Florence, a fine spring morning. The sort of morning on which a red-blooded male might well find his thoughts turning to the romantic side of life. And indeed I must now confess all. I am extremely virile and this fact, together with my arresting good looks – I have red hair of a particularly fiery shade – makes me the centre of a great deal of feminine attention. In my younger days when Carlotta and I conducted our courtship behind the discreetly towering mass of the Palazzo della Signoria, I would ignore the many beguiling glances cast in my direction. But in middle age . . . *scusi*, the temptation became too much and I took a mistress. Yes, there's the truth out. Yet if you saw her I know you would sympathize. She is slim, young, nubile and boasts the most heavenly white fur I have ever seen. To crown all Bianca has the most ravishing pair of blue eyes it has ever been my downfall to gaze into.

Naturally, as a creature of quality, she has a wonderful home. She was noticed as a stray kitten and scooped off the streets by the cook in the Medici Palace kitchens who took her to his work place and there brought her up in comfort. It was whilst visiting the Palace with Grande Mac that I first met her when she was little more than a few months old. Vile seducer I can hear you muttering and yes, I admit that I am somewhat older than she is, though Bianca swears that mature males are more sophisticated and know the ways of the world. And I do treat her well. Though she has no need of delicacies I have been known to drag a whole pigeon all the way from my home to hers in order to give her a tasty morsel. But I still have one more thing to confess to you before I can continue with my tale. Last month our passionate union bore fruit and Bianca gave birth to two kittens, one white, one ginger. I was a father again at forty and delighted with myself.

Anyway, on this particular morning, with all the world in a good mood and the sun dazzling my eyes as I stepped out of the shade of the enclosed passageway of the Ponte Vecchio, I was in the mood for romance and I courteously jumped aside as a pretty little tabby came hurtling out of a butcher's shop on the end of the owner's broom. To show exactly where my sympathies lay I curled my lips back and hissed at him but he booted me up the backside for my pains and the tabby, obviously nervous of an affray, bolted up an alleyway leaving me to gather up the shreds of my dignity and saunter on as if nothing had happened.

Grande Mac was by now out of sight and my nonchalant gait broke into a rapid trot as I endeavoured to catch him up. Then I saw him out of the corner of my eye, just going into the Palace. Determined not to be late I ran swiftly, taking a short cut through the magnificent gardens which lie behind the beautiful Medici home and thus managed to walk through the door and into the kitchens only a few moments after my master. Seeing me, Alessandro, a thoroughly nasty youth if ever there was one, pulled his finger out of the honey pot which he was raiding and fled upstairs to his lessons, shouting to his young kinsmen, 'That miserable moggy's here. Get mobile!'

I sat glowering after him, my tail swollen to the size of a flue brush, not certain which word had irritated me more. Moggy is the very last description to be given to a cat of my social standing, and as for miserable, why I consider myself, though having a serious side of course, to be as debonair and witty and light-hearted as any feline you care to name. Much put out I went to look for Bianca, hoping for consolation and a morsel to eat. However, yet again I was to be disappointed. My mistress greeted me with a toss of her lovely head and a decided narrowing of her china blue eyes.

'*Cara mia*,' I ventured.

She looked wrathful. 'Don't you try your old tricks on me. If you paid a little more attention to your duties as a father, stayed here a night or two in order to discipline your son, my life would be a great deal easier.'

I attempted to look stern. 'You know that isn't possible. I have my master to consider. And, besides, there is Carlotta. What would she say if I didn't come home?'

Bianca flew at me, sizzling. 'There was no mention of her when you stayed here hour upon hour, forcing your attentions upon me.'

'Forcing?' I repeated sarcastically.

'Yes forcing,' she snarled, and boxed my ears, hard.

I have wooed and won many a female in my day, before I became betrothed to Carlotta that is, and there is one thing I have learned from my various experiences. Never argue. Following my own advice, I raised my tail imperiously high and stalked off, nose in air, without saying a word.

One of the scullions, seeing me, laughed. 'Hey, Piccolo, has your lady friend said no? Serve you right, you naughty boy. Come here, I give you a nice bit of chicken to make up for it.'

Somewhat mollified, I took the offering, then purred and rubbed round his legs. But there was nothing more forthcoming and to escape any further confrontation with my mistress I decided to climb on to the windowsill of the school room and eavesdrop on Grande Mac's words of wisdom until Bianca had calmed down. Going back into the garden I swung my finely honed and athletic body up two floors, acutely aware that some hidden observer was watching me, and crept along the various sills until I found the right one. Peering through the glass I could distinctly see all that was going on within. Catherine, as always, was listening to every word my master was saying but Ippolito and Alessandro were comparing lists of girls they had seduced, which was no surprise to me.

A word about these three children if it will not bore you. They are the sole heirs of a once powerful family and have been brought to the Palace to be educated as the future rulers of Florence. Ippolito is the illegitimate son of Guiliano, Duke of Nemours, now deceased, and Alessandro is another little bastard. It would be beneath me to add 'in every sense' so I will refrain from doing so. Anyway, it is officially put about that he is the love child of Lorenzo, Duke of Urbino, also unexpectedly deceased. If this were true it would make the wretched boy half-brother to Grande Mac's star pupil, Catherine, who was neatly born in wedlock. But, and this is where the plot gets really murky, all the cognoscenti of Florence, including and especially my master, know that he is really the child of Pope Clement VII, sired when he was merely Cardinal Guilio de' Medici! *Dio mio*, and they accuse alley cats of being immoral! I wander again, forgive me.

Even though his back was turned Grande Mac was obviously well aware of the two youthful miscreants and their behaviour for he suddenly sprang round and grabbed Alessandro by the wrist.

'If you are to rule Florence one day, my fine young friend,' he hissed, 'it would be as well to pay attention now. Otherwise you might find yourself out on your revolting and grubby little ear. The assassin's knife continually gleams in the darkness, you know.'

Alessandro tried a show of bravado. 'I'll tell the Pope of you.'

My master purred in fine imitation of myself. 'Pray do

so, my dear. He will then, no doubt, for your own protection see that you enter the church.' He cleared his throat. 'Now, the subject of my lesson today is how to influence all around you whilst simultaneously implanting the idea that they are acting entirely of their own free will. You understand me?'

'Oh yes,' answered Catherine, and her dark eyes glistened.

I cocked one ear in the direction of Grande Mac's tutorial but the other had heard a sound below me in the garden and I surreptitiously glanced over my shoulder. I nearly fell off the windowsill at the sight that greeted me. The most beautiful female I had ever seen in my life was staring up at me. Completely amber in shade and fluffy as a ball of wool, her large and limpid eyes, so full of expression and – dare I say it? – desire, were the colour of topaz. I immediately unsheathed my claws and clung to my perch, straining every sinew not to fall off and crash unattractively at her feet. Aware of my unbounded admiration, the stranger lowered her gaze and walked demurely into the undergrowth, tail waving seductively. Now, I have not pretended to you that I am anything but a red-blooded male. With a swift, lithe movement I jumped from the windowsill to the one immediately underneath it and thence to the garden below.

The delicious newcomer was nowhere to be seen but from the depths of a flowering hibiscus came the soft seductive growl of a female in love. With an answering cry and no thought as to the consequences of my actions, I thrust aside the foliage and entered the shadows in which that most beauteous of felines awaited me.

My master always teaches his pupils that there are certain things a gentleman should never discuss. Hints are permissible, sometimes a raised eyebrow, an eloquent shrug, saying far more than words ever could. But, innuendo aside, the secrets of the closed bedroom door and what takes place behind it must remain for ever shrouded in mystery. And as Grande Mac's most loyal admirer who am I to argue with this? Therefore let me simply say that in the shade of that concealing hibiscus there ensued an interlude of the most torrid and passionate nature. Ambra, for that was her name, despite her apparent wide-eyed innocence, was as subtle a mistress of the arts of love as must have been the cats who frequented the court of the Queen of the Nile, the legendary Cleopatra herself. And as I consider myself an ardent and inventive lover I rose to the challenge which she threw down for me. But I am saying too much and disregarding my master's wishes.

I stepped out of the undergrowth half an hour later, tail high, though my legs were a little weak beneath me. And it was then that I saw Carlo, the ugly brute who hangs round the Palace and runs errands for the Medicis' principal cat, Duce. Carlo, who is minus an ear and as thin as an undersized rat, whipped round at my approach, ran his sharp eyes over me, then let them wander to the hibiscus from which Ambra was emerging, looking mightily pleased with herself.

'I think you've got some explaining to do,' he said nastily, his good ear flattening against his head.

I gave him a dirty look. 'What do you mean, mange bag?'

Carlo cocked his head in Ambra's direction. 'Her, that's what.'

'I'm afraid I don't quite follow you.'

'You will in a minute. In fact I think you'd better come along with me. I believe the Duce would like a word or two with you.'

It was a difficult situation. Carlo is a lethal fighter, known for his below the belt bites and scratches. Indeed, I have heard it said that he once aimed his claws so accurately he ruined the chances of the tom-cat attached to the workforce creating the Laurentian Library, a tale much repeated about Florence at the time. Now he was looking at me with a particularly nasty grin on his face, the sort of grin that means trouble for anyone foolhardy enough to ignore it.

'Very well,' I replied with dignity. 'A chat with the Duce is always enlivening.'

And extremely aware of Ambra's gorgeous gaze upon me I sauntered off in Carlo's wake, hoping that I did not look as nervous as I felt.

The sun was by now getting extremely hot and I was therefore not surprised, when shown into one of the Palace's smaller receiving rooms, to see that the shutters had been drawn over the windows to keep it cool. Peering through the gloom I made out the lines of the great red chair, highbacked, with padded velvet arms, which had once belonged to Lorenzo the Magnificent. And much as I suspected, there on the seat was the Duce, head nodding, eyes closed, taking a siesta.

'*Scusi*,' said Carlo, and the principal cat opened one eye.

The Duce was thirteen years old at this time, sixty-five by human reckoning, and his life of power and indulgence was showing clearly upon him. Extremely overweight and big with it, he was a massive tabby, with vast shoulders and a paunch to match. His teeth, too, had seen better days; in fact as he opened his mouth to yawn I observed that several of them were missing, while his breath was enough to cause a lesser cat to faint.

'Piccolo,' he wheezed, shifting slightly in order to release a trapped foot, which came out from under him looking extremely squashed. 'How are you?'

'You might well ask,' interrupted Carlo rudely. 'He's been poaching on your preserves, Duce, that's what.'

The Medici cat shifted his weight once more and opened both eyes. 'What do you mean precisely?'

Carlo showed his lack of breeding. 'He's been sniffing round your lady love, Signor. And not just sniffing either.' He let out a raucous cackle which made me wince.

The Duce stirred himself, heaving his huge hulk into a sitting position. 'Elucidate.'

119

Carlo grinned evilly. 'He was in the bushes with Ambra, Duce, having his wicked way with her.'

The principal cat turned to look at me and I could see that his glinting old eyes had turned to slits. 'Is this true?'

I thought rapidly, wishing that just for a few moments I could own my master's silken tongue. 'Signor,' I said eventually, 'it is true that I had a conversation with your mistress beneath the hibiscus. I believed her to be a stranger on your territory and I was quizzing her about her loyalty to you. You see it occurred to me, albeit briefly, that she might be a spy.'

Carlo cackled again. 'That's a good 'un!'

The Duce raised a paw, motioning him to be silent. 'Go on.'

'It is also true that I found your *inamorata* beautiful, Signor. And not knowing that she belonged to you, I did indeed attempt to woo her, but she spurned me fiercely, saying she loved another. That was the noise Carlo heard. The resounding thwack as Ambra boxed my ears.'

'Um,' said the Duce and I could see that he was considering what I had told him. Yet he was no fool. One does not rise to the position of principal Medici cat by being stupid.

It was at that moment that I was saved by a loud screeching sound on the great marble staircase leading to the upper apartments. Judging by the pitch and tone of the wail it would seem that my young son, as white and blue-eyed as his mother, was in trouble of some kind. Glancing over my shoulder I saw that the door to the room in which I was being interrogated stood open and muttering something unintelligible about going to the rescue, I shot through it, my tail swollen and the hair along my back aloft.

For a moment my eyes were dazzled by the sudden shafts of sunlight coming through the dome high above, and then I saw that the vile Alessandro was using Riccolo as a football and tipping him down one stair after the

other, none too gently at that. I flew through the air, claws unsheathed, and landed on the wretched youth's leg, where I had the joyous experience of sinking my teeth hard into his fleshy thigh. Meanwhile my talons, swift as bolts of lightning, were rending furiously and I was delighted to see a trickle of blood coming from his laddered hose. With a shout of anger, the young man turned his attention to me and Riccolo, seizing the moment, went down the stairs like a white waterfall and vanished in the direction of the kitchens. Spitting and cursing I fought back as Alessandro tried to dislodge my grip. And then the air quivered and stirred as a voice bellowed from above.

'Alessandro de' Medici, I see that you are beyond reasoned thought. Indeed I doubt that you even understand the meaning of the words. Therefore you give me no alternative but to recourse to something that even you will comprehend.'

And with that my master Niccolo, Grande Mac himself, was upon us and had dragged the protesting youth into the room which contained the chair of Lorenzo the Magnificent, scattering the Duce and Carlo as he went, where he undid his belt and gave Alessandro six of the best. During this diversion all three of us, the Duce leading from behind as it were, sped away as quickly as our abilities would allow. As I ran I considered my next move, but even I had to admit that the time had now come for me to beat a tactical retreat. Consequently, I hurtled through the kitchen, looking neither to right nor left, and straight out through the door that led on to the paved courtyard. And then I came to an abrupt halt, for standing directly in my path was Bianca.

'Oh Piccolo, *caro mio*,' she breathed, smiling sweetly.

Somewhat taken aback, I stared at her, wondering what feminine wile she was employing now. But my mistress continued in the same vein.

'Darling, forgive me for being angry with you. Little Riccolo has told me everything. I retract every word I said about you being a bad father. Just stay here tonight and I'll show you how grateful I am.'

I gulped guiltily and at that moment Ambra strolled round the corner, her graceful feline walk turning into a slink as she saw me.

'Who's that?' said Bianca, her voice suddenly cold.

'The Duce's new paramour. A very snooty creature,' I answered. Then, as the eyes of the two females met, added, 'Well, I really must be off. *Ciao*,' and was gone before either of them could make a move to stop me.

The heady relief of leaving the Palace and all its intrigues behind was more powerful than a powder, and I trotted towards my next appointment gleefully, only stopping now and then to look back over my shoulder. But no one was in pursuit and I reached my destination, an alleyway near the Ponte Vecchio, without further difficulty. One or two cats were already there, waiting for me, and I swiftly assumed my place on a high stone block where I could be seen by all those present.

It is at this point that I feel I should give a brief word of explanation. My master's fame being legendary in the fair city of Florence, and the populace knowing that I am his creature in every sense, my own reputation has also spread far and wide. Just as he is looked on almost as a miracle worker in certain quarters, so too am I. Thus, I hold daily audience during which cats, both great and small, rich and poor, bring their problems to me, whilst I, in return for some paltry offering, attempt to solve them. So now, seeing a small crowd of waiting felines and knowing that others would probably follow soon, I got down to business straight away.

First in line was a poverty-stricken widow who offered me a fish bone by way of payment. Naturally I refused it, thus earning a murmur of approbation from those sitting listening. Her story was a sad one, for not only had her elderly husband perished beneath the wheels of a cart but, by a series of misfortunes, her children had either died or gone from home as well. This had left her in charge of one grandson, an unruly ginger tom-kitten who behaved atrociously and refused to listen to her pathetic attempts at discipline. I immediately dispatched Brutus and Caligula, two professional street fighters, who take pleasure in ensuring that erring husbands, sons and so on, are brought back into line. Assuring the worried old lady that they would merely give her boy the mildest form of correction, I sent her on her way looking greatly relieved.

Next to see me was a middle-aged tabby who complained bitterly about a newcomer on his territory. It seemed that he no longer had the strength to see the interloper off and every night there was rape and pillage in the area, in fact no female was safe out after dark.

'He's already got one of my daughters into trouble,' the poor fellow wailed despairingly. I sympathized as best I could, strongly suspecting that in his day the complainant had been just as bad, accepted a piece of steak off him, and promised that that very night Brutus and Caligula would lie in wait, reinforced, if necessary, by Carlo from the Palace. He went away looking duly grateful.

Third to seek my help was a beautiful young woman, not full grown as yet and scarcely more than six months old. She was very much in love, so she told me with a sigh, but because she was so young her owner would not let her mate with her intended and kept her indoors, throwing buckets of cold water over her admirer whenever he appeared. I was very much amused by this story and fought hard to keep a straight face. However, I adopted a serious manner and advised her, for the sake of her health, to wait another six months before embarking on the rigours of married life.

'But how can I stop myself?' she asked piteously.

'Self control,' I answered sternly, 'and allowing your owners to continue their confining tactics. There is no finer way to avoid temptation than not to confront it.'

The virgin lowered her eyes demurely. 'Do you always elude enticement, Piccolo Mac?'

I looked stern. 'I hold court in order to give advice, my dear young lady, not to talk about myself.'

'I see,' she said, but I could have sworn the minx winked at me. And as she hurried away I got the strong impression that she was about to ignore every word I had said and go straight to the arms of her lover. To show my irritation I unceremoniously ate the piece of fish she had brought me.

The court continued and finally the last person to see me made his way to the stone plinth on which I sat. It was Sistine, personal cat of the sculptor Michelangelo, who had been kicked by his fiercely individualistic master the day before and who not so much wanted to complain as talk about it.

'It is the price of working for a genius, alas,' I said soothingly.

'But he is so very temperamental,' sighed Sistine sadly.

'Alas, the decision as to your future lies with you, my friend. Either you stay with him and bask in his reflected glory or you decide to lead a simpler life and pack your bags.'

Michelangelo's cat sighed once more. 'But I'm fond of him, that's the difficulty. It was the chapel after which I'm named that shortened his temper. How would you like to have spent four years flat on your back on a scaffold, painting at great personal discomfort, with your beard turned up to Heaven?'

'I would have hated it.'

'Well then.'

It was my turn to sigh. 'Sistine, it is you who are complaining about your master, not I.'

'You are right. I apologize.'

'Therefore, the best advice I can give you is to utter a pathetic cry when he kicks you next. With his great warm moody heart he is bound to be moved to tears and spend the next few days feeding you with the finest foodstuffs in order to salve his conscience.'

Sistine rubbed his eyes. 'Oh, what a price we pay, those of us who are associated with talent.'

'How very true. Now, if you will forgive me, I really must declare this session to be at an end.'

The afternoon was cooling as I left the alley. The summer was not yet upon us and the fine spring days drew quickly to a close. Glad to be on the move once more, I hastened over the bridge and down the narrow streets leading to my master's home. There, I let myself in by the kitchen door, only to see that Carotta was now asleep by the fire, one eye opening occasionally to check whether supper was ready or not. With a yawn, I settled down beside her comforting amplitude to take a short snooze before the evening's activities.

I awoke to the time of day that I like best of all. Outside the tall timber-framed house night had fallen and candles had been lit in every room. The delicious smell of my master's supper was pervading the atmosphere and Carlotta was already standing near the cooking pots, waiting for titbits. A great sense of ease filled me as I thought of the pleasant evening ahead. For, having dined, it was Grande Mac's habit to retire to his study and it was there, sitting before a roaring fire, that the two of us finally spent some time alone together. And tonight I was not to be kept waiting too long. My master ate his meal quickly, not having any guests, and within an hour I heard his feet ascending the steep wooden staircase as he made his way upwards. This was my signal and I acted accordingly.

Sniffing Carlotta's tail, a duty I am not too happy to perform these days, I hastily bid her *arrivederci* and rushed up the stairs in my master's wake. Then I performed one of my more brilliant tricks. Standing on my hind legs I rattled the handle of his door with my forepaws to show him I was there.

'Enter,' he called, and I completed the feat by pushing the wooden handle downwards.

Grande Mac was seated in a comfortable chair before the

flames, his feet on a footstool, his soft and shapely shoes placed by the hearth. With a loud purr of greeting I leapt on to his lap and indulged in a gallant display of hero worship, pushing up his hand with my head, making dough for all I was worth. Eventually, though, I circled and settled and let his long clever fingers caress my head.

'Well, you old reprobate,' Niccolo chuckled, 'I hear that you were in all kinds of trouble at the Palace today. What with clawing Alessandro and pursuing beautiful females into the bushes. You ought to be ashamed of yourself.' Grande Mac laughed once more. 'But as they both got what they deserved, I can do nothing but praise your actions.'

I purred even more loudly to show my appreciation.

'In fact you're a good boy,' my master went on. 'A very good boy indeed.'

There was a knock on the door and a servant entered with a tray of delicacies – wine and sweetmeats and fruits – for us to share. He set it down on the table beside my master and then stood bowing.

'Will that be all for tonight, Signor?'

'Yes, thank you.'

'And will you send Piccolo Mac downstairs when you've finished with him?'

Grande Mac winked his eye. 'He's had rather an exhausting day. I think just this once I might let him sleep on my bed.'

The servant bowed again. 'Very good, sir.'

'So I'll say goodnight to you.'

The servant went to the door, then turned in the entrance. 'Goodnight, Signor Machiavelli,' he said.

I will leave you at this point, the scene a firelit room inhabited by the cleverest man in Florence and his quick-witted feline companion. As he pours himself a glass of wine and I close my eyes in sleep, all that remains for me to say to you is *arrivederci*, farewell, *ciao*, miaow.

The Cat that Walked by Himself

RUDYARD KIPLING

This befell and behappened and became and was, O, my Best Beloved, when the tame animals were wild. The Dog was wild, and the Horse was wild, and the Cow was wild, and the Sheep was wild, and the Pig was wild – as wild as could be – and they walked in the wet wild woods by their wild lones, but the wildest of all the wild animals was the Cat. He walked by himself, and all places were alike to him.

Of course the Man was wild too. He was dreadfully wild. He didn't even begin to be tame till he met the Woman and she did not like living in his wild ways. She picked out a nice dry cave, instead of a heap of wet leaves, to lie down in, and she strewed clean sand on the floor, and she lit a nice fire of wood at the back of the cave, and she hung a dried Wild Horse skin, tail down, across the opening of the cave, and she said: 'Wipe your feet when you come in, and now we'll keep house.'

That night, Best Beloved, they ate Wild Sheep roasted on the hot stones and flavoured with wild garlic and wild pepper, and Wild Duck stuffed with wild rice, and wild fenugreek and wild coriander, and marrowbones of Wild Oxen, and wild cherries and wild granadillas. Then the

Man went to sleep in front of the fire ever so happy, but the Woman sat up, combing. She took the bone of the shoulder of mutton, the big flat blade bone, and she looked at the wonderful marks on it, and she threw more wood on the fire and she made a magic. She made the first Singing Magic in the world.

Out in the wet wild woods all the wild animals gathered together where they could see the light of the fire a long way off, and they wondered what it meant.

Then Wild Horse stamped with his foot and said: 'O, my friends and my enemies, why have the Man and the Woman made that great light in that great cave, and what harm will it do us?'

Wild Dog lifted up his nose and smelled the smell of the roast mutton and said: 'I will go up and see and look and stay: for I think it is good. Cat, come with me.'

'Nenni,' said the Cat. 'I am the Cat who walks by himself, and all places are alike to me. I will not come.'

'Then we will never be friends again,' said Wild Dog, and he trotted off to the cave.

But when he had gone a little way, the Cat said to himself: 'All places are alike to me. Why should I not go too and see and look and come away?' So he slipped after Wild Dog softly, very softly, and hid himself where he could hear everything.

When Wild Dog reached the mouth of the cave he lifted up the dried Horse skin with his nose a little bit and sniffed the beautiful smell of the roast mutton, and the Woman heard him and laughed and said: 'Here comes the first wild thing out of the wild woods. What do you want?'

Wild Dog said: 'O, my enemy and wife of my enemy, what is this that smells so good in the wild woods?'

Then the Woman picked up a roasted mutton bone and threw it to Wild Dog and said: 'Wild thing out of the wild woods, taste and try.' Wild Dog gnawed the bone and it was more delicious than anything he had ever tasted, and he said: 'O, my enemy and wife of my enemy, give me another.'

The Woman said: 'Wild thing out of the wild woods, help my Man to hunt through the day and guard this cave at night and I will give you as many roast bones as you need.'

'Ah!' said the Cat listening, 'this is a very wise Woman, but she is not so wise as I am.'

Wild Dog crawled into the cave and laid his head on the Woman's lap and said: 'O, my friend and wife of my friend, I will help your Man to hunt through the day, and at night I will guard your cave.'

'Ah!' said the Cat listening, 'that is a very foolish Dog.' And he went back through the wet wild woods waving his tail and walking by his wild lone. But he never told anybody.

When the Man woke up he said: 'What is Wild Dog doing here?' And the Woman said: 'His name is not Wild Dog anymore, but the First Friend because he will be our friend for always and always and always. Take him with you when you go hunting.'

Next night the Woman cut great green armfuls of fresh grass from the water meadows and dried it before the fire so that it smelled like new-mown hay, and she sat at the mouth of the cave and plaited a halter out of horsehide, and she looked at the shoulder of mutton bone – at the big broad blade bone – and she made a magic. She made the second Singing Magic in the world.

Out in the wild woods all the wild animals wondered what had happened to Wild Dog, and at last Wild Horse stamped with his foot and said: 'I will go and see why Wild Dog has not returned. Cat, come with me.'

'Nenni,' said the Cat. 'I am the Cat who walks by himself, and all places are alike to me. I will not come.' But all the same he followed Wild Horse softly, very softly, and hid himself where he could hear everything.

When the Woman heard Wild Horse tripping and stumbling on his long mane she laughed and said: 'Here comes the second wild thing out of the wild woods. What do you want?'

Wild Horse said: 'O, my enemy and wife of my enemy, where is Wild Dog?'

The Woman laughed and picked up the blade bone and looked at it and said: 'Wild thing out of the wild woods, you did not come here for Wild Dog, but for the sake of this good grass.'

And Wild Horse, tripping and stumbling on his long mane, said: 'That is true, give it to me to eat.'

The Woman said: 'Wild thing out of the wild woods, bend your wild head and wear what I give you and you shall eat the wonderful grass three times a day.'

'Ah,' said the Cat listening, 'this is a clever Woman, but she is not so clever as I am.'

Wild Horse bent his wild head and the Woman slipped the plaited hide halter over it, and Wild Horse breathed on the woman's feet and said: 'O, my mistress and wife of my master, I will be your servant for the sake of the wonderful grass.'

'Ah,' said the Cat listening, 'that is a very foolish Horse.' And he went back through the wet wild woods, waving his wild tail and walking by his wild lone.

When the Man and the Dog came back from hunting, the Man said: 'What is Wild Horse doing here?' And the Woman said: 'His name is not Wild Horse anymore, but the First Servant because he will carry us from place to place for always and always and always. Take him with you when you go hunting.'

Next day, holding her wild head high that her wild horns should not catch in the wild trees, Wild Cow came up to the cave, and the Cat followed and hid himself just the same as before; and everything happened just the same as before; and the Cat said the same things as before, and when Wild Cow had promised to give her milk to the Woman every day in exchange for the wonderful grass, the Cat went back through the wet wild woods walking by his lone just the same as before.

And when the Man and the Hose and the Dog came home from hunting and asked the same questions, same as before, the Woman said: 'Her name is not Wild Cow anymore, but the Giver of Good Things. She will give us the warm white milk for always and always and always, and I will take care of her while you three go hunting.'

Next day the Cat waited to see if any other wild thing would go up to the cave, but no one moved, so the Cat walked there by himself, and he saw the Woman milking the Cow, and he saw the light of the fire in the cave, and he smelled the smell of the warm white milk.

Cat said: 'O, my enemy and wife of my enemy, where did Wild Cow go?'

The Woman laughed and said: 'Wild thing out of the wild woods, go back to the woods again, for I have braided up my hair and I have put away the blade bone, and we have no more need of either friends or servants in our cave.'

Cat said: 'I am not a friend and I am not a servant. I am the Cat who walks by himself and I want to come into your cave.'

The Woman said: 'Then why did you not come with First Friend on the first night?'

Cat grew very angry and said: 'Has Wild Dog told tales of me?'

Then the Woman laughed and said: 'You are the Cat who walks by himself and all places are alike to you. You are neither a friend nor a servant. You have said it yourself. Go away and walk by yourself in all places alike.'

Then the Cat pretended to be sorry and said: 'Must I never come into the cave? Must I never sit by the warm fire? Must I never drink the warm white milk? You are very wise and very beautiful. You should not be cruel even to a Cat.'

Then the Woman said: 'I knew I was wise but I did not know I was beautiful. So I will make a bargain with you. If ever I say one word in your praise you may come into the cave.'

'And if you say two words in my praise?' said the Cat.

'I never shall,' said the Woman, 'but if I say two words you may sit by the fire in the cave.'

'And if you say three words?' said the Cat.

'I never shall,' said the Woman, 'but if I do you may drink the warm white milk three times a day for always and always and always.'

Then the Cat arched his back and said: 'Now let the curtain at the mouth of the cave, and the fire at the back of the cave, and the milk pots that stand beside the fire remember what my enemy and the wife of my enemy has said.' And he went away through the wet wild woods waving his wild tails and walking by his wild lone.

That night when the Man and the Horse and the Dog came home from hunting, the Woman did not tell them of the bargain that she had made because she was afraid that they might not like it.

Cat went far and far away and hid himself in the wet wild woods by his wild lone for a long time till the Woman forgot all about him. Only the Bat – the little upside-down Bat – that hung inside the cave knew where Cat hid, and every evening he would fly to Cat with the news.

One evening the Bat said: 'There is a Baby in the Cave. He is new and pink and fat and small, and the Woman is very fond of him.'

'Ah,' said the Cat listening, 'but what is the Baby fond of?'

'He is fond of things that are soft and tickle,' said the Bat. 'He is fond of warm things to hold in his arms when he goes to sleep. He is fond of being played with. He is fond of all those things.'

'Ah,' said the Cat, 'then my time has come.'

Next night Cat walked through the wet wild woods and hid very near the cave till morning time. The woman was very busy cooking, and the Baby cried and interrupted; so she carried him outside the cave and gave him a handful of pebbles to play with. But still the Baby cried.

Then the Cat put out his paddy-paw and patted the Baby on the cheek, and it cooed; and the Cat rubbed against its fat knees and tickled it under its fat chin with his tail. And the Baby laughed; and the Woman heard him and smiled.

Then the Bat – the little upside-down Bat – that hung in the mouth of the cave said: 'O, my hostess and wife of my host and mother of my host, a wild thing from the wild woods is most beautifully playing with your Baby.'

'A blessing on that wild thing whoever he may be,' said the Woman straightening her back, 'for I was a busy Woman this morning and he has done me a service.'

That very minute and second, Best Beloved, the dried horse-skin curtain that was stretched tail-down at the mouth of the cave fell down – *so!* – because it remembered the bargain, and when the Woman went to pick it up – lo and behold! – the Cat was sitting quite comfy inside the cave.

'O, my enemy and wife of my enemy and mother of my enemy,' said the Cat, 'it is I, for you have spoken a word in my praise, and now I can sit within the cave for always and always and always. But still I am the Cat who walks by himself and all places are alike to me.'

The Woman was very angry and shut her lips tight and took up her spinning wheel and began to spin.

But the Baby cried because the Cat had gone away, and the Woman could not hush him for he struggled and kicked and grew black in the face.

'O, my enemy and wife of my enemy and mother of my enemy,' said the Cat, 'take a strand of the thread that you

are spinning and tie it to your spindle wheel and drag it
on the floor and I will show you a magic that shall make
your Baby laugh as loudly as he is now crying.'

'I will do so,' said the Woman, 'because I am at my
wits' end, but I will not thank you for it.'

She tied the thread to the little pot spindle wheel and
drew it across the floor and the Cat ran after it and patted
it with his paws, and rolled head over heels, and tossed it
backward over his shoulder, and chased it between his

hind legs, and pretended to lose it, and pounced down upon it again till the Baby laughed as loudly as he had been crying, and scrambled after the Cat and frolicked all over the cave till he grew tired and settled down to sleep with the Cat in his arms.

'Now,' said the Cat, 'I will sing the Baby a song that shall keep him asleep for an hour.' And he began to purr loud and low, low and loud, till the Baby fell fast asleep. The Woman smiled as she looked down upon the two of them and said: 'That was wonderfully done. Surely you are very clever, O, Cat.'

That very minute and second, Best Beloved, the smoke of the fire at the back of the cave came down in clouds from the roof because it remembered the bargain, and when it had cleared away – lo and behold! – the Cat was sitting, quite comfy, close to the fire.

'O, my enemy and wife of my enemy and mother of my enemy,' said the Cat, 'it is I, for you have spoken a second word in my praise, and now I can sit by the warm fire at the back of the cave for always and always and always. But still I am the Cat who walks by himself and all places are alike to me.'

Then the Woman was very, very angry and let down her hair and put more wood on the fire and brought out the broad blade bone of the shoulder of mutton and began to make a magic that should prevent her from saying a third word in praise of the Cat. It was not a Singing Magic, Best Beloved, it was Still Magic; and by and by the cave grew so still that a little we-wee Mouse crept out of a corner and ran across the floor.

'O, my enemy and wife of my enemy and mother of my enemy,' said the Cat, 'is that little Mouse part of your magic?'

'No,' said the Woman, and she dropped the blade bone and jumped upon a footstool in front of the fire and braided up her hair very quick for fear that the Mouse should run up it.

'Ah,' said the Cat listening, 'then the Mouse will do me no harm if I eat it?'

'No,' said the Woman, braiding up her hair; 'eat it quick and I will always be grateful to you.'

Cat made one jump and caught the little Mouse, and the Woman said: 'A hundred thanks to you, O, Cat. Even the First Friend is not quick enough to catch little Mice as you have done. You must be very wise.'

That very moment and second, O, Best Beloved, the milk pot that stood by the fire cracked in two pieces – *so!* – because it remembered the bargain, and when the Woman jumped down from the footstool – lo and behold! – the Cat was lapping up the warm white milk that lay in one of the broken pieces.

'O, my enemy and wife of my enemy and mother of my enemy,' said the Cat, 'it is I, for you have spoken three words in my praise, and now I can drink the warm white milk three times a day for always and always and always. But *still* I am the Cat who walks by himself and all places are alike to me.'

Then the Woman laughed and set him a bowl of the warm white milk and said: 'O, Cat, you are as clever as a Man, but remember that the bargain was not made with the Man or the Dog, and I do not know what they will do when they come home.'

'What is that to me?' said the Cat. 'If I have my place by the fire and my milk three times a day I do not care what the Man or the Dog can do.'

That evening when the Man and the Dog came into the cave the Woman told them all the story of the bargain, and the Man said: 'Yes, but he has not made a bargain with me or with all proper Men after me.' And he took off his two leather boots and he took up his little stone axe (that makes three) and he fetched a piece of wood and a hatchet (that is five altogether), and he set them out in a row and he said: 'Now we will make a bargain. If you do not catch

Mice when you are in the cave, for always and always and always, I will throw these five things at you whenever I see you, and so shall all proper Men do after me.'

'Ah,' said the Woman listening. 'This is a very clever Cat, but he is not so clever as my Man.'

The Cat counted the five things (and they looked very knobby) and he said: 'I will catch Mice when I am in the cave for always and always and always: but still I am the Cat that walks by himself and all places are alike to me.'

'Not when I am near,' said the Man. 'If you had not said that I would have put all these things away (for always and always and always), but now I am going to throw my two boots and my little stone axe (that makes three) at you whenever I meet you, and so shall all proper Men do after me.'

Then the Dog said: 'Wait a minute. He has not made a bargain with me.' And he sat down and growled dreadfully and showed all his teeth and said: 'If you are not kind to the Baby while I am in the cave for always and always and always I will chase you till I catch you, and when I catch you I will bite you, and so shall all proper Dogs do after me.'

'Ah,' said the Woman listening. 'This is a very clever Cat, but he is not so clever as the Dog.'

Cat counted the Dog's teeth (and they looked very pointed) and he said: 'I will be kind to the Baby while I am in the cave as long as he does not pull my tail too hard for always and always and always. But still I am the Cat that walks by himself and all places are alike to me.'

'Not when I am near,' said the Dog. 'If you had not said that I would have shut my mouth for always and always and always, but now I am going to chase you up a tree whenever I meet you, and so shall all proper Dogs do after me.'

Then the Man threw his two boots and his little stone axe (that makes three) at the Cat, and the Cat ran out of the cave and the Dog chased him up a tree, and from that day to this, Best Beloved, three proper Men out of five will always throw things at a Cat whenever they meet him, and all proper Dogs will chase him up a tree. But the Cat keeps his side of the bargain too. He will kill Mice and he will be kind to Babies when he is in the house, as long as they do not pull his tail too hard. But when he has done that, and between times, he is the Cat that walks by himself and all places are alike to him, and if you look out at nights you can see him waving his wild tail and walking by his wild lone – just the same as before.

The Cat in the Fig Tree

CHARLES MCPHEE

The Great Leader was weary. He ceased to listen. It was so seldom anyone said anything to him any more that he wished to hear. He yawned widely, revealing strong yellow teeth. It was going to be a long day. There was the parade and then the presentation of medals, and then, of course, the speech from the balcony, without which no Nation Day was complete. The Great Leader pushed aside his chair and walked over to the French windows. He had seen a flash of orange in the green of the fig tree and wanted to know what it was. The chief of police was always telling him to keep away from the windows but what was the point of being all-powerful if you could not look through your own windows?

The minister of the interior, who had been addressing him on the water shortage as though he were a public meeting, faltered, lost the thread of what he was saying and came to a halt. He stared vacantly at The Great Leader's back, seeing how the sweat had soaked through his shirt and had stained it. The minister was nervous. It was so unlike the chief to be inattentive and he wondered if he had heard a rumour. He had known him so well and for so long but still he could not always guess what he was thinking. Only a few minutes before, he had been expressing his undying loyalty to The Great Leader whom he had helped to power all those years before, but now he wondered if he had been too fervent, too sincere. He regretted the need to betray him.

The Great Leader did know his old friend was conspiring to kill him. It did not worry him unduly, though it saddened him that even those closest to him were disloyal. There was always someone conspiring against him. The last attempt to assassinate him had been less than a year before and, without knowing he did so, The Great Leader stroked the scar on his hand where he had warded off the knife. It was a fact of life and, in the end, of death that they would try again to kill him.

The chief of police was waiting for the right moment to arrest the conspirators but, in the meantime, The Great Leader thought he would probably be bored to death. There were so many speeches, so many words and really, there was nothing to be done. The water was not his to command, though no doubt he should not have given his mistress a house with a swimming-pool on the hill above the shanty town. They would murder her, the people for whom he had ceased to struggle, and he would be sorry.

The figs on the tree looked purple-ripe and succulent, like so much bruised flesh. He stepped through the windows on to the gravel pathway. He almost stumbled over the slight step and this annoyed him. He was getting old and his bones ached. He walked over to the tree, his feet crunching loudly on the loose stone. He picked one of the figs and bit into it. The red juice refreshed him. He let it dribble down his mouth and chin.

On closer inspection, the orange in the fig tree proved to be a cat. It was a one-eyed brute, probably of great age and scarred by innumerable fights. As he stretched out his hand to it, the cat scrambled down the trunk fluttering the leaves and knocking unripe figs on to the ground. The Great Leader liked cats. They were mostly silent and demanded so little of the humans with whom they chose to lodge. He had an immediate sympathy for this predatory old rogue.

He too was predatory but he wondered for just how long he could be bothered to fight off the young cats who seemed to want so badly to have him dead. In his haste, the cat had dropped a pathetic little bundle of feathers. It had been munching on a fledgling. The Great Leader was not censorious. Was there any difference between the violence of the animal kingdom and the savagery of his own kind? He did not think so. Or rather, at least the cat's mauling of the small bird was dictated by a natural desire to assuage his hunger. His own savagery, he recalled, had been premeditated and in the pursuit of power for its own sake.

Across the city a man, naked to the waist, was oiling a rifle with loving care. As he moved his hand over the black metal, so pure and so cool against his palm, he smelt his own sweat, sour and stale. There had been no water in the apartment for three days and the bottled water, warm and brackish, he reserved for drinking. He could not leave his room during the hours of daylight and, at night, he only dared creep out for a quick breath of fresh air, all the time listening for the armoured police-cars which leaped out of the night without warning, sirens screaming. If it was so hot now in the early morning, surely the heat at midday would be intolerable. He thought he might risk letting in a little air. He cautiously unbolted the heavy wooden shutters. As he did so, a breeze touched his face and cooled his brow. He stepped out on to the balcony, forgetting for a moment the need for secrecy. His room overlooked Freedom Square and was exactly opposite the mausoleum, upon the roof of which The Great Leader would make his speech.

A sudden pain brought his hand to his cheek. Blood trickled warmly between his fingers. For a second he believed he had been shot. Then he saw the cat looking at him with one malevolent eye from across the balcony. Where the other eye had been, there was only an ugly, empty socket. He swore and aimed a kick at it but, tail waving angrily, it evaded his boot and jumped on to the narrow ledge between the man's balcony and that of the apartment next door. He had no idea where the animal had sprung from or why it had attacked him. The city was crawling with wild cats and he knew he should have the scratch dressed in case it became infected. It must wait, of course, until the job was done and he could get out of the city.

The Great Leader dismissed the minister and went back to his apartment to dress. Magnificent though the palace was, the Great Leader's bedroom was cell-like. Apart from the narrow iron bedstead, the only furniture was a wooden rocking chair and a bedside table bearing a ewer of water and a cracked mirror. There was, however, a dressing-room next door where his servant slept. It contained a huge wardrobe with all his uniforms, rank after rank of them. He was not given to introspection but he sometimes wondered why he had collected all these meaningless uniforms, each of which was hung with equally meaningless decorations.

As a child, he had read how the English admiral, Nelson, had insisted on wearing his uniform on the quarterdeck of his ship *Victory* at the battle of Trafalgar. He wore it out of vanity but also to make his presence known to as many of his sailors as possible in the heat of battle. He had read how a French sharpshooter, perched on the mizzen top of the *Redoutable*, had picked him out of the smoke of battle by reason of this peacock display and shot him down. The Great Leader, even when he had first read the story, had been puzzled as to what moral to draw but, from that time, he had eagerly sought out occasions on which he too could wear gleaming medals, gold epaulettes and shiny, black-leather boots. Despite what had happened to Nelson, wearing one of his uniforms made him feel invulnerable.

His servant brought him a dish of eggs and ham, and soft cheese wrapped in vine leaves. He drank moderately of a light dry wine his country exported to many other

countries, one of its few economic achievements. The servant asked him if he wanted a girl but he said he didn't. He would rest for an hour before the duties of the afternoon. The servant was to wake him when it was time to prepare himself. Without taking off his boots, he lay on his bed and, as it creaked under him, the orange cat he had seen in the fig tree dived out from underneath it and came to a shuddering halt by the door. The Great Leader, at first startled and then amused, tried to tempt it with what remained of his meal but the cat arched its back and spat contemptuously. The Great Leader, in his mind, named it Nelson.

After another minute had passed, the cat jumped on to the table, knocking over the wineglass with his tail. Turning round, the cat seemed to understand what he had done and began to lick the wine as it seeped into the linen cloth. The Great Leader filled an ashtray with wine from the bottle and the cat, with evident enjoyment, began to lap at it as though it were milk. 'At least you are not bothered by the water shortage, Nelson,' thought The Great Leader, wryly.

When the wine was finished, the cat stretched and yawned and curled himself up on the little bed and was soon fast asleep. The Great Leader sat in the rocking chair watching the cat and smoking a cigar. Eventually, trying not to disturb the cat, he took off his boots and got under the bed cover. The warmth of the cat on his feet was curiously comforting and The Great Leader, who had the gift shared by many military men of falling asleep whenever he chose, was soon breathing deeply and evenly.

Across the city, the man with the damaged face could not sleep. His face throbbed and he thought he might have a temperature. He peered in the mirror on the wall. The razor-sharp claws had only just missed his eye and had striated his cheek as a butcher might slash porkskin. In the square below, the tarmac boiled and only the noise of the occasional motor car broke the midday silence.

At two, The Great Leader was woken. He noticed with regret that the one-eyed cat had not waited to see him in full fig. He washed and dressed. He wore one of his favourite uniforms, that of Admiral of the Fleet. It particularly appealed to him in this landlocked country to wear the uniform of a non-existent navy. A small group of ministers was waiting for him and he noticed that the minister of defence was sweating heavily and the minister of the interior was rubbing at a pimple on his face with nervous irritation. He smiled and this seemed to make the two men even more uneasy. The Great Leader supposed the chief of police knew what he was doing but, in any case, he was not sure he really cared. There was at least some little excitement in being so much at the mercy of fate.

He got into his black bulletproof limousine and was driven to the stand in the square where he was to take the salute. The crowds seemed thinner and more sullen than usual. Freedom Square was still a furnace. Some soldiers fainted. Nevertheless, other soldiers marched and the tanks, imported from a more developed dictatorship, did not break down. Three obsolete fighter-jets raced above his head. There was only enough fuel for one such demonstration and it was quickly over. The Youth Guard marched past singing. Their optimism struck him as misplaced.

He pinned medals on the breasts of those who had shot dead striking miners in the north of the country, and an 'eagle', the country's highest honour, on the soldier who had helped disarm the knife-wielding lunatic. Each time he attached the shiny medallion which bore a representation of his face in profile to the coarse cloth, he kissed the soldier, first the right cheek, then the left. The smell of garlic and cheap cigarettes which emanated from these loyal veterans choked him.

Then, with his minsters, he walked into the mausoleum which housed the body of the Hero of the Revolution. He climbed slowly up the grand staircase and on to the flat roof. There, behind a balustrade, he stood to attention, his ministers in a line on either side of him. The Great Leader had had to shoot the Hero in the back the day after the Revolution. Though many suspected what he had done, only the chief of police knew for certain. Together, they had dragged the Hero's body into the palace and concocted the story which the children read in the country's history books.

The man in the room across the square sweated. He put the rifle to his cheek and winced from the pain. The scratch made by the cat's claws was beginning to suppurate. He adjusted the telescopic sights. First he saw several men in suits then the all too familiar face: the noble Roman nose, the grey eyes beneath bushy eyebrows, and the small toothbrush moustache. He lowered the rifle half an inch. The medals on The Great Leader's breast filled his vision. There was a noise in the apartment below his and then shouts. He could hear feet on the stone stairs and hoarse voices as he squeezed the trigger.

The Great Leader, standing erect and motionless, wondered if he was going to die. The hairs on the back of his neck stood up and tickled him, always a sign his life was in danger. He glanced sideways at the minister of the interior who was standing beside him. A flash of orange at his feet made him look down. It was the cat. On impulse he leant down to pick it up. He felt the wind as the bullet all but scraped his scalp. He did not see it strike the minister of the interior who had moved to one side, also surprised by the cat's unexpected appearance. He did, however, see him collapse and the phrase that came unbidden into his mind was 'as though all the stuffing had been knocked out of him.'

Letting go of the cat, he knelt beside the dying man and lifted his head off the cold stone. He saw that he was trying to say something and he wondered what words were worth this supreme effort. He lowered his face to his old friend's and saw that he was smiling.

'Curse the cat . . .' whispered the minister. 'Cheek of it . . . mine once . . . followed me everywhere . . . betrayed me . . .'

Then, blood frothed on his lips and trickled down his chin and The Great Leader was reminded of the fig he had eaten in the morning.

The Nine Lives of Impey

ELISABETH BERESFORD

For reasons long since lost and forgotten the rubbish dump on the small island was called The Impot, pronounced Impo. Everything was dumped there from cars to frozen food past its sell-by date. A handful of islanders went there every day, combing through everything and quite often finding a bargain: a portable television which only needed minor adjustments to work perfectly, a pair of blankets never taken out of their wrappings, a catering-sized tin of anchovy fillets. The Impot was a treasure trove for those with the time and the patience. It was said that old Jean Louis had furnished his entire house from the Impot.

At night it was a different story. As the glow from the bonfires died down and the scavenging seabirds returned to their cliffs and rocks, the rats came out. Cautiously at first, noses twitching, eyes red as the sunset, they kept low in the rubbish until they were sure that no human beings were still about. And then they would run, head to tail, leaping and hunting, their only enemies now being the feral cats. They weren't much bigger than the rats, but they were fighters and the rats, at heart, were cowards. The cats would fight anything, biting and snarling and spitting, their long whiskers stiff with blood lust as they ran silently by moonlight.

And then, one full moon, for no apparent reason, the cats left. It was as if a moment's madness had seized them all and they raced over the mounds of rubbish hardly disturbing a tin can or a plastic bottle. They ran for the cliffs, swerved at the very edge and then vanished into the shadows of the Val du Sud. It was a mass migration. But one got left behind.

Impey, for want of a better name, had never been quite like the others. Perhaps one of his parents had been a home cat, one who sometimes had dealings with human creatures. Impey was only young, a black and white kitten with big ears and a thick coat. He had one physical characteristic which showed his background. The long, fierce whiskers of a wild cat.

Impey came out of a deep sleep in a discarded Guernsey sweater, cleaned himself thoroughly, ate the two defrosted fish fingers he'd put aside, brushed up his whiskers, arranged his front paws at quarter to two and looked around for company.

The lights of fishing boats bobbed out at sea, an owl swooped past silently and a rabbit went bounding off into the darkness, but there wasn't another cat in sight. Impey's eyes, turquoise in the half light of a spring evening, searched the shadows, his fur beginning to rise. No eyes gleamed back at him. No voice rose and fell. There wasn't even a hiss. And then his big ears went even further back because he could just hear something else. A scampering on the far side of the dump.

Impey tunnelled back into the old sweater and lay very still. It was coming closer. That scamper scamper scamper and the little whining noises. It was the rats. They were a cowardly lot and they moved cautiously backwards and forwards at first, but as they began to realize that the cats weren't about they grew braver. Their eyes gleamed red in the faint starlight and they fanned out so that the Impot itself seemed to be moving up and down.

Impey had never got on well with the wild cats. He'd

always been on the edge, an outsider. Now he hoped and hoped for their return, but they had gone. Vanished into the spring night. And then one of the leading rats got a whiff of the fish fingers. Impey shrank back as far as he could go, but there was a solid bank behind him now. He was trapped. Wave after wave of rats came out of the darkness. He was only a kitten and they were larger than he was. Any moment now and they might attack. He could see their red eyes and their pointed teeth.

There was only one thing for a fighting Impot cat to do to survive and Impey did it. He took a deep breath, braced himself and sprang. And as he sprang he howled with all his lung power. It wasn't much of a howl, he was only small and he hadn't had much practice, but it had surprise value. The rats fell back, tumbled over each other, biting and scratching in panic in case they had fallen into a wild cat trap. The few seconds of confusion were all Impey needed and he was off as fast as his small paws would carry him. He was in a panic himself because he could sense that the rats had stopped running and were turning back towards him. They were really angry now at having been cheated and they were after blood. Impey's blood.

The Impot covered a large area on one side of the island where the vertical cliffs went down hundreds of feet into the deep black sea. If Impey had turned that way he would have lost all nine lives at once, but some instinct sent him leaping and racing inland. The rats were gaining on him and he was running out of strength, but terror gave him one last burst of energy as he reached the track which lead to the road. A tiny black and white heaving shadow, he threw himself down the bank and fell into the ditch as a car came round the corner with its headlights full on. They were reflected in the eyes of half a hundred rats who turned as one and raced back to the safe darkness of the Impot . . .

One life gone.

150

Impey The Cat Burglar

Impey sat in the shadows and looked at the house. Buildings were strange territories to him. He had never been indoors in his entire short life, but his stomach was telling him that he had to do something desperate very soon. There was no sight or sound of people so he advanced slowly, his whiskers twitching, ears up. And then his black nose picked up something very interesting. A smell of fish. It floated past him and his stomach rumbled more than ever.

Impey began to have a closer look round. The doors were shut and so were all the windows except for one and that was where that wondrous smell was coming from and drifting out into the night sky. Impey measured the distance and sprang. It was perfect. He was teetering on the windowsill and within half a second he had slithered inside. He had no idea it could be so warm, so comforting to be inside something – other than a Guernsey sweater that is – and his fur began to flatten. His nose twitched violently and lead him across the room to a table. And on the table was – was a kipper. Never in his short life had Impey come across a kipper, but he knew at once that it was the most perfect food in the world.

Getting the kipper off the table and across the floor was easy, getting it up to the window was more difficult. For a start it was about half his size and secondly it was kind of unwieldy. It stuck out from the sides of his mouth, it hampered his view and it flapped about when he tried to jump. It took several attempts, but Impey was nothing if not determined. He finally hit the sill sideways on, scrabbled desperately and then more or less fell out of the window and landed on his back, all four paws in the air but with the kipper clenched between his sharp white teeth.

Kipper and Impey vanished into the darkness of the ditch. It took over twenty-four hours for Impey to eat it all and by the finish his stomach was fuller than it had ever been in his entire life. Impey snored, a round black and white furry contented ball. Whiskers just twitching.

The man who lived in the house had scrambled eggs for his supper and thought deeply about the vanishing kipper. Two nights later he put a cod fillet on the table . . .

Impey had a good clean, drank sour milk which some person had kindly put out for the hedgehogs, and decided that this was the place where he could settle down. No rats, good food, a warm ditch, the occasional mouse. No kitten could ask for more. The smell of cod drifted past his nose. Impey stretched, had another good clean and sauntered over to the slightly opened window. He was really pretty pleased with life. He jumped elegantly up on to the sill, paused, sniffed so as to enjoy the moment and then leapt for the table . . .

What exactly happened after that he wasn't too sure. One moment he had landed right by the cod, his mouth open, tail up and the next there was a crash like a thunder clap, some object sailed over his head and clanged into the wall and an enormous roaring creature leapt at him out of the darkness and scared the second life out of him. Impey reacted without even thinking. He shot like a lightning bolt straight from the table, through the open window and halfway across the back garden. He landed in the ditch just as the saucepan yet again came hurtling past him.

'Damned wild cats,' shouted the person. 'Wait until I get my hands on you . . .'

Impey wasn't waiting for anything, he just took to the road until he reached a large tree. He went up it like a squirrel and lay there, shaking and mewing to himself till at last he fell asleep.

Two lives . . .

Impey and the Animal Home

Impey was more cautious for a while, but a stomach has to be fed and the mice seemed to hear him coming. Perhaps he hadn't got the trick of mouse hunting yet. There were a few houses at this end of the island and an old stone fort which was let into four holiday apartments. As it was now late spring there were some holiday makers about. Which meant food scraps from picnics and, if he was very, very careful, some kitchen scraps. It wasn't much, but it was better than nothing for a growing cat. Although rather a thin one.

Twice Impey nearly got caught and then a strange thing happened; a person started being very careless and leaving food about by the side of the fort. Impey perked up. He was an optimist by nature. Maybe this wasn't such a bad place to make a home . . .

He was tucking into some chopped liver – thoughtfully laid out on a cracked plate – and purring to himself when from out of nowhere some kind of thin covering was thrown over him and he was caught. Impey fought like the wild cat he partly was, but it was no good, he was trapped inside a shawl. Kicking, clawing and hissing he was dumped inside a hamper and the lid was closed. His heart hammered very fast indeed. And it got worse because the hamper was put inside some machine which roared and shook. Impey mewed desperately.

'All right, pussy, pussy, pussy . . .'

The noise had stopped and he was being lifted out and spilled from the shawl into a cage. It was quite a big cage, but it was still a prison to a cat who had been free all his young life. Impey sat shivering in a corner. The voices rumbled round his big ears.

'Had several reports of a wild cat down by the Fort. The visitors worry about it attacking their children . . .'

'Not a real feral cat . . .'

'. . . but look at those whiskers! Quite young . . .'

'I suppose if we can tame it a bit somebody might take it in . . .'

The voices meant nothing to Impey. There was food and thin milk and a big ginger cat in the cage next door, but it slept and snored most of the time and the cage on the other side was empty. Persons stopped and talked to Impey, but he sat right at the back of his cage and didn't even look at them. He was desperately homesick for the outside world. Even the rats were better than this prison. He watched and waited, pretending to sleep when they brought him fresh food. Several persons came to look at him and said, 'Pussy pussy pussy. Pretty pussy . . .'

Impey turned his back or pretended they weren't there. His whiskers drooped.

'Nobody's going to take him. He just isn't friendly,' said the Person in Charge. 'We can't keep him for ever. I'm afraid there's only one thing for it, we'll have to put him down . . .'

Impey understood the tone of the words and a chill went through him from nose to tail end. He looked out of the window at the pale early summer sky. He longed with all his being for the outside world and its sights, sounds and smells. He waited.

His chance came on the evening when a young spaniel started baying at the moon and roused every other animal in the Home to do the same thing. The persons were running round and round in circles and one of them didn't close Impey's cage door properly. In thirty seconds he was out and running yet again. Exactly twenty-four hours before his death sentence would have been carried out. It was a very close run thing in deed and it meant . . .

Three lives gone . . .

Impey Goes to Sea

Impey had had enough of persons. He slid through the small town keeping well away from any half-open doors

or windows – they were all traps – until an old familiar smell reached his black nose. The sea. Only this was the sea on the other side of the island. The sea down by the harbour. And floating on that breeze were layers and layers of fish smells. It was like Paradise.

The fishing boats hadn't gone out yet. They were gently tilting backwards and forwards in the slight swell, bobbing to their reflections. The lights of the Harbour Offices gleamed and so did Impey's sapphire eyes. He had been well looked after in the Animal Home and his black and white fur was sleek, his whiskers slightly curled and his tail upright as he moved silently down the quay. He knew exactly what he was looking for. A boat that was not too big – or it might have a cat on board already – but not so small that he would be instantly spotted.

The *Vijon* fitted the bill perfectly. Impey waited for the right tilt and he was on board and under the tarpaulin together with some delectable fish heads and tails. He didn't even stir when the engine chugged into life and the two owners, Pierre and Pete, set out, rounding the end of the harbour wall with its flashing light and then making for the deeper sea. The *Vijon* rocked a bit then, but Impey didn't mind, he dozed on and eventually his patience was rewarded as a great shoal of slippery silver and brown fish came slithering on board. There were crabs too, but he kept away from them as they raised their menacing claws. It was just before dawn when they reached the French market which was noisy with lorries and shouting voices. Impey edged into the dark cavity, cleaned his whiskers and slept.

It was the perfect life. As much as he could eat, no persons trying to trap him, never a rat in sight and not a hint of danger. He learnt to take his exercise and to go off for a drink from a puddle on the quay at dusk, before Pete and Pierre came on board. He learnt to pick out their voices as they came tramping up the quay in their heavy boots. Impey could have settled down happily on the *Vijon* for ever, but he grew fat and careless. He began to leave fish bones lying about.

'Must be the gulls dropping 'em,' said Pierre. 'Geroff!' and he shook his fist at the cirling, crying gulls which followed them far out to sea. The birds laughed back 'heh heh heh'. They were twice the size of Impey but once, when one came boldly on board when Pierre's back was turned and Pete was down below, Impey went for it and saw it off into the evening sky. He was so proud of himself that he forgot caution and Pierre just saw him out of the corner of his eye.

'There's a blessed cat on board,' he shouted.

'Never . . .'

Pete came clumping up and was just taking a cursory look round when there was a massive tug on the nets and he was distracted. But later, when they had sold their catch and were setting out for home, he had another look round and found telltale signs of fur. The wind was getting up and the spray started breaking across the deck which heaved from side to side, the water pouring off it back into the sea. It was the first real storm Impey had experienced and he clung on for dear life. Then they were under the protection of the long harbour wall and the waves became a deep rolling swell. Impey relaxed a shade too soon, the deck was slippery and he slid right to Pierre's boots. Unfortunately, out of sheer force of habit, he had quite a sizeable chunk of conger between his teeth.

'Perishing cat!' shouted Pierre, who was tired and soaked, and he picked up Impey by the scruff of his neck and threw him on to the harbour wall. And missed. Impey had never swum before, but he learnt how to in seconds and fortunately for him the swell picked him up and deposited him on the wall. He was off and into the darkness . . .

Leaving a fourth life behind him . . .

Impey the Explorer

Impey had had enough of the sea. It might provide endless food, but it was also wet and cold and hostile. He preferred dry land. He shook himself over and over again and set off for the middle of the island. He was larger now, no longer a kitten, but not yet a fully grown cat as he made his way up the main street, deserted in the summer dawn, shops shut, windows curtain covered. Not a person in sight.

Impey found a puddle, had a long drink and then left the road, turned down a path and made for the shelter of an old broken stone wall. The grass was long up here and tangled with wild flowers. Sparrows perched on the wall and watched him warily. A lark flew higher and higher, singing its heart out. Impey turned round and round in the long grass and slept till the evening.

He was awake at once when he heard that old familiar hissing and snarling. Rats. He opened his eyes, his fur rising as he slowly edged forwards, but the rats seemed to have shrunk. They were now the same size as he was and when he drew back his mouth and snarled at them, they ran. Impey preened himself. Now it was his turn to hunt the rats. But they were too experienced for him. They knew how to dodge, how to maze him by criss-crossing so he didn't know which rat to hunt. Hunger made him learn and he caught a rabbit, but it was already half dead, its eyes bulging, legs dragging. He killed it and let it lie.

Hunger was becoming a real problem again and the weight he had gained on the boat was going. Then he saw the shrew. It wasn't much, but better than an empty stomach. Impey, legs bent, began to track it. It ran madly backwards and forwards in the pale light of the new moon. Impey judged his moment, sprang as the shrew dodged again, and came down all four paws together, but instead of warm, familiar ground the earth seemed to open up and he went down, down, down, slithering and clawing until he landed with a thump at the bottom of a pothole.

It took Impey all night to struggle back to the surface. But he made it . . .

With his fifth life gone . . .

Farmer Impey

The weather was getting really warm now and as well as food Impey badly needed liquid. His black nose moving backwards and forwards he sniffed his way towards water. The tantalizing smell grew stronger and there were unfamiliar sounds to go with it. Loud, raucous noises rather like the seagulls. Impey crept on and eventually he parted the last of the tall grass and sank down on his stomach. It was a perfect summer's day. That meant nothing to him, but what was important was that ahead and slightly lower down was a great sheet of water. Impey made for it at a bouncing run.

When at last he had finished drinking he brushed up his whiskers, cleaned himself and sat with his front paws at a quarter to two. This was another new world. He was on the edge of a pond. There were bullrushes round one side and from the rushes several sets of curious eyes were watching him. They were all looking at him sideways. Big white birds, much more solid than seagulls. Impey stared back. One of the birds paddled out of cover, put back its head and made the most awful noise. Impey dropped to his stomach. Then all the other birds started. A person came out of a building on the far side of the pond and yelled something. Impey wriggled back into the protection of the long grass.

'Stupid ducks,' the person shouted. 'What's the matter now? Want your dinner then? Greedy birds . . .'

He carried a large sack which he began to empty out by the edge of the water. The ducks paddled over to him, necks outstretched, making more noise than ever. Impey watched them, his own mouth dry, his empty stomach rattling. The person went off and once he was out of sight Impey shot like a black and white arrow to see what he could scrounge. The ducks flapped their wings and hissed a bit, but they didn't seem really to mind this intruder. It was strange-smelling food, but begging cats take what they can get. Impey took.

A kind of tolerance grew up between him and the ducks. They still made a lot of noise and ruffled up their feathers when he came sliding out of cover, but only the drake occasionally went for him, hissing with his neck stretched out. And he never did it for long, but went off to preen his feathers. It was for show more than anything else. It was high summer now and Impey drowsed through the hottest hours of the day as did most of the other wildlife, but he spent the short hours of twilight hunting, turquoise eyes gleaming. It was the perfect life, but he felt a bit lonely at times and when this happened Impey sang to the moon. Sometimes in the far distance his sharp ears seemed to pick up the sound of the feral cats also singing. But it could have been the gannets which covered the western rocks.

It was too good to last and it ended for Impey on the evening of the hottest day of the year. The sea was scarlet as the sun sank towards it and there was scarcely a ripple on the incoming tide. Impey was just rousing himself to get ready for the evening meal when the person came striding towards the pond pushing a barrow with a heaving sack on it. Impey's eyes glinted with curiosity. He parted some grass with his black nose, whiskers stiff.

'There you are, eh,' called out the person to the ducks who had all started to swim towards him, clucking and clattering as usual, 'here's more company for you.' And he up-ended the sack. Out of it stepped the biggest bird Impey had ever seen and it was heavy with it. Twice the size of the ducks, with immaculate white feathers, a very long neck and enormous feet, it glared round at the astonished company. It was obviously bad tempered. Down came the rather snake-like head, the wings rose and it hissed. The ducks ran for it, hissing and screeching. The stranger flapped its wings more than ever and let out the loudest gobbling cry Impey had ever heard. It sent every bird in the neighbourhood flying for cover and the rats, mice, shrews and rabbits as well. The ducks took to the bullrushes. But they were so stupid they forgot their fear within seconds and went back to diving and squabbling between themselves.

Impey's sheer curiousity overcame fear. He stole forward, a black and white shadow. But the newcomer seemed to have a sense of hearing as sharp as Impey's own. Wings beating, head down, great feet hardly touching the ground it went straight for him. Impey's fur, back and tail went straight up.

'Gobble gobble gobble,' shouted the goose.

Whether it intended to gobble him or not Impey didn't pause to find out. He took to the cliffs . . .

Leaving his sixth life behind him . . .

Impey the Great White Mouse Hunter

It had been a late summer, but Impey didn't know that. All he knew was that he was homeless and hungry again. The days were still very warm, but in the evenings a mist had begun to trail across the sea and the swifts and swallows were starting to fly round and round in ever increasing numbers, but Impey's nose was too close to the ground to notice what went on above his black head. No person, albeit unknowingly, brought him food any more. He was on his own again. Even the stupid ducks had been a sort of company. But now he had to hunt in earnest. It was a good season for mice, some of them white with pink eyes. They had come ashore from some foreign ship. There were browns too and the occasional black one. A few rats, the occasional shrew and rabbits, but they ran too fast for him if it was a long chase.

Impey had to hunt so much he was always hungry; the days of drowsing in the sunshine were over. He threaded his way backwards and forwards through the gold corn which covered acres of this part of the island. It even stretched nearly to the cliff edge in places. There were scarlet poppies now, nodding and bending in the hot breeze and at night silent bats hovered backwards and forwards, great eyes gleaming in the moonlight. Impey caught one once, but he let it go because it had bigger claws than he did. There were hedgehogs as well, but they were no good to him because they just rolled up with their spines sticking out stiffly and he couldn't get near them.

It was paw to mouth living, but better than starving until the morning when Impey – and all the other wildlife – heard the terrible noise. It started like a whine and rose to a clatter and then a dreadful roar and over at one side of the cornfield appeared a combine harvester. Every living thing panicked as slowly, inexorably it began to growl round and round, the corn vanishing as if by magic into its entrails and then suddenly reappearing as bales.

The corn field shrank and the animals retreated and retreated into the centre. Oddly it was the rabbits which seemed to be the first to react with some sense. Jumping, bounding, running from side to side they dashed for freedom. The rats followed them, streaking along close to the stubble and after them the mice and shrews. Impey alone seemed transfixed with terror and the great roaring machine was almost on top of him before he suddenly came to his senses. He thought it was chasing him and he was so terrified that he ran straight for the cliff edge, only swerving at the very last second . . .

To leave his seventh life behind . . .

Impey in the Autumn

Impey sat under a gorse bush and watched the feral cats slink past. They were a frightening lot with their cruel flat faces and long coats and whiskers. Occasionally they would turn and snarl at him, or draw back their mouths, showing all their sharp white teeth as they hissed. They lived, moved and hunted as a gang. A closed gang which didn't welcome strangers even if they had all once lived on the Impot together. If Impey caught something and they wanted it he had to give it up. There were twenty, maybe thirty of them and he was not of their tribe so they could turn on him at any moment.

Impey's very well-developed sense of self-preservation told him that he was surviving by the breadth of a whisker and his feeling of being alone grew stronger as the days shortened. The autumn sea mists rolled in, billowing over the sharp top of the cliffs like silent waves. All the animals grew longer coats and the swifts and swallows had long gone. A large white owl passed backwards and forwards and every now and again Impey's sharp ears caught the furious 'gobble gobble gobble' of the goose as the owl floated over the pond.

Then one short evening it suddenly grew colder and

162

the sea mist vanished as the sky cleared and an enormous moon rose slowly into the night sky. It stirred something in Impey's blood and it had a curious effect on the feral cats too. They began to slink towards each other, flitting like shadows from bush to bush as a silver path rippled across the dark sea. They sat and stared at it without moving, their eyes glittering. Impey's own fur rose in spikes. Whatever was happening he didn't like it. He started to slide backwards on his haunches.

One cat began to sing, its voice rising and falling and one by one the others joined in. It was a terrible sound and even the gannets out on their rocks fell silent. Some inner sense in Impey knew that something dreadful was going to happen as he saw the heads begin to turn in his direction, the blank, glittering eyes watching him. As suddenly as the singing had begun it stopped and then, into the silence, came quite a different sound, a farm cart going home.

Impey reacted without thinking. For the first time in his life he made for the protection of a person. A black and white arrow in the moonlight, he raced for his life with the feral cats in pursuit. They were after blood and they meant to have it and they were gaining on him as Impey reached the edge of a high, rocky bank just as the lights of the cart came into sight below him.

Impey didn't stop, he just launched himself into space, a flying cat who landed on the very end of the trailer as it chugged past. It was a spectacular leap which knocked all the breath out of him . . .

And with it went his eighth life . . .

Impey Sits by the Fire

Impey had learnt a great deal since he left the Impot. Stealing didn't pay, the sea was wet and deep, rats were cowardly at heart, geese, combine harvesters and feral cats were to be avoided and it was time he settled down for good. All the wild cat in him had been exorcised. He slid off the trailer as the first outlying cottage came into sight. Then he gave himself a tremendous clean. He was as fully grown as he would ever be and, although on the skinny side, he had a beautiful, velvety coat.

The first cottage had a barking dog which ruled it out at once. The next night he investigated a second cottage, but the smells were all of soap and polish. No animal would be welcome here. The third night he came to a cottage which smelt and felt right and the back door was open. Impey didn't go in, he'd got too wise for that. He just mewed very softly. A man came out and looked at him. He didn't shout at him or shoo him off. He said, 'You're a handsome fellow, but a bit on the thin side. Here . . .'

He went and got two plates. One had scraps on, the other held creamy milk. Impey had never tasted milk like it before, it was like nectar. The man went back inside and shut the door. Impey practically took the pattern off the plates and went to sleep in the garden shed.

The next day Impey went and mewed again, but there was no answer. Very gently he slid through the open back door and looked round. There was some delicious smelling food on the kitchen table and Impey's black nose twitched and his stomach rumbled. But he didn't go near it. He went and curled up in front of the stove. He was fast asleep and snoring softly when the man returned. He looked from Impey to the untouched food and went 'tck tck tck'. Then he picked Impey up very gently and put him outside the back door and gave him two saucers of food and milk. Impey slept in the shed.

The third evening Impey waited just round the corner from the back door. It seemed a very long day, but at last the man came out and looked round.

'Puss, puss, puss . . .' he called. He had the two saucers in his hands. Impey walked towards him very slowly and presented the man with a gift – a very dead mouse which he had found at the back of the shed. He took no notice of the food in spite of his painfully rumbling stomach. He just walked backwards and forwards round the man's legs with his back up and his tail as stiff as a brush. And he purred more loudly than he had ever done in his life before.

The man started to smile and then to laugh.

'Oh, all *right*,' he said, 'you cunning little cat. In you go . . .'

Impey was in front of the stove in half a second flat.

Sometimes, just to make himself useful, he does some mousing or sees off a rat. He patrols round his territory to make sure there are no feral cats or geese about, but he never goes too far. Sometimes he lies dozing on an old Guernsey sweater the man has put in his basket, and his tail and his magnificent whiskers twitch. It's then that he remembers his past eight lives . . .

Impey is planning that his ninth life will go on and

on

and

on

and

on

and

on . . .

The Incomer

BRENDA LACEY

Nobody asked me if I wanted a kitten. I just came in, one Saturday, after a hard day in the garden, and there it was. A little black and white kitten, not much bigger than a ball of wool.

'Look Jason,' Linda said. 'Come and look! See what I've brought us!'

I didn't need to come and look, I could see perfectly well from where I was, and I didn't at all like what I saw. I'm not a great one for kittens, at the best of times: and it can hardly be regarded as the best of times when the kitten in question has been brought into my house, by my girl, and is sitting in my chair, sleeping on my paper – without so much as a 'by your leave'.

I expressed this, in no uncertain terms to Linda.

She laughed. It is a way she has. If I ever protest about anything, you can rely on it. Linda laughs. I have to admit, it works, usually. Linda is perfectly fascinating when she laughs, and usually by the time I have finished thinking about that my irritation, whatever it was, is over.

But not today. She wasn't going to get around me that easily.

Where, I wanted to know, do you think that animal is going to sleep? He isn't going to continue to inhabit my chair, that is for certain. And where is he going to eat? I

166

hope you are not thinking of using one of the plates you use for *us*? And I suppose this will mean papers all over the kitchen floor? You know what messy creatures kittens can be?

Linda looked at me affectionately, and ruffled my hair. 'Oh, what a bad-tempered old thing you are, tonight. I do believe you're jealous!'

Jealous! What a preposterous suggestion. Me, jealous of a little scrap of black and white fur? Of course, I denied it. Vociferously.

She kissed my head. 'Oh, come on Jason,' she said, in her wheedling voice. 'You will get to like him, you know you will. He's ever so sweet really. What shall we call him?'

I looked at the kitten, who had woken up by this time, and was crying plaintively – a pathetic, irritating, mewling whine. 'Yowl?' I suggested, with heavy sarcasm. 'Miaow? Wail? Hiss?'

Linda laughed again. 'Oh, you'll get used to him, in no time. You'll see. Now, come and eat your dinner before it spoils.'

I should have known. I'd been looking forward to dinner. A bit of roast beef, or a spot of cooked chicken. The sort of thing we usually had on Saturday. But not tonight. Oh no. Tonight we had tuna, which I have never cared for particularly. Out of a tin, too. And why? Because the kitten was supposed to like it. It didn't either. Just sniffed it a bit, and then went off and ate some of those moist biscuit things which Linda had put down in a bowl. What a waste.

'Lucky' she called it. Well, it didn't seem particularly lucky to me. Quite the opposite.

All right – so I was jealous. I could see it was stupid, even then. But Linda and I had been together almost longer than I can remember. Even when I was very young she was there, next door, and I adored her even then – though she hardly noticed me in those days. Later, there was always a string of bright young men waiting to take

her out, here there and everywhere. But I watched, and waited, and in the end she did turn to me. Pretty soon we were inseparable, and then we moved in together – into our own place on the other side of town, and when I saw the bright young men I would smile to myself. Linda was mine. Until this kitten turned up.

We had done everything together. Watched television. Listened to music. We even shared our hobbies, though we were completely different in our interests. I took an interest in her handiwork, and she took an equal interest in my sporting trophies. That was how we were. Slept together, ate together, shared our dreams. And then this wretched kitten arrived from nowhere, and suddenly she seemed to spend all her time looking after it. No time to talk, relax. Worse still, no time for love.

I think matters really came to a head the night the kitten came and slept on our bed – *between* Linda and me. And when I protested, Linda picked up the kitten and started petting it. That was it! I stormed out, and went to sleep on the sofa. She came after me, of course, but I wouldn't even look at her. Just turned over and pretended to be asleep.

After that, things seemed to go from bad to worse. I took to ignoring Lucky. Whatever he wanted – to come in, go out, eat or drink – I ignored him. This was Linda's folly, she could do the looking after. I refused to have anything to do with it.

She tried to wheedle me. 'Oh come on Jason, darling. You're being silly.'

And so I was, but I wasn't going to admit it. My pride was at stake, by this time. She was babying that kitten, I told myself. And that was what hurt. Just because I couldn't have children. But she'd known that, before she moved in with me. It got to the stage that, whenever Linda took Lucky on her knee, I sat and glowered.

In the end, it got to her. I could see it. I knew Linda of old. And then I heard her talking to one of her friends on the telephone. 'Yes, little black and white kitten, ever such a sweet little thing. But really, it hasn't worked out. Jason hasn't taken to him at all. I'd thought he'd come round, in the end, cause he's an affectionate creature really, and I thought he'd really enjoy having a kitten around the place. Be a bit of company for him, when I was out, too. But there you are. Jason comes first, obviously. So if you know anyone who might give a kitten a good home, let me know.'

I was triumphant. 'Jason comes first!' That kitten would have to go. For more than an hour I walked around with my head in the clouds.

And then, of course, I began to have second thoughts. You couldn't help feeling sorry for the kitten, really. He hadn't asked to come, after all. And he didn't really take up all that much room. I looked at him, sitting on the hearth-rug by the fire. He'd given up sitting in my chair, and the paper was all my own. He was, I supposed, quite a pretty little thing. Quite cute really.

I waited until Linda went out of the room to make some

coffee, and then I made my move. Went over to the kitten, and very gently fondled its fur. Lucky opened one eye and looked at me. And purred. I did it again. The purr got louder. I could feel a great stupid grin of satisfaction sweep over me. It was, after all, quite an agreeable kitten. If you liked that sort of thing. I sat down beside it, listening to the purr.

And that was where I was when Linda came back into the room. If I'd heard her coming, I would have moved, of course, but I was too interested in the kitten. She opened the door, and by that time it was too late. Caught in the act.

Linda looked at me, and smiled. A slow, delighted smile.

'Hey Brian!' she called to one of the bright young men who was drinking coffee with her in the kitchen. 'Come in here and have a look at this. Curled up together like a pair of old pals. And I thought it would never happen. Oh, Jason.' She came and put her arms around me, and lifted me to her shoulder, 'You silly old pussy cat. Why couldn't you have done that all along?'

Lucky Cat

CHARLOTTE WALLACE

Gerald Fawnsley was unhappy and a little drunk as he came back to the flat about two in the morning. He threw down his coat which was sleek and black just like Basil's. 'Well old fellow,' he said, gathering him up into his arms and nuzzling his cheek against the cat's fur, 'I made a fool of myself tonight. You remember that girl who said you gave her asthma and that, if she married me, you would be the first thing to go? She's just said she never wants to see me again as long as she lives. She told me I had to choose: her or "that bloody cat". I don't know why but, at that moment, I knew there was really no competition. I chose you. She burst into tears and said she hated me and that was that.'

Basil couldn't understand it. He knew he was supposed to be lucky, being so black, but anytime Gerald got keen on a girl, he seemed quite unwittingly to break up the relationship. For instance, there was the French girl Marie-Claire who was such a good cook Gerald began to get fat and Basil, on the leftovers, grew so rotund he could barely jump up on to the sofa. One evening – it must have been the young lovers' third month together – as Marie-Claire was cooking, she confessed to Basil, she was going to make Gerald ask her to marry him.

When Gerald got back from work, he was greeted by

171

Marie-Claire's loving kiss and would have been happy to have tumbled into bed with her. His heart rather sank when he saw the candlelit table, the single rose in its elegant little vase, the gleaming silver. Obviously, he was in for a special meal and, though he loved good food, he had eaten an awful lot recently and it had so happened he had had to take some clients out to lunch. The curry he had eaten with so much gusto three hours before was still very much 'in situ' but he had a suspicion that that might not be the case for long.

Still, he dutifully sat down to salmon mousse. Basil could never resist salmon mousse, particularly one as good as Marie-Claire's. He made to leap on to Gerald's lap but, being much less agile than he remembered, he missed Gerald and had to make a grab at the tablecloth. The tablecloth, the salmon mousse, the white wine, the rose, the silver followed Basil on to the floor. It did not need Marie-Claire's shrieks to warn Basil he was going to be unpopular. He got to his feet and made for the door but he was still embraced by the tablecloth. However much he thrashed about he could not get free. When at last he managed to poke his head out, he saw that Gerald was laughing fit to burst but Marie-Claire was crying with rage. She grabbed the saucepan off the stove and threw it at Basil missing him by miles. She had forgotten there was still sauce in the pan and this now spotted Gerald's Charvet tie and splashed down his trousers. Gerald's laughter now turned to rage and so sudden was his change of mood, it precipitated digestive revolt; he shot the whole of his curry down his already pink-sauced suit.

'She had no sense of humour,' Gerald confided to Basil later. Anyway, I could never have married her. I would have had a heart attack by the time I was forty.'

Still, Basil had felt a bit guilty. Half a dozen other promising romances followed, none of which survived Basil's efforts to be helpful, courteous and kind. He really did want his master to marry and be happy.

172

The idea eventually came to him to go out and find someone to suit his master. It was self-evident that Gerald was not himself capable of finding a mate, so the responsibility lay with his friends to do it for him. He took his quest seriously, often spending nights away from home much to Gerald's concern. 'Where *have* you been, Basil?' he cried in alarm after the cat had returned from one such trip, scarred and weary, his usually sleek fur bedraggled and dull. Of course, Basil could not explain but he looked so sorrowfully at his master, Gerald, misunderstanding, said: 'Don't worry old fellow, I'll never leave you. We'll be two crusty bachelors together and women can go hang. But I think I will put a collar and address on you, just in case you get lost again.'

Although he spoke with spirit, Basil thought he could detect a tremor in his voice. He noticed his master was looking almost as bedraggled as himself. His suit was crumpled. He hadn't brushed his hair and his eyes were rather glassy. He was clutching a glass of whisky which he refilled far too frequently. Basil had tasted whisky once, thinking it was water, and he knew it was poison. 'I can't bear it if you aren't here when I come in, Basil. If you go and if I lose my job, which seems quite on the cards, I think I'll commit suicide.'

Basil was seriously worried. On none of his trips had he seen anyone he remotely liked the look of. After all, human-beings weren't prepossessing at the best of times.

Dolefully, Basil slunk out of the flat and straight into the path of a hurrying girl. She tripped over him and fell heavily. The noise brought Gerald out on to the landing. 'Basil!' he yelled. 'What have you done?' Rushing to the young lady's side he gently cradled her in his arms. She had been momentarily stunned but now her eyes opened. As Gerald met her gaze he fell utterly, hopelessly, in love.

As she tried to get up, she let out a cry of pain. 'Oh, my ankle!' she gasped, catching hold of Gerald for support. 'I think it must be broken.'

173

'Here let me help you into my flat and then I'll call the doctor,' urged Gerald solicitously.

'Oh but I'm late already. I really must be going.'

'I'm afraid, thanks to Basil here, you can't go anywhere,' said Gerald firmly, drinking in the loveliness of the young goddess who had fallen into his arms as though she were a gift from heaven. 'I'm Gerald Fawnsley. Who were you going to see, Miss . . . Miss . . . Let me ring and explain.'

'Ouch!' the girl ejaculated, proving Gerald's point. 'I was meeting my father. He hates me to be late. He's such a busy man, when he makes the time to see me, I feel I have to . . .'

'Please, don't distress yourself,' said Gerald wretchedly, as the girl began to cry again. 'Do you know what his telephone number is?'

'Oh yes. I have it here in my diary. But . . . where is my handbag?' she wailed.

Then followed a mad hunt by Gerald for the bag which was eventually found two flights of stairs down. It had burst open and much of what it contained, which seemed an unbelievable amount to Gerald, had spilled down a further flight. At last, however everything had been gathered up and the diary located.

'730 234,' she read out to Gerald.

'Who shall I ask for?' he queried as he dialled.

'My father, of course!' she answered crossly.

'Forgive me,' said Gerald humbly, 'but I don't know his name.'

'Oh sorry, yes . . . but I quite forgot we were strangers.' She flashed him such a brilliant smile his heart turned a couple of somersaults. 'I'm Caroline Spry and my father is Sir Godfrey Spry,' she said.

He could not prevent his surprise showing on his face. The goddess's father was one of the best-known industrialists in England. Gerald was a little down-hearted. She must be an heiress and her father would want something better than a not very successful stockbroker as a son-in-law. Oh God! he checked himself. There he was again, rushing ahead of himself. He was already imagining asking Sir Godfrey for his daughter's hand and he had only known her five minutes.

'Oh yes,' said the girl dryly, 'everyone knows my father, except me I sometimes think. I really should not say this to a complete stranger but my father is someone I hardly know at all. That is why I am so anxious about not missing my appointment with him.'

By this time Gerald had got through on the telephone to a fierce sounding lady who said she was Miss Walmsley, Sir Godfrey's personal assistant. When Gerald had finished telling her about Caroline's mishap there was a silence.

'Hello? Are you still there?' asked Gerald. 'Oh yes,' said the woman, 'I'm here but I'm afraid Sir Godfrey isn't. He is in Geneva. He had to go quite suddenly and I'm afraid he quite forgot he had asked Miss Caroline to lunch. She is in the room with you now, is she?'

'Yes indeed,' said Gerald uncomfortably.

'Perhaps,' said Miss Walmsley, 'it would be better if you did not say her father had forgotten she was coming today.'

'Can I speak to Daddy?' demanded Caroline from the chair.

'I don't think . . . I mean . . .' stammered Gerald. The girl, suddenly resolute, hopped across the room and seized the telephone out of his hands. 'Miss Walmsley? It's Caroline Spry here. May I speak to my father?' Gerald could not hear what Miss Walmsley answered but the girl suddenly seemed to crumple. Gently, Gerald took the telephone out of her hand and helped her back to the chair. 'He had forgotten all about me,' she said in little more than a whisper. Suddenly, theatrically, she bent her face to her hands and sobbed wildly.

'Please Miss . . . please Caroline . . .' said Gerald going down on his knees. 'Please don't cry. Why don't I ring your mother?'

Caroline gulped down her sobs and tried to pull herself

together. 'I am sorry Mr Fawnsley,' and even at that moment Gerald could not help a leap of pleasure to find she had remembered his name, 'You must think me such a fool. I don't know why I'm crying. It must be delayed shock or something. I'm afraid I haven't got a mother. She died when I was five, but I'm quite all right, honestly.'

'No please, Miss Spry . . . Caroline, Basil and I will look after you. You have had a horrid shock and it was all my fault or rather Basil's.' He scowled at the cat but Basil could see he wasn't really cross. 'Let us escort you to your flat and settle you in. You have taken the flat above this one, haven't you?'

'Yes, number 5. I have only been here a week and you are the first resident I have met. I hope all the others aren't as dangerous as you,' she smiled. 'Ought I to take out medical insurance, do you think?'

Basil and Gerald helped her back to her own flat and Caroline, catching sight of herself in the mirror exclaimed: 'Oh dear! I look like something the cat brought home.' Then, seeing Basil, added quickly, 'I'm sorry Basil, I was only joking. I love cats and I think we are going to be great friends.'

Basil purred appreciatively. He liked this girl. She sat in a big armchair with her leg on a stool and Basil sat in her lap and she stroked him. Gerald stood at the door and was jealous.

Several weeks passed. Things seemed to be getting better at work and Gerald had even been commended for sorting out a particularly complicated problem connected with a client's off-shore fund. In fact he was so busy he was often not home until after nine in the evenings. Basil spent most of his time with Caroline. She was mobile now but did not go out much during the day. It was Gerald's habit to knock on Caroline's door, maybe have a drink and then take Basil down to have their supper together unless Caroline had a date. At weekends Caroline

went away to stay with friends of whom, rather to Gerald's chagrin, she seemed to have a large circle.

Coming back from work one Monday about a couple of months after the accident, Gerald went as usual to pick up Basil. He was rather put out to find Caroline with a glass of wine in one hand, her other arm round a good looking young man whose face was disfigured, in Gerald's eyes, by a grin of self-congratulation. 'I have just come to pick up Basil,' said Gerald uncertainly.

'Oh, Gerald,' Caroline trilled as Basil leapt into his arms, 'come and be introduced to my fiancé.'

Gerald could remember nothing of what followed except that the man he now hated most in all the world was called Monty Braggot. Caroline's fiancé! The word with its frenchified coyness made him want to vomit. Oh God! Why had he not spoken of his love before? Now it was too late. No gentleman could speak of love to a girl who had introduced him, without a trace of embarrassment, to her fiancé. But it had always been impossible. Of course he had loved the girl from the first moment he had seen her lying on the floor half-stunned but somehow, despite the propitious circumstances of their first meeting, the relationship had never developed. As far as Gerald knew, she looked on him as just a kindly neighbour with a cat to trip over.

As the days passed, Basil became increasingly concerned at his master's downward spiral through self-pity to depression. The wedding, to which Gerald had been invited, was scheduled for early March and, as the day approached, Gerald went into something worse than mere depression. Caroline was hardly in the flat, she was so busy with preparations for her great day. So, evening after evening, Gerald sat in his chair staring glumly into space, hugging Basil. He did not eat or wash or even sleep.

One such evening, two or three days before the wedding, when Gerald had at last fallen into an uneasy doze, Basil slipped out of the flat with no object in view except to get some air and maybe forage for some food. In his grief, Gerald had forgotten to feed him. Two blocks away there was a particularly toothsome dustbin which he had often visited before. He was just preparing to leap on to it and push off the lid to see what good things it held – he thought he could smell sardines – when he noticed, going into the house next door, the man who had, to his disgust, won the affections of his beloved Caroline. He knew that the girl was adored by his master and that this man was the cause of his master's sadness.

On a whim, he turned from the dustbin and walked over to the door through which he had seen his master's enemy, and therefore his own, disappear. The door was firmly closed but at a glance he saw that for a cat of his agility there would be no difficulty in gaining entrance by a half-open window on the first floor. After thinking about it for a few minutes, he leapt softly on to a convenient drainpipe and from thence through the window. The room into which he had jumped was a bedroom and in the bed were two humans. They were so tangled up in the sheets that he could only see a bare arm and a shapely leg and then a mop of golden curls. After a moment, the girl stopped wrestling with the bedclothes and, glancing towards the window, saw Basil. 'Why, Monty!' she cried. 'There's a lucky black cat. It must have got in by the window.' The other person in the bed reluctantly raised his head from the girl's breast. His eyes met Basil's and his face went bright red. 'Monty darling,' said the girl, 'why are you blushing? Do you recognize the cat?'

'Of course not!' said Monty sulkily, 'and I'm not blushing.'

'Yes you are,' insisted the girl. 'You do know this cat. I'm sure of it. Why does he bother you?'

'I tell you,' said the wretched Monty getting up from the bed, 'I've never seen the bloody cat in my life and now I am going to throw it out.'

'Oh no you're not,' said the girl jumping up. She looked

quite ravishingly beautiful in her nakedness and for a moment Basil could see what Monty could see. He allowed the girl to pick him up in her arms and read the label on his collar. 'He lives just round the corner. When you've gone I will take him back to his home.'

'Oh, for God's sake, Sukie,' cried Monty impatiently, 'leave the cat alone. It doesn't need you to take it home. Come back to bed, there's a good girl! I've only got five minutes then I have to be going.'

'Well,' said the girl hotly, 'you can bloody well spend the five minutes playing with yourself. I refuse to be a quickie for you, my lad.'

'Come on Sukie, I didn't mean it that way,' he coaxed. 'I just meant we haven't got much time and . . . Oh, to hell with it then.'

Seeing there was no chance of persuading the girl back to bed, he got up and began dressing himself. Putting on his tie, he said carelessly, 'Give the cat to me. I'll take him home.'

'No,' said the girl still naked, hugging the cat to her breasts, 'I don't trust you, Monty. I will do it. You get on back to the office. Isn't your "meeting" supposed to be over by now? We don't want didydums to get into trouble do we?'

A little later, the girl, now dressed in expensive jeans and a man's shirt which seemed to emphasize just those attributes it might have been supposed to have concealed, rang the bell of Gerald's flat. Gerald was out at work but Caroline happened to be coming down the stairs. 'Were you looking for Mr Fawnsley?' she asked. 'Ah, is that Basil?'

'You know the cat?' said Sukie. 'Yes I found him in my flat and I thought I would bring him home.'

'How very kind of you,' said Caroline. 'He belongs to my neighbour, Gerald Fawnsley. He – Basil I mean, not Gerald – is always gallivanting. I know Gerald will be so pleased to have him back. Why don't you bring him up to my flat? Perhaps you have time for a coffee?'

The two girls cooing over Basil went into Caroline's flat and Caroline went into the kitchen to put on the kettle. While she was out of the room Sukie glanced at the framed photographs on the mantelpiece. She immediately noticed the photograph of Monty who had been caught by the photographer in the act of kissing Caroline. It was Caroline's particular favourite. As she came back into the room Sukie said: 'What a small world! I see you know Monty. When was that photo taken?'

'Oh, a month ago. Why, do you know my fiancé?'

'Your fiancé,' exclaimed Sukie. 'You must be mistaken! Monty and I have been together for a year now and we are planning to get married next August.'

Caroline dropped the coffee.

Basil left them to sort it out and they did not notice him leaving. 'Another human relationship I have put an end to,' he growled to himself. 'I don't think I can be a lucky cat.'

'He was only after my money,' said Caroline, snuggling into Gerald's shoulder. 'I see that now.'

It was six months later and they were honeymooning at Lake Garda. It had all been so simple in the end. Gerald had come back to find Caroline in tears sitting hunched up on the stairs outside his flat. He had lifted her into his arms and comforted her. She had told him what Basil had done and Gerald had said that he had never liked the look of the man – he could not bring himself to give him a name. Gerald, breathing in her scent as though it were nectar, and knowing that it was wrong to take advantage of her distress, told her he loved her and said she should marry him instead. She must, he opined, know he loved her, always had and always would. He said much else but nothing that Basil could listen to without embarrassment.

She replied she had always loved him but had never suspected . . . And then he stopped her speaking with kisses.

And so there they were: married and in bliss. 'Your father was awfully good about it in the end,' Gerald murmured, generous in victory. 'He might have cut up a bit rough.'

'Oh,' said Caroline in a small voice, 'I don't think he minded as long as I was off his hands.'

Gerald hardly heard her. 'I wonder how Basil's getting on without us,' he said, letting his hand travel down her flat stomach. 'I expect he's destroying somebody's love affair.'

She turned and nestled deeper against his chest. 'He brought us together,' she went on comfortably. 'For us he is a lucky cat and always will be.'

The Kitten's Tailor

PEGGY BACON

Once there was a young tailor's apprentice with blue eyes and brown hair, who in due time became a tailor, and delightedly acquired a small shop of his own, with a green door and a shiny window and a real sign outside in red and gold. Inside this establishment were a small room with a counter, and a still smaller room with a shelf. And here, when the day arrived, came the tailor with a kitten and a thimble; and having arranged upon the shelf the mug and plate that were his, and the bowl that was the kitten's, he composed himself to wait for a customer.

It was not long before one came – a very grand gentleman – and the tailor's heart gave an important throb as he hurried in to take his first order. There was a fine suit to make, of white satin and silver lace, and the gentleman was eager to have it the day after next. So when he was gone, down sat the tailor to his work, and down sat the kitten beside him.

While his master was busy snipping, the kitten played with the thimble; what mattered it, since the tailor was not using it then? And when he finally needed it, the thimble was soon found. But when the young man began to sew, he could not help wishing that the kitten would not squeeze quite so close to his right elbow, though the

little creature obviously sat there because of a very flatter-
ing interest in the work.

In fact, from time to time it would reach out a tentative
paw towards the long thread with which the tailor was
stitching. But the latter always managed to elude it until –
quite suddenly – the kitten made a little lunge, caught the
thread, and gave it such a pull that the seam puckered and
the tailor must rip out and start afresh. Upon a repetition
of this offence, he removed the animal to the back room.
But there the kitten felt so lonely and wailed so piteously
that the tailor let him in again, rebuking it, however, with:
'Crumpet, be good!' Whereat the kitten sat down at a little
distance from the tailor and looked wistfully at the thread.

Noticing the disconsolate air of the kitten, the tailor
tossed it an empty spool; and while Crumpet played, the
young man worked on busily, letting his thoughts wander
to the baker's daughter, who, for some inexplicable
reason, refused to marry him. He had gone to see her
only the day before, hoping that since he was become a
real tailor with a new shop – and such a nice one – she
would at last accept his proposals. But, though she
admitted her love for him, she still refused, and he came
away disappointed and puzzled.

The young man was soon roused from these thoughts
by sounds from the table; and looking up, discovered to
his excessive annoyance that Crumpet, having unwound
a skein of silk, was at the moment engaged in tangling the
silver lace. Dodging the now almost angry tailor with
mischievous agility, the kitten sprang to the bale of white
satin, swiftly sharpened its claws therein, and then rolled
over on its back with disarming coyness, batting a derisive
paw at his friend. But, steeling his heart, the latter opened
the shop door, and depositing Crumpet with all possible
gentleness in the street without, he returned hastily to his
work. As the day was chilly, Crumpet clambered on to the
window-ledge, mewing sadly and pressing an impotent
little nose against the pane; so that the tailor, conscience-

stricken, opened the door and recalled the kitten, who charged in wildly, and then, recollecting itself, halted just in time to wash its face. After which, with an air of virtuous reform, it curled up in a corner and went to sleep.

The tailor surveyed his work. The suit was indeed barely started, owing to constant interruptions; and when he considered the bale of satin, pricked and pulled by the naughty claws, the silk hopelessly snarled, the silver lace torn and bitten, he was forced to admit that much damage had been done that morning. And as it was now noon, he left his work, laid out the mug, the plate and the bowl, and summoned Crumpet. Together they ate their meal of bread and milk, then speedily set to work again, the tailor endeavouring to make up for the loss of the morning, the kitten slyly rooting in the button-box, which, of course, soon upset, and cost the poor man some thirty minutes of angry grubbing.

During the remainder of the day the kitten was expelled from the room four times and four times recalled in recognition of its hearty protests. Its offences were varied, for it distributed its attentions impartially among the spools, the scissors and the beeswax, which last it evidently fancied edible, chewing it up very small and spitting it out disappointedly with much coughing and choking, thereby causing the tailor no little anxiety for its windpipe. The tray of pins that the tailor always kept within convenient reach was soon overturned, and the contents scattered far and wide. Indeed, if there had been six little kittens, the pins could not have been scattered further, for the tailor found them in the far recesses of the room.

It is hard to punish a fat little kitten – 'And that kitten an orphan!' so thought the tailor with a sympathetic pang. And the end of the day found a very discouraged young man and a not very chastened puss. As the occurrences of the first day were repeated the next, it is easy to see that the suit was not nearly ready when the fine gentleman called for it. Excuses were in vain; abuse was heaped on the head of the poor tailor, and the gentleman stormed himself off.

That evening the tailor faced the facts with a serious mind, and after a small struggle with himself, decided to give up the thought of being a tailor; and as a grocery is a pleasant place for a kitten, being always warm and full of amusement, he determined to turn grocer. Acting on this resolution, he sought out his uncle who owned a large grocery store in the next street. 'Splendid!' cried the old man, upon hearing the tailor's plan. 'I have long been wanting a partner in my business, and who could be a fitter one than my own nephew?'

And so the young tailor became a young grocer, and he and the kitten went to live in the grocery store. As they were both very fond of cheese, they easily reconciled themselves to the change, and very comfortable they were to be sure. Crumpet could sleep on the flour bags, on the counter, in the sunny window, or in his own soft basket behind the stove, and he soon cultivated a taste for dried fish. There were plenty of potatoes and walnuts for him to play with and as he grew older he learned to appreciate the rats and mice.

As for the tailor, or rather the grocer, he presently plucked up courage to ask again for the plump hand of the baker's daughter, and this time to his great joy it was not denied him. 'Now that you are a grocer, my love,' cried she, 'I have no objections at all; but I would never marry a tailor. To sit like a Turk is undignified and barbarous, and I have heard it makes them bowlegged.' And so they were married.

Dick Baker's Cat

MARK TWAIN

One of my comrades there – another of those victims of eighteen years of unrequited toil and blighted hopes – was one of the gentlest spirits that ever bore its patient cross in a weary exile; grave and simple Dick Baker, pocket-miner of Dead-Horse Gulch. He was forty-six, grey as a rat, earnest, thoughtful, slenderly educated, slouchily dressed and clay-soiled, but his heart was finer metal than any gold his shovel ever brought to light – than any, indeed, that ever was mined or minted.

Whenever he was out of luck and a little down-hearted, he would fall to mourning over the loss of a wonderful cat he used to own (for where women and children are not, men of kindly impulses take up with pets, for they must love something). And he always spoke of the strange sagacity of that cat with the air of a man who believed in his secret heart that there was something human about it – maybe even supernatural.

I heard him talking about this animal once. He said:

'Gentlemen, I used to have a cat here, by the name of Tom Quartz, which you'd 'a' took an interest in, I reckon – most anybody would. I had him here eight year – and he was the remarkablest cat *I* ever see. He was a large grey one of the Tom specie, an' he had more hard, natchral sense than any man in this camp – 'n' a *power* of dignity –

he wouldn't let the Gov'ner of Califorhy be familiar with him. He never ketched a rat in his life – 'peared to be above it. He never cared for nothing but mining. He knowed more about mining, that cat did, than any man *I* ever, ever see. You couldn't tell *him* noth'n' 'bout placer-diggin's – 'n' as for pocket-mining, why he was just born for it. He would dig out after me an' Jim when we went over the hills prospect'n', and he would trot along behind us for as much as five mile, if we went so fur. An' he had the best judgment about mining-ground – why, you never see anything like it. When we went to work, he'd scatter a glance round, 'n' if he didn't think much of the indications, he would give a look as much as to say, "Well, I'll have to get you to excuse *me*" – 'n' without another word he'd hyste his nose in the air 'n' shove for home. But if the ground suited him, he would lay low 'n' keep dark till the first pan was washed, 'n' then he would sidle up 'n' take a look, an' if there was about six or seven grains of gold *he* was satisfied – he didn't want no better prospect 'n' that – 'n' then he would lay down on our coats and snore like a steamboat till we'd struck the pocket, an' then get up 'n' superintend. He was nearly lightin' on superintending.

'Well, by an' by, up comes this yer quartz excitement. Everybody was into it – everybody was pick'n' 'n' blast'n' instead of shovellin' dirt on the hillside – everbody was putt'n' down a shaft instead of scrapin' the surface. Noth'n' would do Jim, but *we* must tackle the ledges, too, 'n' so we did. We commenced putt'n' down a shaft, 'n' Tom Quartz he begin to wonder what in the dickens it was all about. *He* hadn't ever seen any mining like that before, 'n' he was all upset, as you may say – he couldn't come to a right understanding of it no way – it was too many for *him*. He was down on it too, you bet you – he was down on it powerful – 'n' always appeared to consider it the cussedest foolishness out. But that cat, you know, was *always* agin' new-fangled arrangements – somehow he never could abide 'em. *You* know how it is with old habits. But by an'

by Tom Quartz begin to git sort of reconciled a little
though he never *could* altogether understand that eternal
sinkin' of a shaft an' never pannin' out anything. At last
he got to comin' down in the shaft, hisself, to try to cipher
it out. An' when he'd git the blues, 'n' feel kind o' scruffy,
'n' aggravated 'n' disgusted – knowin' as he did, that the
bills was runnin' up all the time an' we warn't makin' a
cent – he would curl up on a gunny-sack in the corner an'
go to sleep. Well, one day when the shaft was down about
eight foot, the rock got so hard that we had to put in a blast
– the first blast'n' we'd ever done since Tom Quartz
was born. An' then we lit the fuse 'n' clumb out 'n' got off
'bout fifty yards – 'n' forgot 'n' left Tom Quartz sound
asleep on the gunny-sack. In 'bout a minute we seen a
puff of smoke bust up out of the hole, 'n' then everything
let go with an awful crash, 'n' about four million ton of
rocks 'n' dirt 'n' smoke 'n' splinters shot up 'bout a mile
an' a half into the air, an' by George, right in the dead
centre of it was old Tom Quartz a-goin' end over end, an'

a-snortin' an' a-sneez'n, an' a-clawin' an' a-reach'n' for
things like all possessed. But it warn't no use, you know,
it warn't no use. An' that was the last we see of *him* for
about two minutes 'n' a half, an' then all of a sudden it
begin to rain rocks and rubbage an' directly he come down
ker-whoop about ten foot off f'm where we stood. Well, I
reckon he was p'raps the orneriest-lookin' beast you ever
see. One ear was sot back on his neck, 'n' his tail was stove
up, 'n' his eye-winkers were singed off, 'n' he was all
blacked up with powder an' smoke, an' all sloppy with
mud 'n' slush f'm one end to the other. Well, sir, it warn't
no use to try to apologize – we couldn't say a word. He
took a sort of disgusted look at hisself, 'n' then he looked
at us – an' it was just exactly the same as if he had said –
"Gents, maybe *you* think it's smart to take advantage of a
cat that ain't had no experience of quartz-minin', but *I*
think *different*" – an' then he turned on his heel 'n'
marched off home without ever saying another word.

'That was jest his style. An' maybe you won't believe
it, but after that you never see a cat so prejudiced agin'
quartz-mining as what he was. An' by an' by when he *did*
get to goin' down in the shaft agin', you'd 'a' been
astonished at his sagacity. The minute we'd tetch off a
blast 'n' the fuse'd begin to sizzle, he'd give a look as
much as to say, "Well, I'll have to git you to excuse *me*,"
an' it was surpris'n' the way he'd shin out of that hole 'n'
go f'r a tree. Sagacity? It ain't no name for it. 'Twas
inspiration!'

I said, 'Well, Mr Baker, his prejudice against quartz-
mining *was* remarkable, considering how he came by it.
Couldn't you ever cure him of it?'

'*Cure him*! No! When Tom Quartz was sot once, he was
always sot – and you might 'a' blowed him up as much as
three million times 'n' you'd never 'a' broken him of his
cussed prejudice agin' quartz-mining.'

The Spirit of the Hearth

ANN GRANGER

They moved into the house on a Monday, early in the Spring. The cat arrived the following Saturday morning. As Margot opened the kitchen door, a dark shape, crouched low, squeezed past her and ran under the table. Startled, she let out a shriek.

Duncan shouted 'What he devil – ?' and began to chase the animal round the table. The cat nipped in and out of Duncan's feet and the furniture legs until Duncan stumbled and cracked his knee. He began to swear and curse in language which surprised Margot. Normally he had an unimaginative turn of phrase.

Eventually the cat streaked out through the door again.

'Poor thing, you frightened it!' said Margot reproachfully.

'Good!' retorted Duncan nastily, rubbing his bruised knee.

During the chase the porridge had congealed and the bacon burned to a crisp beneath the grill. It wasn't a good start to the weekend. But it was, thought Margot as she scraped the porridge pot, par for the course. But then, she hadn't wanted to move to this isolated house in the first place. A desolate neck of the woods it appeared to her, offering not a soul for company. She clanged the pan against the side of the sink with unnecessary force.

The cat hadn't gone away. It crouched in the drizzling rain under the eaves of one of the two stone barns on the property, its eyes fixed on the house.

From the window, Margot asked, 'I wonder where it came from?'

Duncan, stomping around with hammer and nails, growled, 'I don't care. Just chase the brute away!'

'He's not a brute,' she said. 'He's rather handsome.'

DIY carpentry was Duncan's hobby and a new home offered him endless scope to indulge it. He specialized in putting up shelves, whether new shelving was needed or not, only satisfied when every available wall space bristled with lengths of pinewood. Margot pointed out that the shelves collected dust and made it impossible to reposition the furniture. But he ignored her.

When the rain stopped, and distant hammering indicated her husband was safely occupied, Margot went out and made friendly overtures to the cat.

He – for the newcomer was clearly a feline gentleman-adventurer – was black all over without a single white hair. He was fully grown and strongly made. If he had a fault, it was that his head was oddly shaped, broad and flat, and his smallish ears stuck outwards, on either side of his face, like a pair of lip handles on an urn. In compensation he had magnificent topaz eyes, gleaming against his jet fur.

Otherwise, he was in a sorry state. His coat was unkempt, he limped and looked as if he'd been living wild.

Throughout the day he continued to try to get into the house, growing ever more ingenious and desperate. Around four o'clock they were seated in the drawing room having a cup of tea. Duncan had just said, 'I could put some shelves either side of that hearth . . .' when they were startled by the shrill screech of claws scraping on glass.

Duncan nearly jumped out of his skin. A black shadow slithered through the open transom window and dropped to the floor with a thud. Enterprisingly, the cat had leapt from an emptied packing case deposited outside, to grab the window frame and scramble through the narrow aperture.

There was another Keystone Cops pursuit during which a Victorian card table which had belonged to Duncan's grandmother was knocked over and slightly marked.

The cat, ejected again, retired under the barn eaves and lay siege to the back door.

Eventually Margot took pity on him. She hunted in the larder for something a cat might eat and – while Duncan was measuring up for additional shelving in the linen cupboard – took a saucer of tuna fish outside. The cat watched her approach with suspicion, but he could smell the fish. As she put it down, he rubbed his wet fur against her leg before inspecting the offering. Then he ate it all. Margot felt absurdly pleased, like a mother whose infant had just managed a new skill.

'I do wish I knew where you came from,' she told him.

He gave her a cursory glance and set about cleaning himself up. He'd lost his air of desperation and there was a certain permanence about him, sitting there, polishing his whiskers. Wherever he'd come from, clearly he now meant to stay here.

He hung about for the next few days out of doors. Duncan swore at him and shied the occasional missile which the cat dodged. Margot surreptitiously bought cat food on her next shopping foray and fed him behind Duncan's back. The cat recognized her now and, when he saw her coming, would walk to meet her uttering chirrups of greeting. She called him 'Puss', because she didn't know what else to call him. She'd never kept a cat. Duncan disliked the idea of animals around the house.

They only ever did as Duncan wanted. Like moving to the Highlands. She'd been quite happy in Perth. But then Duncan had bought this former farmhouse, its stone outbuildings now converted in to garaging. It was situated between Pitlochry and Aberfeldy and he announced he would commute from here into Perth, despite the long drive.

And all this, mind you, without a word of consultation. It didn't seem to occur to him that he took Margot away from all her friends, the many charitable concerns with which she'd been involved, the shops she knew and any form of entertainment, and plonked her down here in the middle of nowhere. On weekdays she was totally alone from after breakfast when he left till he returned for his supper in the evening. She could drive into either of the two towns, but they were small places and it would be difficult to spend more than an hour in either one of them.

At night, during much of the following week, the cat sat on a barn roof and yowled. The sound echoed eerily around the surrounding braes, sometimes sounding like a baby in distress and sometimes low and ominous as if some ancient being had stirred and called out to know who disturbed the sleep of centuries.

'Will you listen to that?' Duncan muttered, thumping the pillows. 'Like a blasted banshee!'

Margot crept out of bed and stood at the window. The sky was overcast but, as she watched, a paler, ink-blue patch lightened and the cloud cover slid aside to reveal a dead-white moon. In the pale light she thought she could distinguish a small shape perched on a ridge tile.

'He wants to come indoors,' she said.

'Over my dead body!' retorted her husband from the bed behind her.

The next morning, as Margot was settling the week's account with the milkman on the doorstep, the cat strolled round the corner of the house.

The milkman, a shaven-headed youth with an earring, said, 'Hullo, Hamish! I see they left you behind!'

'You know him?' Margot exclaimed.

'Aye. It's Mrs Frayne's cat, the lady who lived here before you.'

'But she moved miles away! He must have found his way back!' Margot stared at the cat, marvelling.

'Canny beasts, cats,' opined the milkman.

'Well, write to her!' Duncan ordered. 'Tell her we've got the creature and we'll put it in a basket and send it along by train.'

Margot wrote. Mrs Frayne wrote back to say she was glad Hamish was safe. She'd been worried. He'd run off from his new home within twenty-four hours. There didn't seem any point in returning him. He'd only run away again. Surely his attachment to his old house ought to be rewarded? Would they like to keep him?

'No!' snapped Duncan. 'Can you believe the effrontery of the woman?'

Margot heard herself say, loudly and firmly, 'I would like to keep him. He'll be company for me while you're away. In fact, I think I shall keep him.'

Duncan stared at her in surprise. She so seldom opposed him. This time some new note in her voice told him her mind was made up.

'All right,' he said grudgingly. 'But keep it out of my way!'

Duncan needn't have worried about Hamish keeping out of his way. The cat refused to go anywhere near him. If Duncan came into the drawing room, Hamish would rise from his favourite place before the wide stone hearth, and stalk out, quivering disapproval. If forced to share room space with Duncan, Hamish could crouch immobile except for the very tip of his long black tail. This would twitch from time to time as if pent-up rage sent an electric charge running down his spine.

Having Hamish around made all the difference to Margot. She began to talk to him as she would a human companion. Every morning, just like a pair of human friends, they had elevenses together. Margot had coffee and Hamish had a saucer of milk. She had always bought semi-skimmed milk because Duncan worried about his cholesterol. But Hamish didn't care for semi-skimmed, so Margot began to buy one pint of full cream milk per week, just for Hamish.

She also bought a book on 'Caring For Your Cat'.

To her alarm, the writer of the book was stern on the subject of feeding milk to cats. He insisted it was a food, not a drink, and played havoc with a cat's diet. He was against giving mature cats milk.

Margot read this bit out aloud to Hamish. He sat on a chair opposite her across the kitchen table, watching her with his tawny eyes and listening. When she'd finished, he directed a withering look at the book and his whiskers bristled. 'Much that fellow knows about cats!' he seemed to be saying. 'Calls himself an expert?'

As summer passed, Margot forgot Perth and her resentment at being removed from her former home. She began to understand Hamish's attachment to this present one.

The house was very old and built of a grey granite which, if you looked closely, was infused with shimmering echoes of slate-blue and mauve-pink.

Its great hearth, where Hamish liked to snooze, still had an iron hook from which a cauldron had once been suspended. The brickwork at the back of it was as black as Hamish's fur from a couple of hundred years of scorching flames.

It was beneath the stone flags of such hearths that, in olden times, the spirit of the house dwelt. The origins of this belief are long lost. Perhaps the spirit was a fire god. Or just a household deity of the sort worshipped from ancient Rome to the Far East. But he kept a watchful presence over his domain and could not be separated nor driven from it. Each new owner had first to placate him with small offerings of food and drink. Failure to do this would have resulted in ill fortune befalling the household for the spirit, true to his fiery nature, was easily made angry.

Perhaps, too, at some time the memory of the hearth spirit became confused with the legend of St Nicholas. Even now, hopeful children leave out offerings of mincepies and glasses of sherry for Father Christmas who, clad in his flame-red suit, enters the house via the chimney and will reward those who are true to him.

As for the house's twisting wooden staircase, that creaked with age as if its bones had set. Its bannister was worn smooth by countless hands and its treads had warped and were uneven.

'This all needs replacing,' said Duncan, a manic gleam in his eye.

'Don't you dare!' cried Margot.

She was standing up for herself more and more these days and it seemed to puzzle him.

On the landing at the top of the stairs stood an ancient cupboard. Across the upper frame in brass studs was emblazoned the date 1788. Mrs Frayne had left it behind because, she said, it had been there when she came and as far as she knew, had always been in the house. The top of this cupboard was another of Hamish's favoured retreats. He reached it by leaping first on to the newel post at the head of the stair and thence to the cupboard top. Margot put a piece of old blanket up there for him.

Sometimes she and Hamish went for summer walks, climbing the steep path beside the rustling, plashing burn. Great boulders had rolled down from far above, who knew how many centuries before, and now lay strewn about. Densely growing trees shut out the sky. Hamish walked a little behind her in stately fashion and kept well clear of the water. If they met anyone – especially someone with a dog – he scrabbled up the nearest tree until the intruder had gone away. Dogs skirted the tree and Hamish with respect, very often in a shame-faced sort of way with their tails drooping. Only the bravest gave a nervous bark. Such was the power of Hamish's baleful topaz glare.

As Autumn approached the trees turned to glorious shades of flame-red, pale orange and golden-brown. It was so beautiful all around that every morning, when she got up, Margot threw open the window and just stood there, wondering at it all.

She realized she'd fallen in love for the very first time in her life. She was in love with this old house, the surrounding mountains and forests, everything. She loved it far more than she'd ever loved Duncan or anything else. She never wanted to leave it. She belonged here, just as Hamish felt he did. She and the cat together.

But something was going on. It had been going on all summer. To be quite honest, it had started before they left Perth, but Margot had ignored the signs.

More and more often, Duncan stayed late in Perth 'at the office'. But on several occasions, when she rang to see what she should do about supper, she only got the office cleaner who told her everyone had gone home ages earlier.

Then he began to ring late in the day to say he wouldn't be home at all that night. The pressure of work meant he had to stay on and it made better sense for him to stay over and return the following evening.

Next he bought some expensive new shirts and two or three rather bright ties, quite unlike his usual sober choice. He also took to using a scented aftershave.

At weekends – for goodness sake – he started jogging. For this he bought a royal blue tracksuit with a white flash on the jacket. Clad in this startling outfit and large, clumsy white trainer shoes, he puffed up and down the hills and returned alarmingly purple in the face and sweating.

'Got to keep in trim!' he said. But didn't say why.

After a couple of weekends of this, his ankles ballooned

and he developed painful shin splints. By Monday morning he could only hobble to the car, watched by Margot and Hamish in silence.

Then there were the phone calls. They came when Duncan was at home and he always dashed (or limped very fast depending on his fitness régime) to answer before she could get there. If she did pick the phone up first, the caller rang off as soon as Margot said, 'Hullo?'

'Hamish,' she said to the cat one morning across the kitchen table, 'A person can only be a fool for so long. He's got Another Woman!'

Hamish blinked his topaz eyes and looked wary.

'How long's it been going on, I wonder? Quite a while, I shouldn't be surprised. That's why he brought me all the way up here away from Perth! So as I shouldn't find out and he could have his fun undisturbed! I expect she's young and pretty. What on earth does she see in him?' Margot added in wonder.

He was, after all, of dour disposition and his sole passion to her knowledge had only ever been woodwork. Perhaps with his new lady-friend he was the life and soul of the party. It was hard to imagine. But on the other hand, perhaps she oughtn't to be surprised.

Margot was forty-six. Some women looked younger than their age but Margot had always looked hers. Even as a child she'd looked a year or two older than she was. ('Only five? And such a – er – bonnie lassie!') The spectacles didn't help. She'd always been short-sighted. She'd tried contact lenses but hadn't got on with them. Fashionable clothes looked nothing on her and she stuck to skirts and sweaters. So that was it. Middle-aged, bespectacled and plain.

'And about to be dumped!' she informed the cat. 'Traded in for a newer, flashier model, Hamish!'

Hamish looked as if he might argue.

'Now, I know what you're thinking,' Margot told him, 'but you're wrong. I don't mind Duncan finding me dull.

Let the old goat make a fool of himself. I don't actually want him. What I do want is my home, here, and if I don't watch out, I'll lose it! And so, Hamish, will you! Both of us, out on our ears.'

Perhaps Hamish was sensitive about his rather small and oddly placed ears because he lowered them at this, and looked huffy.

But she'd told him the truth. She could lose the only thing she had which she loved with passion, the house. She had no money of her own. She had never had a career because Duncan hadn't wanted her to work. (A wife with a successful career, she had realized too late, would have been a threat to his ego.) They had no children. Everything was Duncan's.

She supposed, if they divorced, their finances would be divided but knowing Duncan, he'd manage to fiddle it to his advantage. He was a lawyer, for goodness sake. Even if she could persuade him to let her have this house, she wouldn't be able to afford to live here. Only think of the heating costs and the general maintenance! And she'd need to keep her little car, living way out here and the bus service so scarce. Soon it would be winter and the snow would lie on the ground. Then she'd really be cut off.

'When the weather turns bad, he'll get fed up with trying to commute to Perth. That's when he'll leave,' she said to the cat. 'We've got to do something before that, Hamish!' But she really didn't know what.

In the meantime, she polished and dusted and kept the old house immaculate. The fierce possessiveness grew in her. She wouldn't let it go, she wouldn't!

The phone continued to ring at intervals and when she answered, the line, as before, went dead. Duncan, heaven help them, bought a pair of jeans.

He also refused to eat red meat and took to crunching Ryvita instead of toast at breakfast.

'That, Hamish,' said Margot, 'is so that he can squeeze

into the jeans! She'll be the death of him if he goes on like this.'

Hamish yawned widely, stretching his jaw and rolling back his upper lip to reveal needle-sharp teeth and a curled pink tongue. It was the nearest thing to a cat-sneer she'd ever seen.

One morning, when there was a real bite in the air, the milkman told her that snow had fallen the night before on the high ground. Winter was on its way.

Duncan announced that he had to go away for the weekend, to a business conference, in Edinburgh. But when she went into the bedroom on Friday morning he was packing his bright ties and expensive shirts and the jeans.

She hadn't meant to accuse him, because she had no real proof. But somehow, perhaps it was sight of those hopelessly inappropriate clothes, she couldn't help it. It all poured out. She told him she knew he had someone else.

He didn't deny it. He just agreed, in a serenely pompous way, that he did. Fiona, her name was. She wasn't long out of law school, a bright girl and utterly charming. He told Margot all this with a smirking pride which was both repellent and ridiculous.

'And what,' asked Margot scornfully, 'does a bright, charming girl want with a humourless, balding, middle-aged man?'

Fiona, it seemed, found older men more interesting. She had told Duncan that she had never even considered a partner in her own age group. Young men were callow. Older men had experience.

'The only partnership she's interested in,' said Margot, 'is in the firm!'

Duncan said that was an unworthy remark. But, as it happened, he meant to offer Fiona a partnership in everything. Yes, he wanted a divorce. He trusted they could come to an agreeable settlement.

'Oh, do you? And what,' demanded Margot, her voice

on edge, 'does an agreeable settlement mean? Agreeable to whom?'

Duncan said he hoped she wasn't going to be mean-spirited. She ought not to deny him and Fiona happiness just because she was so discontented. He was disappointed she was being difficult. Perhaps she ought to see her doctor and get some pills or something? It was probably the menopause.

Margot rode roughshod over this. 'What about this house?' she asked, her voice cracking.

'We'll sell it, naturally,' Duncan said. 'And divide the money. You'll have enough to buy yourself a little flat somewhere.'

'I don't want a flat!' she yelled. 'I want my home!'

He said, 'Don't be silly. What would you do in a great empty house like this?' And with that, he walked out of the room on to the landing.

She flew after him and grabbed his arm. He tried to shake her off but Margot clung, shouting at him.

'For twenty years I've kept house for you, an unpaid housekeeper! For twenty years nothing but cooking and cleaning and shopping! A roof over my head is the only thing I had – and even then I had to earn it! What kind of partnership did you ever offer me? Our house wasn't something I shared with you! It was the place where I was employed – to look after you! Now you tell me it's something you think you can take back when you feel like it! Just as you took away my home in Perth, so now you want to take away this one, too! You shan't, do you hear? I won't let you, I won't!'

Duncan snapped back that it wasn't his fault if she hadn't found her life fulfilling. He'd always assumed she was perfectly happy and if she hadn't been, well, that wasn't his responsibility.

'Hypocrite!' she yelled, at which he uttered an exclamation of disgust and gave her a violent shove which loosened her grip and sent her spinning back.

She struck the wall behind her and slipped, ending up sitting on the floor with one leg crooked up and one out straight. Her glasses had fallen off and she had to scrabble around for them before she could do anything else. When she got them back on her nose, she saw that Duncan had started to walk downstairs, ignoring her plight. His back view was rigid with self-righteousness.

Neither of them had noticed the cat, so taken up were they with their own quarrel. Hamish had been crouched on top of the old cupboard on the landing as they argued, his ears flattened and his tail lashing. Now, without warning, he leapt.

To Margot, still sitting on the floor, the creature which launched itself from the cupboard wasn't Hamish at all. It was bigger, enormous, its jet fur bristling, yellow flames shooting from eyes like pits of molten gold, its sharp white teeth bared in a ferocious snarl. Its front legs were outstretched like bat's wings and, as it hurtled through the air, it let out a dreadful, blood-curdling hiss such as she'd never imagined from man or beast.

Duncan heard it and turned. For a second, only a brief moment, his face registered horror. He raised his arm to protect his face, but too late. The cat wrapped itself around his head. Scarlet lines appeared across the man's cheeks and brow. Blood spurted from the skin where the sharp claws dug in. Duncan staggered on the uneven old stairs as he tried simultaneously to push away the cat and grab at the banister.

He achieved neither. He fell, crashing down the whole length of the stair, his body sliding helplessly from tread to tread, his head banging on the banister, man and cat locked together in an awful embrace.

They landed with an impact which made the whole stairway and landing shudder. Then there was silence which was even worse.

Margot scrambled to her feet and hurried down the stair. 'Hamish? Are you all right? Where are you?'

A low growl answered. She saw topaz eyes gleaming in the far corner of the hall. The cat crouched there, fur still bristling and tail thumping the ground. Duncan lay at the foot of the stair, half turned on to his back. She knelt over him.

His eyes flickered up at her and his mouth moved but no sound came out. Thick, dark blood began to trickle from one ear and then from his nostrils and finally from his mouth. He made a sound at last, an indistinct mumbling. A desperate urgency entered his eyes but he didn't, or couldn't, move.

She jumped up and ran to the telephone. As she picked up the receiver, she heard another warning growl. From the corner Hamish's topaz eyes were fixed on her with mesmeric power, as if forbidding her to summon aid.

Obediently she put back the receiver and sat down on the chair by the telephone table. She sat there for perhaps a quarter of an hour. Then Hamish uncoiled himself and strolled away into the drawing room. Margot rose stiffly and went to where Duncan lay. His eyes gazed up, sightless.

She went back to the telephone and dialled for the ambulance.

Duncan was declared dead on arrival at hospital. A little later in the day, two police officers came, a man and a female colleague. Both were very kind, but asked a lot of questions in a gentle, probing sort of way.

'The gentleman's face was severely lacerated,' the woman officer said. She glanced at Hamish who reclined in a shaft of pale sunlight, blinking sleepily. 'They appear to be animal claw marks. Is the cat – er – vicious?'

'Certainly not!' Margot said firmly.

'Could you tell us exactly what happened?'

'Unfortunately,' Margot began. 'I can't tell you exactly because I wasn't there when the accident occurred.'

What was this? She was the most truthful woman alive!

How could she lie so easily? She heard her own voice, but somehow, it wasn't she who spoke. It was someone else who spoke through her, using her vocal cords. She wondered what on earth she was going to say next.

'What I suspect may have happened is this,' a voice – her voice – said. 'My husband was very fond of the cat . . .' The voice broke realistically. 'It used to ride round on his shoulder. It also sleeps on top of the cupboard up there on the landing. I think it must have been up there when Duncan started to go downstairs and it jumped on to his shoulder. Duncan hadn't expected it and reacted violently. The cat panicked and clung on and – and poor Duncan fell.'

The police officers exchanged glances. They asked if they might examine the staircase. She could hear them talking to one another as they did. The man said, 'The old stair's a death trap! It's a wonder one of them hasna' taken a tumble afore now!'

They came back and the woman observed, 'I see there's a suitcase by the bedroom door.'

'Yes, my husband was about to go on a business trip.' Margot's voice trembled. 'This has been such a terrible shock. We were married twenty years.'

They were very sympathetic. They made her a cup of tea and asked if there was anyone they could telephone who might come and stay with Margot.

'Because you shouldn't be alone, you really shouldn't,' the young woman officer said.

'I have friends in Perth,' Margot told her. 'I can ring one of them, if I find – if I find it too lonely.'

Hamish, before the log fire in the wide stone hearth, rolled on to his back and stretched himself into an elongated band of black fur.

The young woman went on hesitantly, 'I wonder if we could borrow the cat for a few hours? We'll take great care of him and bring him back tonight.'

They hadn't a cat basket so Margot found a wicker

picnic basket and Hamish was shut up in that despite his plaintive miaows.

They brought Hamish back as promised. 'Forensics just wanted to take a wee look at his paws,' they explained.

Hamish had not enjoyed being transported in the picnic basket. He bristled ruffled dignity and turned his back to Margot for almost an hour. Even so, she could see where a little fur had been clipped from between the pads of his paws. She supposed the police were looking for traces of Duncan's blood and wondered if they'd found any.

Very late that evening, after the police had gone, the phone rang and, when Margot picked it up, the line went dead, as before.

'She's wondering why he hasn't turned up, Hamish!' Margot said to the cat.

Hamish, the memory of the picnic basket fading, and feeling peckish after all the excitement, walked out into the kitchen and sat down before his dish. Margot gave him half a Weetabix mashed in tepid milk, a little treat to which he was partial.

The police returned the next morning and said they were sorry to bother her like this, but they'd like to take one more look. They climbed up to the top of the cupboard and saw Hamish's blanket. They measured the staircase. At last they expressed themselves satisfied.

'A tragic accident,' the male officer said. 'And to think the poor gentleman was so fond of the cat, too.'

Over the weekend, the phone rang three more times. The last time, when Margot picked it up, she didn't say 'hullo'. She just said, 'He won't be joining you. He's dead.'

There was a sharp intake of breath at the other end of the line. But Margot hung up before the caller could ask any questions.

'So, Hamish,' she said. 'That's that. Now we have the place to ourselves.'

With the cat at her heels, she went into the drawing room. There Margot settled with notepad and biro before the fire. It had occurred to her that the house, in such a picturesque tourist area, would be ideal for a summer bed-and-breakfast business. As she scribbled and planned, Hamish took up his rightful place before the hearth. The logs crackled and spat a little, but otherwise all was peace.

The Slum Cat

ERNEST THOMPSON SETON

LIFE I

The little slum kitten was not six weeks old yet, but she was alone in the old junk-yard. Her mother had gone to seek food among the garbage-boxes the night before, and had never returned, so when the second evening came she was very hungry. A deep-laid instinct drove her forth from the old cracker-box to seek something to eat. Feeling her way silently among the rubbish she smelt everything that seemed eatable, but without finding food. At length she reached the wooden steps leading down into Jap Malee's bird store underground at the far end of the yard. The door was open a little, and she walked in. A Negro sitting idly on a box in a corner watched her curiously. She wandered past some rabbits; they paid no heed. She came to a wide-barred cage in which was a fox. He crouched low; his eyes glowed. The kitten wandered, sniffing, up to the bars, put her head in, sniffed again, then made straight toward the feed-pan, to be seized in a flash by the crouching fox. She gave a frightened 'mew', and the Negro also sprang forward, spitting with such copious vigour in the Fox's face that he dropped the kitten and returned to the corner, there to sit blinking his eyes in sullen fear.

209

The Negro pulled the kitten out. She tottered in a circle a few times, then revived, and a few minutes later, when Jap Malee came back, she was purring in the Negro's lap, apparently none the worse.

Jap was not an Oriental; he was a full-blooded Cockney; but his eyes were such little accidental slits aslant in his round, flat face that his first name was forgotten in the highly descriptive title of 'Jap'. He was not especially unkind to the birds and beasts which furnished his living, but he did not want the slum kitten.

The Negro gave her all the food she could eat and then carried her to a distant block and dropped her in an iron-yard. Here she lived and somehow found food enough to grow till, weeks later, an extended exploration brought her back to her old quarters in the junk-yard and, glad to be at home, she at once settled down.

Kitty was now fully grown. She was a striking-looking cat of the tiger type. Her marks were black on a pale grey, and the four beauty spots of white, on nose, ears and tail-tip, lent a certain distinction. She was expert now at getting a living, yet she had some days of starvation and had so far failed in her ambition to catch a sparrow. She was quite alone, but a new force was coming into her life.

She was lying in the sun one September day when a large black cat came walking along the top of a wall in her direction. By his torn ear she recognized him at once as an old enemy. She slunk into her box and hid. He picked his way gingerly, bounded lightly to a shed that was at the end of the yard, and was crossing the roof when a yellow cat rose up. The black tom glared and growled; so did the yellow tom. Their tails lashed from side to side. Strong throats growled and yowled. They approached with ears laid back, with muscles a-tense.

'Yow – yow – ow,' said the black one.

'Wow – w – w – ' was the slightly deeper answer.

'Ya – wow – wow – wow – ' said the black one, edging up an inch nearer.

'Yow – w – w – ' was the yellow answer, as the blond cat rose to full height and stepped with vast dignity a whole inch forward. 'Yow – w,' and he went another inch, while his tail went swish, thump, from one side to the other.

'Ya – wow – wow – w,' screamed the black in a rising tone, and he backed the eighth of an inch as he marked the broad, unshrinking beast before him.

Windows opened all around, human voices were heard, but the cat scene went on.

'Wow – yow – ow,' rumbled the yellow peril, his voice deepening as the other's rose. 'Yow,' and he advanced another step.

Now their noses were but three inches apart; they stood sidewise, both ready to clinch, but each waiting for the other. They glared at each other for three minutes in silence, and like statues, except that each tail-tip was twisting.

The yellow began again. 'Yow – ow – ow,' in a deep tone.

'Ya-a-a-a-a,' screamed the black with intent to strike terror by his yell, but he retreated one-sixteenth of an inch. The yellow walked up a whole long inch; their whiskers were mixing now; another advance, and their noses almost touched.

'Yo – w – w,' said yellow like a deep moan.

'Ta-a-a-a-a,' screamed black, but he retreated a thirty-second of an inch, and the yellow warrior closed and clinched like a demon.

Oh, how they rolled and bit and tore – especially the yellow one!

How they pitched and gripped and hugged – but especially the yellow one!

Over and over, sometimes one on top, sometimes the other, but usually the yellow one, and over they rolled till

211

off the roof, amid cheers from all the windows. They lost not a second in that fall into the junk-yard; they tore and clawed all the way down, but especially the yellow one; and when they struck the ground, still fighting, the one on top was chiefly the yellow one; and before they separated both had had as much as they wanted, especially the black one! He scaled the wall and, bleeding and growling, disappeared, while the news was passed from window to window that Cayley's 'Nig' had been licked by 'Orange Billy'.

Either the yellow cat was a very clever seeker, or else slum Kitty did not hide very hard, for he discovered her among the boxes and she made no attempt to get away, probably because she had witnessed the fight. There is nothing like success in warfare to win the female heart, and thereafter the yellow tom and Kitty became very good friends, not sharing each other's lives or food – cats do not do that much – but recognizing each other as entitled to special friendly privileges.

When October's shortening days were on an event took place in the old cracker-box. If 'Orange Billy' had come he would have seen five little kittens curled up in the embrace of their mother, the little slum Kitty. It was a wonderful thing for her. She felt all the elation an animal mother can feel – all the delight – as she tenderly loved them and licked them.

She had added a joy to her joyless life, but she had also added a heavy burden. All her strength was taken now to find food. And one day, led by a tempting smell, she wandered into the bird cellar and into an open cage. Everything was still, there was meat ahead, and she reached forward to seize it; the cage door fell with a snap and she was a prisoner. That night the Negro put an end to the kittens and was about to do the same with the mother when her unusual markings attracted the attention of the bird man, who decided to keep her.

LIFE II

Jap Malee was as disreputable a little Cockney bantam as ever sold cheap canary birds in a cellar. He was extremely poor, and the Negro lived with him because the 'Henglishman' was willing to share bed and board. Jap was perfectly honest, according to his lights, but he had no lights and there is little doubt that his chief revenue was derived from storing and restoring stolen dogs and cats. The fox and the half a dozen canaries were mere blinds. The 'Lost and Found' columns of the papers were the only ones of interest to Jap, but he noticed and saved a clipping about breeding for fur. This was stuck on the wall of his den and, under its influence, he set about making an experiment with the slum cat. First he soaked her dirty fur with stuff to kill the two or three kinds of creepers she wore and, when it had done its work, he washed her thoroughly. Kitty was savagely indignant, but a warm and happy glow spread over her as she dried off in a cage near the stove, and her fur began to fluff out with wonderful softness and whiteness. Jap and his assistant were much pleased. But this was preparatory. 'Nothing is so good for growing fur as plenty of oily food and continued exposure to cold weather,' said the clipping. Winter was at hand, and Jap Malee put Kitty's cage out in the yard, protected only from the rain and the direct wind, and fed her with all the oil cake and fish heads she could eat. In a week the change began to show. She was rapidly getting fat. She had nothing to do but get fat and dress her fur. Her cage was kept clean, and Nature responded to the chill weather and oily food by making Kitty's coat thicker and glossier every day so that, by Christmas, she was an unusually beautiful cat in the fullest and finest of fur with markings that were at least a rarity.

Why not send the slum cat to the show now coming on?

"T'won't do, ye kneow, Sammy, to henter 'er as a Tramp Cat, ye kneow,' Jap observed to his help; 'but it kin be arranged to suit the Knickerbockers. Nothink like a good noime, ye kneow. Ye see now, it had orter be "Royal" somethink or other – nothink goes with the Knickerbockers like "Royal" anythink. Now, "Royal Dick" or "Royal Sam": 'ow's that? But 'owld on: them's tom names. Oi say, Sammy, wot's the noime of that island where you were born?'

'Analostan Island, sah, was my native vicinity, sah.'

'Oi say, now, that's good, ye kneow. "Royal Analostan," by jove! The onliest pedigreed Royal Analostan in the howle sheow, ye kneow. Ain't that capital?' and they mingled their cackles.

'But we'll 'ave to 'ave a pedigree, ye kneow;' so a very long fake pedigree on the recognized lines was prepared.

One afternoon Sam, in a borrowed silk hat, delivered the cat and the pedigree at the show door. He had been a barber, and he could put on more pomp in five minutes than Jap Malee could have displayed in a lifetime, and this, doubtless, was one reason for the respectful reception awarded the Royal Analostan at the cat show.

Jap had all the Cockney's reverence for the upper class. He was proud to be an exhibitor but when, on the opening day, he went to the door he was overpowered to see the array of carriages and silk hats. The gateman looked at him sharply but passed him on his ticket, doubtless taking him for a stable boy to some exhibitor. The hall had velvet carpets before the long rows of cages. Jap was sneaking down the side row, glancing at the cats of all kinds, noting the blue ribbons and the ends, glancing about but not daring to ask for his own exhibit, inwardly trembling to think what the gorgeous gathering of fashion would say if they discovered the trick he was playing on them. But he saw no sign of slum Kitty.

In the middle of the centre aisle were the high-class cats. A great throng was there. The passage was roped and two policemen were there to keep the crowd moving.

Jap wriggled in among them; he was too short to see over, but he gathered from the remarks that the gem of the show was there.

'Oh, isn't she a beauty!' said one tall woman.

'Ah! what distinction!' was the reply.

'One cannot mistake the air that comes only from ages of the most refined surroundings.'

'How I should like to own that superb creature!'

Jap pushed near enough to get a glimpse of the cage and read a placard which announced that 'The Blue Ribbon and Gold Medal of the Knickerbocker High Society Cat and Pet Show had been awarded to the thoroughbred pedigreed Royal Analostan, imported and exhibited by J. Malee, Esquire, the well-known fancier. Not for sale.' Jap caught his breath; he stared – yes, surely, there, high in a gilded cage on velvet cushions, with two policemen for guards, her fur bright black and pale grey, her bluish eyes slightly closed, was his slum Kitty, looking the picture of a cat that was bored to death.

Jap Malee lingered around the cage for hours, drinking a draught of glory such as he had never before known. But he saw that it would be wise for him to remain unknown; his 'butler' must do all the business.

It was slum Kitty who made that show a success. Each day her value went up in the owner's eyes. He did not know what prices had been given for cats and thought that he was touching a record pitch when his 'butler' gave the director authority to sell the cat for $100.

This is how it came about that the slum cat found herself transferred to a Fifth Avenue mansion. She showed a most unaccountable wildness, as well as other peculiarities. Her retreat from the lap dog to the centre of the dinner-table was understood to express a deep-rooted, though mistaken, idea of avoiding a defiling touch. The patrician way in which she would get the cover off a milk-can was especially applauded, while her frequent wallowings in the garbage-pail were understood to be the manifestation of a little pardonable high-born eccentricity. She was fed and pampered, shown and praised, but she was not happy. She clawed at that blue ribbon around her neck till she got it off; she jumped against the plate glass because that seemed the road to outside; and she would sit and gaze out on the roofs and back yards at the other side of the window and wish she could be among them for a change.

She was strictly watched – was never allowed outside – so that all the happy garbage-pail moments occurred while these receptacles of joy were indoors. But one night in March, as they were being set out a-row for the early scavenger, the Royal Analostan saw her chance, slipped out of the door, and was lost to view.

Of course there was a grand stir, but pussy neither knew nor cared anything about that. Her one thought was to go home. A raw east wind had been rising and now it came to her with a particularly friendly message. Man would have called it an unpleasant smell of the docks, but to pussy it was a welcome message from her own country. She trotted on down the long street due east, threading the rails of front gardens, stopping like a statue for an instant, or crossing the street in search of the darkest side. She came at length to the docks and to the water, but the place was strange. She could go north or south; something turned her southward and, dodging among docks and dogs, carts and cats, crooked arms of the bay and straight board fences, she got in an hour or two into familiar scenes and smells and, before the sun came up, she crawled back, weary and footsore, through the same old hole in the same old fence, and over a wall into her junk-yard back of the bird cellar, yes, back into the very cracker-box where she was born.

After a long rest she came quietly down the cracker-box towards the steps leading to the cellar, and engaged in her old-time pursuit of seeking for eatables. The door opened and there stood the Negro. He shouted to the bird-man inside:

'Say, Boss, come hyar! Ef dere ain't dat dar Royal Analostan comed back!'

Jap came in time to see the cat jumping the wall. The Royal Analostan had been a windfall for him; had been the means of adding many comforts to the cellar and several prisoners to the cages. It was now of the utmost importance to recapture Her Majesty. Stale fish heads and other infallible lures were put out till pussy was induced to chew at a large fish head in a box trap. The Negro, in watching, pulled the string that dropped the lid, and a minute later the Analostan was again in a cage in the cellar. Meanwhile, Jap had been watching the 'Lost and Found' column. There it was: 'Twenty-five dollars reward,' etc. That night Mr Malee's 'butler' called at the Fifth Avenue mansion with the missing cat. 'Mr Malee's compliments, sah.' Of course, Mr Malee would not be rewarded, but the 'butler' was evidently open to any offer.

Kitty was guarded carefully after that but, so far from being disgusted with the old life of starving and glad of her care, she became wilder and more dissatisfied.

The spring was on in full power now and the Fifth Avenue family were thinking of their country residence. They packed up, closed house and moved off to the summer home some fifty miles away, and Pussy, in a basket, went with them.

The basket was put on the back seat of a carriage. New sounds and passing smells were entered and left. Then a roaring of many feet, more swinging of the basket, then some clicks, some bangs, a long, shrill whistle, and doorbells of a very big front door, a rumbling, a whizzling, an unpleasant smell; then there was a succession of jolts, roars, jars, stops, clicks, clacks, smells, jumps, shakes, more smells, more shakes, big shakes, little shakes, gases, smoke, screeches, door-bells, tremblings; roars, thunders, and some new smells, raps, taps, heavings, rumbling and more smells. When at last it all stopped the sun came twinkling through the basket lid. The Royal Cat was lifted into another carriage and they turned aside from their past course. Very soon the carriage swerved, the noises of its wheels were grittings and rattlings, a new and horrible sound was added – the barking of dogs, big and little, and dreadfully close. The basket was lifted, and slum Kitty had reached her country home.

Everyone was officiously kind. All wanted to please the Royal Cat, but, somehow, none of them did, except possibly the big, fat cook that Kitty discovered on wandering into the kitchen. That greasy woman smelt more like a slum than anything she had met for months and the Royal Analostan was proportionately attracted. The cook, when she learned that fears were entertained about the cat's staying, said: 'Shure, she'd 'tind to thot; wanst a cat licks her futs shure she's at home.' So she deftly caught the unapproachable Royalty in her apron and committed the horrible sacrilege of greasing the soles of her feet with pot grease. Of course, Kitty resented it; she resented everything in the place; but, on being set down, she began to dress her paws and found evident satisfaction in that grease. She licked all four feet for an hour, and the cook triumphantly announced that now 'shure she's be apt to sthay'; and stay she did, but she showed a most surprising and disgusting preference for the kitchen and the cook and the garbage-pail.

The family, though distressed by these high-born eccentricities, were glad to see the Royal Analostan more contented and approachable. They guarded her from every menace. The dogs were taught to respect her; no man or boy about the place would have dreamed of throwing a stone at the famous pedigreed cat, and she had all the food she wanted, but still she was not happy. She was hankering for many things, she scarcely knew what. She had everything – yes, but she wanted something else. Plenty to eat and drink – yes, but milk does not taste the same when you can go and drink all you want from a saucer; it has to be stolen out of a tin pail when one is pinched with hunger, or it does not have the tang – it is not milk.

How pussy did hate it all! True, there was one sweet smelling shrub in the whole horrible place – one that she did enjoy nipping and rubbing against it; it was the only bright spot in her country life.

One day, after a summer of discontent, a succession of things happened that stirred anew the slum instincts of the Royal prisoner. A great bundle of stuff from the docks had reached the country mansion. What it contained was of little moment, but it was rich with the most piquant of slum smells. The chords of memory surely dwell in the nose, and pussy's past was conjured up with dangerous force. Next day the cook left through some trouble. That evening the youngest boy of the house, a horrid little American with no proper appreciation of Royalty, was tying a tin to the blue-blooded one's tail, doubtless in furtherance of some altruistic project, when pussy resented it with a paw that wore five big fish-hooks for the occasion. The howl of down-trodden America roused America's mother; the deft and womanly blow she aimed with her book was miraculously avoided and pussy took flight, up-stairs, of course. A hunted rat runs downstairs, a hunted dog goes on the level, a hunted cat runs up. She hid in the garret and waited till night came. Then, gliding down-stairs, she tried the screen doors, found one unlatched and escaped into black August night. Pitch black to man's eyes, it was simply grey to her, and she glided through the disgusting shrubbery and flower-beds, had a final nip at that one little bush that had been an attractive spot in the garden, and boldly took her back track of the spring.

How could she take a back track that she never saw? There is in all animals some sense of direction. It is low in man and high in horses, but cats have a large gift, and this mysterious guide took her westward, not clearly and definitely, but with a general impulse that was made definite because the easiest travel was on the road. In an hour she had reached the Hudson River. Her nose had told her many times that the course was true. Smell after smell came back.

At the river was the railroad. She could not go on the water; she must go north or south. This was a case where her sense of direction was clear: it said 'go south'; and Kitty trotted down the footpath between the iron rails and the fence.

LIFE III

Cats can go very fast up a tree or over a wall, but when it comes to the long, steady trot that reels off mile after mile, hour after hour, it is not the cat-hop but the dog-trot that counts. She became tired and a little footsore. She was thinking of a rest when a dog came running to the fence near by and broke out into such a horrible barking close to her ear that pussy leaped in terror. She ran as hard as she could down the path. The barking seemed to grow into a low rumble – a louder rumble and roaring – a terrifying thunder. A light shone; Kitty glanced back to see, not the dog, but a huge black thing with ablazing eye, coming on yowling and spitting like a yard full of tom cats. She put forth all her power to run, made such time as she never had made before, but dared not leap the fence. She was running like a dog – was flying, but all in vain: the monstrous pursuer overtook her, but missed her in the darkness, and hurried past to be lost in the night, while Kitty sat gasping for breath.

This was only the first encounter with the strange monsters – strange to her eyes – her nose seemed to know them, and told her that this was another landmark on the home trail. But pussy learned that they were very stupid and could not find her at all if she hid by slipping quietly under a fence and lying still. Before morning she had encountered many of them, but escaped unharmed from all.

About sunrise she reached a nice little slum on her home trail and was lucky enough to find several unsterilized eatables in an ash-heap. She spent the day around a stable. It was very like home, but she had no idea of staying there. She was driven by an inner craving that was neither hunger nor fear, and next evening set out as before. She had seen the 'One-eyed Thunder-rollers' all day going by, and was getting used to them. That night passed much like the first one. The days went by in skulking in barns, hiding from dogs and small boys, and the nights in limping along the track, for she was getting footsore; but on she went, mile after mile, southward, ever southward – dogs, boys, roarers, hunger – dogs, boys, roarers, hunger – but day after day with increasing wariness on she went, and her nose from time to time cheered her by confidently reporting, 'This surely is a smell we passed last spring.'

So week after week went by, and pussy, dirty, ribbonless, footsore and weary, arrived at the Harlem Bridge. Though it was enveloped in delicious smells she did not like the look of that bridge. For half the night she wandered up and down the shore without discovering any other means of going south excepting some other bridges. Somehow she had to come back to it; not only its smells were familiar, but from time to time when a 'One-eye' ran over it there was the peculiar rumbling roar that was a sensation in the springtime trip. She leaped to the timber stringer and glided out over the water. She had got less than a third of the way over when a 'Thundering One-eye' came roaring at her from the opposite end. She was much frightened but, knowing their blindness, she dropped to a low side beam and there crouched in hiding. Of course, the stupid monster missed her and passed on, and all would have been well but it turned back, or another just like it, and came suddenly roaring behind her. Pussy leaped to the long track and made for the home shore. She might have got there, but a third of the red-eye terrors came roaring down at her from that side. She was running her hardest, but was caught between two foes. There was nothing for it but a desperate leap from the timbers into – she did not know what. Down – down – down – plop! splash! plunge – into the deep water, not cold, for it was August, but oh! so horrible. She spluttered and coughed and struck out for the shore. She had never learned to swim, and yet she swam, for the simple reason that a cat's position and attitude in swimming are the same as her position and attitude in walking. She had fallen into a place she did not like; naturally she tried to walk out, and the result was that she swam ashore. Which shore? It never fails – the south – the shore nearest home. She scrambled out all dripping wet, up the muddy bank and through coal-piles and dust-heaps, looking as black, dirty and unroyal as it was possible for a cat to look.

Once the shock was over the Royal pedigreed slummer began to feel better for the plunge. A genial glow without from the bath, a genial sense of triumph within, for had she not outwitted three of the big terrors?

Her nose, her memory and her instinct of direction inclined her to get on the track again, but the place was infested with the big thunder-rollers, and prudence led her to turn aside and follow the river bank with its musky home reminders.

She was more than two days learning the infinite dangers and complexities of the East River docks, and at length, on the third night, she reached familiar ground, the place she had passed the night of her first escape. From that her course was sure and rapid. She knew just where she was going and how to get there. She knew even the most prominent features in the dogscape now. She went faster, felt happier. In a little while she would be curled up in the old junk-yard. Another turn and the block was in sight –

*

222

But – what – it was gone. Kitty could not believe her eyes. There, where had stood, or leaned, or slouched, or straggled – the houses of the block – was a great broken wilderness of stone, lumber and holes in the ground.

Kitty walked all around it. She knew by the bearings and by the local colour of the pavement that she was in her home; that there had lived the bird-man, and there was the old junk-yard; but all were gone, completely gone, taking the familiar odours with them; and pussy turned sick at heart in the utter hopelessness of the case. Her home love was her master mood. She had given up all to come to a home that no longer existed, and for once her brave little spirit was cast down. She wandered over the silent heaps of rubbish and found neither consolation nor eatables. The ruin had covered several of the blocks and reached back from the water. It was not a fire. Kitty had seen one of these things once. Pussy knew nothing of the great bridge that was to rise from this very spot.

When the sun came up Kitty sought cover. An adjoining block still stood with little change, and the Royal Analostan retired to that. She knew some of its trails, but once there was unpleasantly surprised to find the place swarming with cats that, like herself, were driven from their old grounds, and when the garbage-cans came out there were several cats to each. It meant a famine in the land and pussy, after standing it a few days, set out to find her other home in Fifth Avenue. She got there to find it shut up and deserted, and the next night she returned to the crowded slum.

September and October wore away. Many of the cats died of starvation or were too weak to escape their natural enemies. But Kitty, young and strong, still lived.

Great changes had come over the ruined blocks. Though silent the night she saw them, they were crowded with noisy workmen all day. A tall building was completed by the end of October, and slum Kitty, driven by hunger, went sneaking up to a pail that a Negro had set outside. The pail, unfortunately, was not garbage, but a new thing in that region, a scrubbing-pail – a sad disappointment, but it had a sense of comfort: there was a trace of a familiar touch on the handle. While she was studying it the Negro elevator boy came out again. In spite of his blue clothes his odorous person confirmed the good impression of the handle. Kitty had retreated across the street. He gazed at her.

'Sho ef dat don't look like de Royal Ankalostan – Hya, pussy – pussy – pussy – pus-s-s-y, co-o-ome – pus-s-s-y, hya! I specs she's sho hungry.'

Hungry! She had not had a real meal for a month. The Negro went into the hall and reappeared with a portion of his own lunch.

'Hya, pussy, puss – puss – puss.' At length he laid the meat on the pavement and went back to the door. Slum Kitty came, found it savoury; sniffed at the meat, seized it, and fled like a little tigress to eat her prize in peace.

LIFE IV

This was the beginning of a new era. Pussy came to the door of the building now when pinched by hunger, and the good feeling for the Negro grew. She had never understood that man before. Now he was her friend, the only one she had.

One week pussy caught a rat. She was crossing the street in front of the new building when her friend opened the door for a well-dressed man to come out.

'Hell, look at that for a cat,' said the man.

'Yes, sah,' answered the Negro; 'dat's ma cat, sah; she's a terror on rats, sah. Hez 'em 'bout cleaned up, sah; dat's why she so thin.'

'Well, don't let her starve,' said the man, with the air of a landlord. 'Can't you feed her?'

'De liver-meat man comes reg'lar, sah, quatah dollar a

week, sah,' said the Negro, realizing that he was entitled to the extra fifteen cents for 'the idea'.

'That's all right; I'll stand it.'

Since then the Negro has sold her a number of times with a perfectly clear conscience, because he knows quite well that it is only a question of a few days before the Royal Analostan comes back again. She has learned to tolerate the elevator and even to ride up and down on it. The Negro stoutly maintains that once she heard the meat man while she was on the top floor and managed to press the button that called the elevator to take her down.

She is sleek and beautiful again. She is not only one of 400 that form the inner circle about the liverman's barrow, but she is recognized as the star pensioner as well.

But in spite of her prosperity, her social position, her Royal name and fake pedigree, the greatest pleasure of her life is to slip out and go a-slumming in the gloaming, for now, as in her previous lives, she is at heart, and likely to be, nothing but a dirty little slum cat.

Mildred

ERA ZISTEL

The two women bent over the box in which the mother cat lay.

'I'll let her keep the white one, and the black, I think.'

'And kill all the rest? How can you?'

'I've got to. Where would I find homes for six?'

'That cute little patchwork one? You won't keep that?'

'The calico?' She reached down and picked it up by the nape of its neck, while the mother cat followed each movement, her eyes large with worried pride. 'No, I don't think so. It's a female. I don't know anybody would take a female.'

'I will.'

'Are you crazy? What do you want with a cat?'

'Well – I think it's cute. And I don't want it to be killed.'

The woman put the kitten back into the box, and the mother washed it vigorously.

'You'd better think it over. I'll keep it until tomorrow.'

'I don't have to think it over.'

'You really do want her, then? You won't change your mind?'

'I never change my mind. I said I'd take it, didn't I?'

Thus, by a whim, Mildred's fate was settled. She was destined to live.

*

The first night she spent in her new home she cried and kept her mistress awake the whole night long, and this was responsible for a certain quarrelsome tendency that marked her dealings with the butcher, baker and candlestick maker all through the following day. The next night she started to cry again, but then found the bed where her mistress lay, and once snuggled down into it, just below the pillow, where the heavy, sweet warmth enveloped her like an overpowering drug, she began to forget that other warmth from which she had been taken.

'Good little Mildred', her mistress murmured, stroking the small body of her companion with a lethargic, possessive hand. 'Sweet dreams, my sugarplum!'

Mildred got used to answering to 'Sugarplum' and to any number of other pet names as well. Even 'my little grapefruit', spoken in a certain tone of voice, would cause her to cock an attentive ear and, with just a little more added to that certain tone of voice, she'd go bounding over, her tail high, her front and back paws running on different tracks, to wherever her mistress might be.

She had no fault, nor any fault to find. She adored her mistress and her mistress adored her. And in such an abnormal state of perfection they lived for four months and a little more, until another personality and another pet name entered upon the scene.

The first few times Mildred heard 'Harry, darling' spoken in that certain tone of voice, she went bounding over to her mistress only to receive no more than an absentminded pat. Thereafter, she merely cocked an attentive ear. Ignore it entirely she could not, for since it had been hers for so long, there was always the chance that it might be again.

After a while she figured it out. It belonged to Harry when he was there. It belonged to her when he was gone. She hated Harry.

She hated him for more reasons than that one. He was the sort who would, without a 'May I?' or an 'I'm sorry' or even a 'Shoo!' push her with a casual hand into sudden wakefulness and clumsy exit from the chair he wanted to occupy. She hated him, not for his cruelty, for he never really hurt her, but for his indifference. She hated him because not even her most loving gaze which, with brazen duplicity, she bestowed upon him at first, could lure him away from other absorptions; because not even her most complicated caper could make him smile and hold out a friendly hand. She hated him because he made even her mistress forget, while he was there, and sometimes for hours after he had left, that there was a Mildred in the house. But most of all she hated him because she felt the strength of his purpose and desire to have the sole possession of what had been, up to the time of his arrival, solely hers.

Sometimes, while he sat in her favourite chair calmly reading a newspaper, and she sat on the floor, her back turned to him, calmly washing her face, while in the bedroom her mistress was getting ready to go out, she would be aware of the hidden, silent war that was going on between them. Perhaps he was aware of it, too. For occasionally, when she turned her head with a swift movement to give her tail a few nervous licks, she would see that the hand holding the newspaper had relaxed and the eyes were staring at her. Then a ridge of bristling fur would appear along her spine.

Finally she began to fear him. That was when she realized that his attitude toward her was no longer one of indifference.

When Harry was angry he paced the floor.

The woman watched him and, from a far corner of the sofa where her safety seemed most certain, Mildred watched him, too. The movement of the two pairs of eyes was thus so co-ordinated by the human pendulum going to and fro that it looked as if they might be watching a slow-motion tennis match.

'I won't have it!' Harry said, pacing back and forth in

the small room that could not give sufficient range for his wrath to dissipate itself. 'Not in my house, I won't. Furniture torn to shreds. Cat's fur all over the place. Every time I sit down on one of these damned chairs of yours it takes a week of brushing to get the stuff off my pants again. And all this fuss, fuss, fussing over her all the time! God, the way you talk sometimes you'd think it was a baby you had here and not a cat. It's disgusting.

'Oh, dear, it's time for Mildred's dinner!'; he mimicked derisively. 'Sorry, I've simply got to rush away . . . Oh, do hurry, hurry, hurry; My precious Mildred will be starved. She won't know what's happened to me. She'll be worried, she'll be hungry, she'll be lonesome . . .

'Oh God. Keep that up much longer and you'll have me nutty, too. If it was at least a dog, then maybe I could understand. But to make such a fuss over a cat, and nothing but a lousy little alley cat at that . . .'

He kicked at the edge of a rumpled rug, found satisfaction in the action and kicked at it again on his way back.

'It seems to me you're the one that's making the fuss, Harry', the woman ventured timidly. 'If only I knew what to do with her – '

'Do with her? Give her away. Throw her out. Anything. Just get rid of her, that's all. It's her or me, do you understand? I love you. I'm asking you to marry me. But I'll be damned if I'm going to marry that cat of yours, too.'

The woman felt herself weakening, and burst into tears.

Mildred, sitting on the very edge of the sofa, was aware of the tension between the two she was watching, and felt the first flicker of fear. It was just at this moment that her mistress, reaching over suddenly, caught her up in her arms and held her tight, so tight that it hurt, and let the wet drops fall on her immaculate fur. Mildred found this not only painful but obnoxious. A peculiar, hitherto unknown mixture of revulsion and terror urged her to fight free from the convulsive tightening of the possessive arms, the sticky wetness and the horrid noises her mistress was making. She fought. There was the sound of ripping cloth, an exclamation of dismay, an oath from Harry. Then she was under a chair in the corner of the room, licking the salt of the tears from her fur and a few drops of blood from her sharp claws.

It had been the wrong thing to do. She knew almost immediately that she had lost ground in her subterranean battle with Harry. Because, even though he cursed her, he was no longer angry. He was pleased and triumphant.

Thereafter, whenever the same scene occurred, as it did more and more frequently, she allowed herself without protest to be clutched and mauled and squeezed and sobbed over by her distraught mistress, enduring it stoically, her body limp, her eyes closed, everything except the beating of her heart held in suspension until that moment when her mistress would turn and throw her arms around Harry instead. Then she would jump down from the lap that had temporarily forgotten her, to spend the next deliciously quiet hour smoothing her rumpled fur and scrubbing away the salty moisture.

This went on for some time before she made her next and final mistake. That was when her mistress began to cry in bed at night. After over four months of the same routine, Mildred was convinced that the night was meant for sleeping. So when her mistress snatched her out of her pleasant descent into oblivion, pressed her to her breast, shook the bed with her sobbing, released her to blow her nose, then held her tight again, Mildred found it disagreeable and incomprehensible. She waited quietly, patiently, until the next time her mistress found it necessary to free her to search for a handkerchief. Then with a quick leap she was off the bed. Ignoring the plaintive voice that called and begged her to return, she spent the rest of the night curled up on her favourite chair in the living room.

And that was the end.

The next day her mistress was changed. In the morning

she ignored Mildred. Then, imitating Harry, she paced the floor for a while, after which she sat down and cried, then took Mildred on her lap. Cupping the small head in her hands, she forced Mildred to look into her eyes. Mildred hated that. She loved looking into her mistress' eyes, but only when she felt like it, not when she was forced to do it. So she twisted her head this way and that, trying to pull away, until at last her mistress had to let her go, but not before she had given a slap with her hand that startled more than it hurt.

Confused and resentful, Mildred retired to her chair and with an impatient tongue repaired the damages to her toilet. Her mistress was still crying, but after a time she quieted down, and finally became quite calm. Infinitely relieved, Mildred relaxed, folded her paws under her trim little chest and drifted off into a pleasant daydream. But soon she became aware of the fact that something else was going to happen. Her mistress began to walk to and fro again, but more purposefully this time, as if she was preparing to go out. That in itself was not unusual. But there was something in the way she walked, something in her grim silence, something in the air . . .

When she approached Mildred again it was merely to tie something around her neck. No word was spoken. The eyes were remote, unfriendly, the hands indifferent as those of a stranger. Mildred looked down at the thing that was hanging around her neck, tried to get rid of it with her tongue, but discovered it wouldn't wash away.

Then suddenly, without warning, those indifferent hands snatched her up and carried her across the room to the one door beyond which she had never been since she had entered it too long ago for her to remember. It opened, and closed again behind her with a loud and definite bang. On the other side of it was terror and madness, roaring, hooting, screeching, clattering, shouting madness. Mildred fought silently, wildly, without restraint, digging her claws deep into whatever they found to cling to, but she could not free herself from the tentacles that held her.

After a time another door opened and closed, and everything was quiet again. Terror receded, to be replaced by exhaustion. She was safe, she was being held by arms that she knew, and for the moment that was sufficient. But now her mistress was putting her down, into the surrounding unfamiliarity. Terror returned. She tried to claw her way back up into the arms, only to be brushed off and shoved away. Then again a door opened and closed, and she was left alone.

For a moment she could comprehend neither her surroundings nor what had happened to her. As if held suspended in time, she stayed where she had been put, absolutely still, not a muscle moving, her eyes staring at nothing. Then quickly she turned and clawed at the door through which her mistress had so suddenly vanished. It would not open. She sniffed at it, tried to thrust a paw through a narrow crack, worked with swift, violent energy to enlarge it, gave up and turned again to examine the strangeness around her.

She was in a small, bare hall, from which a long flight of stairs extended upward. Both hall and stairway were empty of sound and movement, but for sensitive nostrils odours were plentiful. She went around the circumference of the cubicle, sniffing carefully the walls, the floor, and all along the first step. Much of life had been recorded there, but most of it, being outside the realm of her experience, meant nothing to her.

When she had finished her inspection she sat down again in a corner and waited. She waited for a long time. The thing around her neck began to annoy her. She scratched at it, stretching her neck and showing the tip of her pink tongue, but it merely went around and around; she couldn't get it off. She shook her head and gave her ear a few scrubs with her paw, got up and sat down again. A dim memory began to form, a memory of kittenhood, when she was lost in the vastness of the room, and cried, and her mother came running to her, crooning, to show her the way back to their box.

It was a wonderful memory that made her glow and relax in the comfort of it. She opened her mouth and the little sound came out, the call of the lost kitten. Her comfort increased. She repeated the call, louder and louder and louder. At last there was an answering sound from the head of the flight of stairs.

The woman knocked, waited, then knocked again. The door opened.

'Excuse me', the woman said, 'but – is that your cat down in the hall?'

The other woman turned and looked behind her.

'No,' she said, 'mine is right here.'

'Oh, then forgive me. There's a cat crying down there and I thought – '

'In the hall? Oh yes, now I hear it, too.' She closed the door and the two of them started down the stairs.

Mildred heard them coming, looked up and swiftly climbed the first flight of stairs to meet them. On the landing she paused, sat down and waited for them. She opened her mouth, but made no sound now. Her call had been answered in a way.

'Well!' one of the women said, 'Hello there, kitty. How did you manage to get in here?'

Mildred stood up, her tail high and straight as a flagstaff, then abruptly sat down again. She blinked, and again opened her mouth without making a sound. Her round eyes appealed first to the one, then to the other of the two women.

'It must be somebody's pet. Look how friendly it is.'

Stooping down, the woman stroked the cat's head. Her hand paused, then explored.

'Wait a minute. There's something tied around her neck. 'Well . . . what's this?'

Mildred sat very still.

'My name is Mildred', the woman read, then turned over the paper disc and saw the words on the other side. 'Please be good to me!'

'Somebody must have put her in here, then.'

'Yes. I suppose they tried the door and found it unlocked, so they just shoved her in and left her.'

'That's what happened? They didn't want you any more, poor Mildred? I wonder why. You're such a pretty little thing.'

Mildred stood up at the sound of her name. Hearing it pleased her, but the way the two women looked at her brought back uneasiness. This was a crisis of some sort and she didn't known how to meet it. Delicately, with arched back, she went from one to the other, rubbing her body against their legs, feeling their kindness and their pity, but knowing also that something else, what she most needed, was being witheld. Finally she sat down in front of them again, neatly, her little paws primly placed side by side, her tail curved to fit snugly against her body, putting everything that she felt into her eyes and gazing up at them. But still they were silent.

'What do you think we ought to do with her?' one of them said at last.

'I don't know. If I didn't have a dog – '

'If I didn't have a cat of my own I'd take her. But mine would tear her to pieces.'

'So would my dog.'

'We can't send her away to be killed?'

'She's such a cute little thing. And so gentle.'

'Yes, it would be a pity, but . . . what about Larry?'

'Oh, Larry would take her, I think.'

'We might ask him in the morning.'

'Yes but what can we do with her tonight?'

'We could let her stay out in the court. It's a dry night. I could put an old blanket near the window and give her some milk and food.'

'Let's do that, then.'

Mildred looked at them eagerly. A decision had been reached, that much she knew. Were they going to take her home? She allowed herself to be picked up and carried away to whatever their decision might be.

The night was meant for sleeping. So she had been taught. But this night was different. Its vastness and strangeness terrified her. No night had ever before had such a high ceiling, nor walls that were so far away. Where was the bed of her mistress? And her mistress, where was she? Where was the sweet, heavy, comforting warmth, the possessive hand, the voice that sleepily called her Sugarplum?

She drank a little of the milk that had been left for her, a great deal of the water and, after sniffing at it, left the food untouched. Then she huddled against the window through which she had been carried into this vast, unknown and threatening night, shrinking away from it as much as possible, waiting to be taken in and back to her mistress again.

She waited a long time, until the time became too long. Then she cried. Only now it was not the wail of the lost kitten. She called as she used to when she had been accidentally locked in the clothes closet, a call that always brought her mistress running to open the door and let her out and make a big fuss over her because she had been shut up. She called now because she was locked out, because she wanted the window opened, because she wanted her mistress to pick her up and carry her home, and this time make even more of a fuss over her than usual, because this was much worse than being shut up in the closet.

But suddenly she was quiet again. She lifted her head and searched the air with her nostrils. Her ears tilted to catch an elusive sound, flattened, then were brought forward again. What was it? Danger? She didn't know.

She bunched herself up still tighter, made herself as small as possible, pressed against the pane of glass. A shadow some distance away detached itself from the rest of the night, came slowly and stealthily toward her, straight toward her, with ominous purposefulness.

Making no movement, she shrank away from it. Momentarily distracted by the plate of food, it stopped, then advanced again, until it was no more than a few inches away. It, too, searched the air with its nostrils, came closer still until she felt its hot breath on her body. She did not move. The nose of the shadow touched hers, snuffled at her eyes, her ears, along the entire length of her body. She did not turn her head, did not even blink her eyes, but kept them focused on some distant spot even when the dark head in front of her was all that she could see.

Finally the shadow turned away. It went back to the plate of food, ate noisily, glaring at her and growling. Then it drank her milk, disdained the water and slowly, sedately padded off.

Mildred unbunched herself and stretched and yawned with relief. It was her first meeting with Blackie.

Blackie was Larry's cat. Mildred became his 'Other Cat.'

In the morning, very early in the morning, Larry would let himself into the cellar carrying a great box of rubbish that he would place in a corner, then he would fumble in his pocket and pull out a paper parcel.

'Heah Blackie, heah Blackie!' he would call. 'Wheah is you, boy? Come get yo breakfass, Blackie.' Then he would remember, and add: 'Come on, you Other Cat. Heah yo, breakfass now.'

Mildred learned to answer that call, although the voice was not that of her mistress, and did not call her Mildred, or even Sugarplum. She got used to being just plain Other Cat, she got used to Larry and even, upon a few occasions, allowed herself the luxury of rubbing against human legs. Sometimes, then, he would stoop down and pat her head, and offer her a morsel of food from his hand. This she accepted greedily, for it was usually all she got. The next moment Larry would be off again, shouldering mop and broom, and she would be left alone with Blackie, who growled and spat and clawed at her if she came anywhere near the food.

However, it wasn't so bad as it might have been. Up there on the window-sill where she had spent the first night of this new life of hers, and where during the day Blackie never dared go, she would find more food, on a plate, as she was accustomed to it, and a small saucer of milk.

She got used to looking for her food there, and accepting whatever she found. She got used to the woman standing behind the closed window watching her eat, as she often did, and to the cat that sometimes was with the woman, also watching her eat, but growling and hissing and spitting with such ferocity that occasionally, even after she was used to it, Mildred would still start and let the food drop from her mouth and make a bolt for home.

She got used to thinking of home as the cellar in which she now slept, on a pile of empty crates, in a corner behind the furnace, on top of the coal pile, anywhere where she might be out of Blackie's way. She got used to having her formerly immaculate coat grimy with coal dust and sticky with the various exudations of the cellar. She no longer washed herself; it was sickening and useless. She got used to the rustling of the great cockroaches and the squeaking of the mice, and to hearing Blackie pounce and growl as he played with a rat he had caught. She got used to the darkness, the dampness, the filth and the loneliness. It was not a good life, but she lived.

Larry, entering the room, put down his bucket, his cloth and his newspapers and stared through the window he was just about to clean.

'Hey, you!' he shouted through the glass, 'what you doin' up heah?'

Mildred raised her head to look at him, then calmly went on eating. She didn't like Larry particularly, but she wasn't afraid of him. Sometimes he still gave her that pat on the head and a morsel of food from his hand. Sometimes, but not often. Big Blackie was his favourite.

But suddenly the window was thrown open, and something struck her cross the face. Startled, blinded for a moment, she hissed at whatever it was, then, as the roll of newspapers threatened to descend again, jumped down from the window-sill and sped away.

'*Larry!*'

'Ma'am?'

'What were you doing to that cat?'

'Jes chasin her, ma'am. Ah didn't hurt her none. That ma otha cat, ma'am. She got no call to be up heah. She belong down in the cellar.'

'Isn't that the cat we found on the stairs?'

'Yes, ma'am, ah thinks so, ma'am.'

'Well, she just comes up here to eat. She doesn't do any harm. I've been putting out food for her every day.'

'Yes, ma'am. Ah sees that, ma'am. An ef you don mind, ah wishes you wouldn't, ma'am. Ain't no need foh you to be puttin' stuff out foh her. Jes draws bugs an' flies an' things. Tenants goin start complainin, next thing ah knows ah gots the lanlord after *me*.'

'But she's hungry, Larry.'

'No, ma'am. Couldn't be she hongry, ma'am. Ah feeds her mahself every day.'

'Are you sure?'

'Yes ma'am. Swear to God. Ah feeds her good, both her an Blackie. Ah feeds em good, ma'am, don't you worry. Every mornin. Liver ah gives 'em, an all stuff like that.'

'Well . . .'

Larry took in the dishes, the plate of food half eaten, the saucer of untouched milk, and handed them to the woman. Then he began to clean the windows.

It was almost a week before Mildred dared go up there

again. But hunger finally drove her back. The window-sill was bare. No plate of food, no saucer of milk. The cat on the other side of the glass spat and tried to tear its way through with furious claws. The woman was not there. Mildred sat down for a moment, ignoring the noise, paying no attention to the raging of the cat on the other side of the pane. She put her head down and sniffed at the place where the food had always been. Then, with a last glance back, to the spot just behind the cat where the woman usually stood. She jumped down and went away. Not until she was back in the safety of the cellar did she cry. And then not for long, because Blackie came stalking toward her.

Now she no longer ran with Blackie to greet Larry in the morning. Remembrance of the stinging blow across her face would come back each time she caught sight of him.

'Heah Blackie, com on, boy!' Larry would call. 'Heah you breakfass. Come on, you Other Cat!'

Sometimes even now he would approach her, holding out a morsel of food, and her nostrils would catch the delicious scent; but then she would recall how that same hand had struck her with the roll of newspapers, and she would shrink away.

'What the mattah with you, Other Cat?' Larry would say. 'Why you ain't never hongry no more? Cotchin too many mice and rats, ah bet. Heah Blackie, you always hongry, ain't you?'

From her corner Mildred would watch until Larry left; then she would dart in and seize a piece of the meat, sometimes dodging the quick claws tht raked out, sometimes feeling them gouge a burning track across her nose.

She began to hunt mice, but she was not good at it. She had none of Blackie's skill, nor his patience. For him it was a game. For her it became a matter of life or death. So she fumbled, miscalculated, lost her prey because of the very hunger it was meant to appease. Sometimes, surfeited and content, Blackie would go off and leave a dead mouse or a mutilated rat lying where his worrying paw had tired of it. And these chance discards became her sole subsistence. They kept her alive. But always the hunger gnawed.

She dreamed of fine big bowls full of milk. She would approach them and sniff at them and put her tongue down into the creamy whiteness, and then she would be awake again. She cried. Hunger and something else, something that gnawed and fought within her much like the hunger, made her restless. She prowled around ceaselessly, crying and hunting for whatever it was that would bring her peace. When she saw Blackie following her, she turned and hissed at him, flew at him as she had never dared to before, trying to bury her claws in his flesh. He dodged skilfully, then leapt upon her, fastening his teeth in the back of her neck. Squirm and howl and fight as she might, she could not free herself.

In the end she let him have his way with her, as he had had his way with the food.

The hunger changed from a gnawing in her stomach to an insidious pain that crept over her whole body. As her belly swelled, her frame became more gaunt. Even her head shrank, until it seemed to be made up of no more than ears and mouth and enormous, staring eyes. From a distance those great, hungry eyes watched Larry's every movement in the morning, watched his brown hands producing and unwrapping the paper parcel and putting it down on the floor, watched while he held out the bit of food for her.

Then the mouth of the death's-head would open, and a pitiful cry would issue from it. She couldn't help it, she had to cry. Even Larry was shaken by the desolate sound. 'Come heah, Other Cat', he would say to her. 'Come get some breakfass now. Ah declare, sompn wrong with you sure. You jes worryin yoself to death. Come heah, now, come heah. Ah gonna take you away an have you put out yo misery.'

But she would not go to him.

One day he went after her and tried to catch her. Clumsy as she was, her legs weak and trembling, her sides swollen, nevertheless she managed to elude his grasping hands and flee. The cellar, piled high with boxes, old broken furniture and kindling wood, offered many recesses to hide in. At last Larry gave up looking for her and went away.

The following morning he brought two strangers with him. Mildred came crying, as she always did when she saw Larry now, and waited for him to take the paper parcel out of his pocket.

'Better try now', Larry said. 'She never come no closer'n that.'

The two strangers approached her, holding out their hands, coaxing. She retreated. Then suddenly they tried to throw something over her. But she was too quick for them. A scream, a mad scrambling, a clatter of falling boxes, and she was away from them, safe in her hiding place. The two strangers cursed, laughed, and started working on something they had placed on the floor of the cellar.

'Don't you all cotch my Blackie, now', Larry said, as he started up the stairs, carrying his mop and broom. 'Ah very fond of that cat.'

'Don't worry, we ain't gonna cotch nothin. We'll leave all that to you', one of the men called back to him. 'That ought to get her', he said then to the other man. 'Bet you he'll have her inside of an hour.'

Whatever it was they put on the floor has a delicious aroma. Mildred's nostrils flared. She raised her head and sniffed, then mewed soundlessly. Her mouth open, her breathing quick and laboured, she eased herself out of her hiding place. The strangers were gone. Larry was gone. The thing that smelled so good was inside a wire box. She went over to it cautiously.

But Blackie had also caught the scent. With a snarl he came bounding over. She retreated, watching enviously while he inspected the box, then crawled inside and snatched the food. Something snapped. Blackie looked up, startled, gave a warning growl, and returned to his feast. Mildred looked on while he ate, washed briefly around the corners of his mouth, then tried to find his way out of the box. It seemed he couldn't. He was imprisoned.

All through the rest of the day and the night that followed he howled and fought and tore with claws and teeth at the wire mesh of the box. But when morning came and Larry's feet descended the cellar steps he was still a captive, only quiet now, exhausted and defeated.

Larry took one look at the trap and his mouth fell open.

'Well . . . Ah'll be . . . Doggone! Ah done fergit all about it!'

Blackie, hearing his master's voice, found energy for one last long howl of desperation and rage. Then Larry exploded. He began to howl, too. He laughed until the tears came to his eyes, until he doubled up and his knees gave way. Sitting on the floor holding his sides, he continued to howl, while Blackie behind his bars and Mildred in her hiding place listened and looked on in amazement.

Then at last, with still an occasional explosive guffaw, he got up and went over to Blackie.

'Doggone! We sets a trap to cotch the other one, an heah you'se the one that gits cotched. Blackie, you a fool. You jes nothing but a great big black old fool. What for you wants to go an git yosef cotched like that? You wants you should git put out yo misery, now?'

Chuckling, he opened the door of the trap. Blackie took one look at freedom, and like a streak of black lightning shot away into it.

'Hey, Blackie, heah Blackie! Come back heah, Blackie, heah you breakfass, boy!'

Larry called in vain. For once in his life, Blackie had had enough. Finally Larry put the food on the floor and left, and on that one morning Mildred had all she wanted to eat. But soon after, because her stomach was no longer accustomed to being given what it demanded, she was sick.

Before he went away that evening, Larry returned to the cellar and set the trap again. No Blackie was to be seen, but he talked to him anyway.

'You stay away from heah now, Blackie, you heah me? This for that Other Cat. You stay away and let her git cotched, and tomorrow ah takes her away. Then you gits twice as much to eat. How that, Blackie, huh?'

Blackie stayed away from the trap. So did Mildred. The next morning Larry had a fine big rat to dispose of. Whereupon, at his request, the two strangers came back and removed the trap.

Mildred wandered around restlessly, hunting for something she could not find. With difficulty she climbed the cellar stairs, stopping frequently with her front paws on one step, her haunches on another, her heavy belly sagging. She was at the end of her strength. She was almost finished. She was going to die, but an inexorable law of nature decreed that first she must give birth. She reached the courtyard and slowly went prowling across it, still hunting, still not finding.

A bright ray of sunshine lay slanting across the yard. When she came to it and felt its warmth caressing her swollen body, she began to purr. But then suddenly she was still again, immobile as if the yellow light had frozen her in its path. Someone was calling her by her own name, not Other Cat, but that almost forgotten name she had not heard for so long.

'Mildred!'

There it was again. She lifted a paw in preparation for flight back to the darkness and safety of her corner behind the boxes in the cellar. Yet she felt drawn toward the familiar sound. And she was tired, much too tired to run. She raised her head, looked toward the voice and wailed.

'Here, Mildred!'

It was the woman at the window who used to put out the plates of food for her. She was calling and patting the sill with her hand. Mildred looked at her, then at the window ledge, and cried. The woman continued to coax.

Of the three memories associated with the woman and the window, the snarling, spitting cat on the other side of the glass and the hand holding the newspaper that had slapped across her face slowly dimmed and receded, while the saucer of milk became almost a reality as she stared at the spot where she had found it waiting for her in the past. It was toward that illusion that she leapt, forgetting her weakness and her fears, even the heaviness of her belly that made her jump almost too much for her. Scrabbling on the rough stone surface with her claws, she managed somehow to pull her body up over the edge of the sill, then lay there exhausted, breathing heavily, unable to defend herself.

The woman put a hand toward her. She winced, but could not withdraw. Then the hand did not strike her after all. It gently stroked her head.

Peering into the room, Mildred's wide eyes sought the other remembered danger, her sparse fur stiffening with fear, her sides heaving in anticipation of the sudden vicious attack and the retreat she knew she could not make. But nothing happened. There was no movement in the shadows, no sound, and gradually her fear ebbed away. The cat that belonged to the woman was gone.

Two memories thus dismissed, the third became a reality. The woman disappeared for a moment, and when she came back it was to put a small saucer of milk on the window ledge. Greedily Mildred lapped up the milk, washed the saucer and watched the hand reach out and take it away again.

The hand did not go far away. Mildred turned to look down into the courtyard, then back at the floor of the room, and again at the hand that held the saucer. For a moment she stood uncertainly balanced on the ledge between two worlds. Then she jumped to the floor and followed the saucer as it was carried across the room.

*

She was Mildred again. She was no longer the Other Cat, had never been the Other Cat except in a bad dream, and that was over now.

In the box she had been given she lay still and listened while the woman talked.

'My cat is dead', the woman was saying. 'That's why I called you, Mildred. She was going to have babies just like you, but something went wrong and she died. I was crying when I went to the window, but then I saw you, and it was just as if . . .'

Mildred didn't understand a word of what the woman was saying. But she understood she had come home again.

Tomorrow she would clean herself up, wash away all the grease and grime of the cellar to make herself worthy of that home.

In the meantime . . .

She sighed deeply and closed her eyes.

Acknowledgments

All possible care has been taken to make full acknowledgment in every case where material is still in copyright. If errors have occurred, they will be corrected in subsequent editions if notification is sent to the publisher. Grateful acknowledgment is made for permission to reprint the following:

THAT DAMNED CAT by Teresa Crane, copyright © Teresa Crane 1995, reproduced by permission of the author.

THE SUBURBAN LION by Stella Whitelaw, copyright © Stella Whitelaw 1995, reproduced by permission of the author.

OLLY AND GINNY by James Herriot from *JAMES HERRIOT'S CAT STORIES* (Michael Joseph Ltd) reproduced by permission of David Higham Associates. Copyright © by James Herriot 1994.

THE WOLF AND THE CATS by Jane Beeson, copyright © Jane Beeson 1995, reproduced by permission of the author and Andrew Mann Ltd.

CAT TALK by Lynne Bryan, copyright © Lynne Bryan 1993, *New Woman* 1993, *Envy at the Cheese Handout* 1995 published by Faber and Faber.